JEAN GIONO

TWO RIDERS
OF THE STORM

Translated from the French by
Alan Brown

PETER OWEN
LONDON AND CHESTER SPRINGS

To Colette and Jean-Pierre Rudin

PETER OWEN PUBLISHERS
73 Kenway Road, London SW5 0RE

Peter Owen books are distributed in the USA by
Dufour Editions Inc., Chester Springs, PA 19425-0007

Translated from the French *Deux Cavaliers de l'orage*
© Editions Gallimard 1965
English translation © Peter Owen 1967
This paperback edition published 2002

ISBN 0 7206 1159 8

A catalogue record for this book is available from
the British Library.

Printed and bound in Great Britain by
Bookmarque Ltd, Croydon, Surrey

History of the Jasons

The Jasons are not exactly from the High Hill country: at least it's no trouble to trace their ancestors who came from the valleys, down behind. In 1793, the valleys having asked for a guillotine, they were sent one. It was a Jason, Old Jason, who opened the crates, unpacked the machine, set it up and put it to work across the countryside. It was shortly after this that the Jasons were obliged to go into the High Hills. They became the Jasons of Grangias—for they had settled on Grangias farm—until the time of Jason the Artist.

He was the one who first began as a mule-dealer. One Saturday evening, just before the fair at Lachau, he left in his tilbury with three mules and two she-mules in tow, the finest brutes even seen. He left ten others in the stable, plus his wife, a certain Mathilde from Grange-Neuve farm, and his mother, who had one foot in the grave, and, finally, Grangias with its reaches. He was going to the fair. He came back nine years later. He was great friends with Siméon Pierre-à-Feu. Siméon had not thought of him for a long time. He had, in fact, grown deaf, when one evening there's a man's voice outside the door asking to be let in. The hired man first takes the rifle, then opens up. Siméon had his back turned and heard nothing.

'Well?' demanded the hired man, keeping the other on the threshold of the night at gunpoint.

The women looked on, silent. Luckily Siméon turned and despite the nine years said:

'It's Jason! Come in!'

It was Jason. He was forty-two. His mother was dead. The oddest thing was about Mathilde, his wife. She had always been easy-going and a bit simple. She had left for the plains, and they said that there, in a part of the world where there were convents for women, she had become what they called a lay-sister, cooking, cleaning vegetables: in any case, disappeared. As for Grangias, it would take a hundred years to work it up again. Here, if the wild growth is not held in check it will eat up man's property with the swiftness of the sea. But that seemed not to trouble Jason much. At any rate, here is what had happened:

He went off to the fair, and his mules had been a tremendous success down there. There was no price prime enough for animals of that quality. After the banquet the Councillor kissed him, weeping with wine, and the Councillor's wife kissed him, saying it was only proper. About one in the morning he recovered all his woodsman's vigour, in better form than if he had been eating pot roast with rough wine. He gambled his mules. He won. He gambled his winnings and his tilbury. He didn't know how much he was up. He stuffed a handful of crowns in the lap of the Councillor's wife.

Well, by daylight he had won fair and square perhaps ten thousand francs, maybe more. Cool as your eye. Chilled and on edge from thirty-odd years of solitude in the High Hills and his Jason blood that was slowly stirring certain devilishly splendid embers in his body. But easy on!—never losing his head, doing everything by the book with an iron system that nothing, not the most cunning bailiff, could undo again.

The Councillor's wife watched him with tired eyes, the

dark circles beneath them sagging to her cheekbones, but with a touch of down-boy in her look: and there was her mouth, full, red and glossy, over which she ran her tongue from time to time. Quite a change from a thing like Mathilde of Grange-Neuve farm.

As for the Councillor, he was put to bed in a room on the second floor of the Maltese Cross. And the Councillor's wife took our Artist to the best clothier in the High Street for a complete suit of nankeen plus a Cronstadt hat which settled just a shade to one side on those curling Jason locks above a rugged face that was hungry as a wolf. They didn't pay their respects—"Greetings, chief!"—until almost evening to a slightly be-puked Councillor, and their plot was all worked out. He had sold all his animals and had kept only the tilbury and the she-mule, Anatole.

'And now he's coming with us to la Sigouyère'—which was this blesséd Councillor's chateau—'and he'll stay with us for a while, just until he can buy Sainte-Roustagne next door, and he'll be a good neighbour for us, won't he, darling?'

'Good idea she's got, what do you say to it, chief?'

Bugger! What was there to say? And so:

'All aboard, madame, up you go, chief!'

He was a man well over fifty who had to be given a hand under the arms after country fairs. And away to la Sigouyère! His wife would have been somewhere between twenty-five and twenty-eight, not tall, but very straight.

'I stayed there five years.'

'Did you buy Sainte-Roustagne?'

'No.'

And then (he brushed it all away with a sweep of his arm then told the story of the five years and the whole falderal) . . . . Then he left, just like that. Oh, but they'd had some feasts!

'One time, sixteen woodcocks and forty plovers on a single table. And wine that they brought us in a boat up the Rhone, from a foreign country with two X's in the name.'

After that, no one knew what he had done. He himself declared that he had done nothing. At the time there was a man called Bordier, known as Fly-by-Night, who stopped travellers on the highways, from Tain down to the sea— with a band that galloped like a dust-storm. They were no sooner the talk of the walnut groves Grenoble way than they were cleaning out a tax-collector or two somewhere by Toulon. And quite often there were a few deaths in the process. Jason's role? Not a word! Some said his job had been the supply of fresh horses for this special cavalry. Others, on the contrary, maintained he had been up to all kinds of devilment. He himself said:

'I did nothing. They stopped me on the way and kept me with them.'

Whether it had been because of a woman, or money, or the threat of the rope, one thing was sure: he'd been a member of the band, for shortly before his return to the High Hills the said Bordier had been found stone-dead across a highway. Just the other side of Apt in the Vaucluse, at the meeting of five roads that lead off in all directions. This Bordier had been tidily strangled with such force that he had died standing up and without a fight, though he had two loaded pistols, one in each hand. And had them still, stretched out there on the icy road, having been given time neither to defend himself nor call on Mary. For the whole of the High Hill country the sudden brutality of this had the Jason touch. He made no secret of it. He had been pursued at the same time by the gendarmes and the bandits, they both mounted and he on foot, all through the forests of Muirol which he knew like his own pocket.

'Where you couldn't get through, over by Frégate, you'd

take to the road again and damn!—there was a tricorn every time. No need to know if it was a gendarme or one of the others. They were both wearing tricorns. And then you'd cut back towards Loubillon by the broken passes where you have to know what you're doing.'

To know was so needful that one of the first nights two gendarmes broke their necks, horses and all, in the cliffs of Goirand. But the best of all was when the bandits tried a little brutally to go warm their hands in a woodman's cabin. The fog had hidden some ten other cabins from their view. They thought they were the masters with only one man to face, despite his gun. At the very first shot scores of others pooped off from all sides. As if this peppering were not enough, the gendarmes, attracted by the noise, sabred the survivors next morning by the first light as they dragged their wounds through the mist.

It was then that Jason arrived at the home of Siméon Pierre-à-Feu, not too haggard, casting scarcely one little glance too many over his shoulder. The foresters of the High Hill country found that very flattering.

Jason, who didn't yet have his nickname, the Artist, was not a man for regrets. He sold Grangias without seeing it again and came to the village. He liked company. As for the sequel to that cavalcade of gendarmes, he had composed a letter to the Councillor in a large and fancy hand, and had come, twirling his moustache, to hand it over to the postman. He had taken a great barn of a place, an old four-storey house, and had given it the name, 'Hotel of the West.'

Of course there was no question of expecting travellers on these roads that lie in the High Hills. No, but there are always a few woodmen suddenly taken by desire for a proper bed, and there are always men with a thirst, and young people beginning to want to dance on Sundays.

No one knew how, but Jason had come back able to play the cornet.

'I've done lots worse,' he said.

They had a township surveyor who played the clarinet. And above all there was the word 'West' on the sign. Here, the West is that sunken gorge through which the wind comes in to play on your nerves, where you can lean out above the grey plain from among the splendid, black leafage of the oaks, and be possessed of the strong desire to stay here and live with your own joys.

Jason the Artist was by now a good forty-four years old, and his hair was still black and full of curls, scarcely the least bit thinner. The skin had grown tired beneath eyes that were hungry as ever but more tender. They hinted that now the sweetmeats would be left the pleasure of deciding where and how they would be eaten. His moustache was long, soft and very docile: he would lift it to crush his red lips against the cornet's mouthpiece. For two years now it had been common knowledge that Mathilde was dead.

Who mentioned Ariane of Pavon to him? Perhaps no one, perhaps everyone. This Ariane was the very youngest at Pavon farm. Of that whole farm, with its sixteen carts and as many teams, and of the fifty peacocks on which it was forbidden to lay a hand, either to sell them or to eat them, Ariane would never have any share: she was the last. But she managed to make her own name just by being what she was. She was twenty, blonde, with a round face that had light golden down on the lower part, a few freckles under her blue eyes, arms like iron, breasts like iron, thighs like iron, doing alone on the wide lands of Pavon the work, as they said, of three grown men and two she-mules. And whenever a man spoke to her of something else she would stand there, red as a rooster, breathless, expecting anything, quick now, her eyes beseeching. Yet there it was: they all said,

'If ever she pulls herself together she'll let you have one that'll turn your head back to front, even if it's all in fun.' And as a rule that was the end of it.

When they told the Artist about her he stood for a long time stroking his moustache.

'Tell her,' he said, 'that if ever I lie on top of her they'll find her next day as flat as a cigarette paper.'

They all laughed, but of course they went off to give her the message.

'Tell him,' she said, 'that if I catch him he'll rue his life, man and all that he is.'

The following Sunday she was there, planted before the two musicians. The Artist attacked a polka, but he barely had time to count one-two: he got his glass of wine right in the face. He leapt from the stand. The whole crowd of dancers, screaming like a flock of chickens, rushed for the doors and looked in through the windows. He hurled himself at her with all his might, crushing her in his two arms below her breasts to lift her and throw her down. Without budging she struck him a key-blow just at the base of the kidneys and above the buttocks; in a flash he straightened up like a steel spring and let her go. This was enough to make you think. She made him think still more with a man's blow straight to the chin. From that moment on he made no allowance for the fact that she was a woman, and tried coldly to knock her out on the spot.

Three months later they were married. No one knew that in the meantime they had fought twice more, alone in the woods: once, when she had torn a lump out of his arm with her teeth and he had left on her belly a bruise shaped for all the world like a shoe; and another time when he half-ripped off one of her ears, but she laid him out properly for a good minute or two with a kick between the legs.

The master of Pavon gave a hundred crowns. Everyone was surprised. Nobody puts himself out for the youngest. But the master longed to see an end to the business, and he would have paid much more to see it end this way. The night of the wedding the Artist, who had had a drop to drink for the occasion and held it not quite so well as fifteen years before, began to laugh, saying, 'See, I won after all!' Ariane cracked a bottle of wine over his head and this was why he was obliged to wait another day to have the first of her.

People said they continued from time to time to take each other's measure, but the proof that they didn't spend all their time fighting is that they had two children, one after the other: Marceau and Marat. And seventeen years after Marat, Ariane, who everyone thought was finished, had a third: Ange—the one the two brothers called 'Notre Cadet'.

The Artist kept on the Hotel of the West. Around 1902, 1903, when the smuggling of lucifer matches was a going concern, it had even become an inn that made money during the night hours, after closing. Smugglers had it all their own way through the High Hills. It's dream country: there's cover for doing anything you like to name.

Le Féli, a tall scarecrow that they called Chinless, was often seen coming out of the West. He had nothing but forehead prolonged into a sharp nose, and tiny fox-eyes that shone brightly but were very sad. He walked softly on cord-soled shoes, without a sound, always close to the walls. He was a poor man, widower and all—one, that is, who not only loses everything he has, but loses it wretchedly. At the end of 1903 the two squads of gendarmes from the valleys down behind, plus our nasty little bit of a squad from the

High Hills, received the strictest orders to put an end once and for all to this kind of work.

It was in that same year as well that Jason the Artist, paralyzed in his armchair for the last six months, realized that he would never walk again, and that the great open paths through the forests were now closed forever. He could already feel the catch beginning in his throat, and when he was alone he tried to count the words that he could no longer pronounce.

One evening—it was an hour after midnight—there's a knock at the door: 'Open, in the name of the law!' There was no light in the front room of the inn, but there was in the cellar. Ariane shuts the cellar door, lights the oil lamp.

'My poor little pet,' said the Artist, 'I can't be any help to you.'

'Don't worry your head,' said she.

And she opened the door after a 'Who's there?' that boded ill for someone. In the Artist's prime no gendarme would have dared come in. They came in: six of them, carbines in hand.

'Are you off to the war?' demanded Ariane.

They told her which war they were off to, but a little louder than if they had really felt at ease. In his armchair the Artist had closed his eyes.

'Have a little drink,' said Ariane. 'It's icy cold in here.'

She set six small glasses before them. She went to the table at the back to fetch the brandy. At this time she looked as she was to look until her death. She had lost her womanly roundness; she was tall, lanky, she walked slowly on the flat of her feet, her torso like cast iron.

She came back to them with a three-gallon demi-john which she carried by the neck. With just one hand, with a simple movement of her wrist, she raised it, tipped it, slowly, held it tipped without trembling, without leaning back, without watching what she did, during the whole time it took to pour, very slowly, six little glasses full, and fill them exactly to the brim without spilling a drop. As if it had been a quart bottle, and even then you couldn't have done it as neatly. And all the time she looked at them with her cold, blue eyes under the cold, white hair of an old woman who has nothing to lose.

That went on for a good long minute, and the room was so still that Jason the Artist opened his eyes: 'I thought they'd all gone up in smoke.' She hadn't even had time to say 'To your health!' when they wished her a good night and went. No one had so much as mentioned matches. She emptied back in the demi-john the six little glasses which they had not touched. And no one ever did mention matches, from that time on.

The Artist died a few years later. When all he could move was his eyes, his son Marceau gave him his final pleasure. Marceau had begun to take up his father's first profession: he was a mule-dealer, but, like a young man, more for the splash he made than for the money. And one summer afternoon he came with a new string of mules beneath the great oak where they had the old man resting. He said not a word, for there would have been the frightful affliction of being unable to answer; he did not even look at his father; he made as if there were nothing on all this earth but Marceau Jason and his mules. Thus the old man could feel himself quite free for one last time.

Marceau made the animals walk up and down before his father, and they were fine brutes, almost as fine as the ones at the fair that time, if not finer! He had chosen them, he made them walk, trot and caper. Then he went off with them. As it was a rather misty summer day he had not far to go before the fog and the last tears made him disappear as if he had been nothing but a freak of magic.

Marceau at twenty-six, with not a pinch of fat on him, weighed sixteen stone, and Marat, two years younger, weighed almost as much. They were like two bears, but quick and alert: they whirled suddenly on their heels, they walked swiftly; there was no trace of stiffness in anything they did—for example, their arms were not only free from fingertip to armpit, they seemed to be prolonged with all their liberty of movement right into the muscles of their shoulders. Every move they made seemed easy; they themselves gave a strong impression of lightness, of suppleness. Since, despite all this, you couldn't help seeing their well-hewn bulk and their strength, the effect was of something wild, in the sense the word has in the High Hills, that's to say the impression a wolf gives when you surprise him in his daytime bed and he gets up and moves off step by step, looking back just a little. In deep winter, when the two brothers took a spite at a tree, the two axes flew in a figure-eight with the sound of a flight of partridge.

Only Marceau went by his given name, and on great occasions his father and mother called him Jason, the family name to which he had the right as firstborn. When people referred to Marat they said 'the middle one'. And when it was Ange, they said 'Notre Cadet', for the two brothers together called him 'Our Junior'.

As soon as the two brothers began to live a man's life they couldn't get on without the child. When he was perhaps seven, blond like Ariane but with curls like the Artist's, Marceau and the middle one were hungry for him. They dragged him along on all their tours about the countryside.

There is a great bitterness in these vast forests that freeze where they stand without ever stirring, and again without stirring put on in spring their enormous cover of dark fur.

When the bitterness takes hold of a Jason he grows impassioned, but a Jason can feel passion only for a Jason: that was what had ruled them all until now.

Marceau would set the child on the backs of his quieter mules, but when he lifted the little body in his great hands it seemed to him that all his strength dissolved in joy. He was always afraid of letting him fall. He chose the quietest of his animals. He stayed close beside it.

If the mule caught a foot and stumbled over hidden branches as they traversed the great stretches of dead leaves, Marceau would abuse it, screaming in the voice of his rage, shrill as the squeal of a swine. He revelled in being there to worry that something might happen. There was no need to worry with him there beside the mule; and Notre Cadet, if he didn't show the beginnings of shoulders like those of his brothers, was none the less clever with his limbs and, in fact, stronger than you'd think. But how beautiful he was! He had a little mouth as full as a red acorn, and eyes so soft that when he rubbed too hard at the glaze below his running nose he brought tears to them at once, even though a moment before he had been laughing like a real horseman on his gentle mule, rasped by the cold and gloriously pink beneath his transparent skin.

The middle one, Marat, was killed in 1917 in the course of small, everyday skirmishes, in the mud by Suippes. When the war was over Marceau found his way back to his countryside heavy with trees, high in the sky, mute with a great silence. His first act was to de-baptize Notre Cadet. He called him 'Mon Cadet'. Then, he got married.

Caresses

By then Ange was sixteen. He had filled out, but in no way could he be compared with Marceau. Everyone remembered that at the same age the elder brother was already a sort of miracle. Not Ange. He was sturdy, fairly broad, agile. He had a way of looking that was dark and direct.

It had always been Marceau's ambition to go down and do business in the valley of the Rhone; the kind of business he had at once begun with a great grin the moment his good name was established: that is, superciliously offering animals riddled with faults, impossible to sell, and selling them by dint of browbeating, self-assurance and guile.

The river banks were famous as the country of connoisseurs of horses. Marceau had heard so much about the fine studs that were said to gallop about down there in the shade of the elms and plane-trees, that he was tormented by the desire to go and play his arrogant game among such beauties. Time and again he had started off to try his luck, along with Marat. But each time they had been just a little intimidated by the greenness. They had gone right to the verge of the valley, leaving the black forests, descending the wooded paths for three, four days, and then the moors. But when they came to the last knolls that overlooked the flat-lands they had been stopped by a spectacle whose magnificence left them helpless.

They had an aerial view of a great expanse of parks and green pasture. Enormous plane-trees sheltered fountains, water ran in canals. Châteaux seated on fine, round lawns contemplated their powdered façades in outlandish pools. A fantastic thing: under the shade of the trees there were women doing nothing, sitting in armchairs!

To afford whims of this kind, these people must surely be possessed of redoubtable powers. The wind, moreover, though it blew strong enough, did not indulge down here in trouble-making or blind rage as in the mountains. It tumbled the great, green masses of supple foliage with an anger that was a good imitation, but in which Marceau, who was nobody's fool, quickly recognized the precautions fine gentlemen take with each other when they play a little rough. What was more, the trees did not groan as the oaks did, they were content to purr like cats. Marceau realized that in these parts broad shoulders were not of much avail. One had to hold the trumps of that other game.

You couldn't help being delighted by everything the show-off stallions did. Their life was one of tremblings, of volts and leaps among the shining grasses. Your eye was caught by a whirl of delicate legs, of thighs, of manes, turning ceaselessly in the wind and in a frenzy of joy through the lights and shadows. Purple glints flashed from the animals' gold. Foals with their tufted hair still clinging went tangling their heads with grasshoppers and their hooves with yarn among the rocking chairs and fine robes. The mares came licking them until the women's hands could touch them. In this frenetic peace there was a fascinating restfulness.

Whenever Marceau looked at Ange and saw him, he felt a restfulness like this in his heart. What in the child had made him hungry enraptured him in the adolescent. The

boy forced on one an impression of pure and frozen seren-
ity. A certain slowness of the eyes which thus gave a long
stress to their coal-black gaze made of them a thing almost
divine. He was starting to show a trace of golden down
above his lips. His cheeks were perfect ovals, slightly pointed.
His hair, curled and fair as wood-shavings, welled above his
forehead and his temples. The skin of his face was satiny
and brown as the shell of a hazel-nut. In all this dazzling,
cheating beauty that beguiled and played with life, his chin,
solid and strong-willed, was always still. This, then, was
how Marceau had found him on his return. Just as he had
left him, he would say. For, used to the immense bulk of
Marat, Marceau saw nothing of Mon Cadet's broad
shoulders, formed in elegance, nor of his supple, free-
moving body which could indeed have been encircled by
the elder's two enormous hands.

Marceau's guile and greed quickly perceived that he had
here an incomparable high card for his game in the great
estates below.

They left one day in June, and this time Marceau cast
not one glance down from that last hillock where he had
so often stopped with Marat. They took the last slope and
plunged boldly into the promised valley. They were leading
a string of six brutes that you could have called the devil's
castoffs. If the thing was worth risking, you might as well
go the whole hog. That was Marceau's way. He had three
she-mules and three mules. Of the three she-mules two were
underhand biters, snapping like fox-traps with unpredict-
able treachery. Apart from that, they had splendid hides and
were very fat, precisely because of the fact that no one dared
to work them. The third was mad. And the worst of it was
that she succeeded at times in dissembling the fact. As for
the he-mules, the Pope himself could have made nothing

out of them. They were liars. The whole time they did nothing but pretend. You thought they were leaning with all their weight into their collars, but nothing moved until a lead-horse was hitched in front of them. So what use were the mules? Here, their necks unencumbered and the cart-prop before their noses, they strolled peacefully through the good smell of crushed thyme. When it was a case of taking a little jaunt like a millionaire they never raised objections.

They passed the great gates of several estates in this way before they could make up their minds. Then, suddenly, at first sight, Marceau led the whole lot in a driveway to a place belonging to some sort of baron who at once burst out laughing. His legs were bowed as barrel-staves in his tight breeches, and he wore a horseshoe pin stuck in his hunting cravat. He saw through the trickery in a flash, that one did. 'The only thing that interests me,' he said, 'is to see the boy ride this mad she-mule.' He spoke to Mon Cadet. 'How would that suit you?' 'Fine,' said Mon Cadet. 'You'd gallop her in the pasture?' 'Of course,' said Mon Cadet. 'Why not?' 'This isn't a circus,' said Marceau. 'We'll be on our way, child.' They reined about. And as he turned Mon Cadet took his time and as if it were nothing at all made his mule perform a little Spanish step of which he had the secret. 'Hey there!' said the baron. 'Not so fast! That boy interests me, by Jove!' 'You're not the only one,' said Marceau.

They went on a little farther to a grove of plane-trees, and while the animals drank at a fountain Marceau wound up his proud reflections by affirming aloud that they might be in luck after all.

In fact, a few hours later they had sold the whole pack. It had gone like a breeze in those domains where the women spend their afternoons in wicker armchairs following the

course of the clouds sailing above the sycamores. Mon
Cadet's beauty had been an instant sensation, like a house
on fire. He had appeared on the verges of the parks like a
boon, and had ridden up to the fine folk as if he were the god
of mules. The fact is, Marceau himself was flabbergasted.
Where the devil had the boy picked it all up? You couldn't
tell if he was punishing the brute with the bit, or if he knew
a spell to dominate it, but once up on the most refractory
of the mules he made it caper and dance and perform. That
mule lost Marceau a hundred-sou piece, for he'd bet that
four men couldn't hold it. You had to laugh. Strangest of
all, for a moment Mon Cadet even seemed to let go the
reins. Marceau was speechless. 'The glory's gone to his
head,' he said to himself. But not at all. If it was brag-
gadocio (and to be sure it was nothing else) it was in any
case backed up by a profound knowledge of what was possible, for the she-mule, though she looked from the corner
of her eye and laid back her ears, meekly continued her
volte, with such simple sweetness you would gladly have
taken her head in your arms and kissed her muzzle. 'Watch
it!' shouted Marceau to a woman who was about to do precisely that. He caught himself. 'Excuse me,' he said, 'it's
not that the animal's mean, but she's a mule, and you
always have to keep your distance.' To himself he said,
'The little bugger's making them take dynamite for kindling
sticks. Just as well I won't be around when it blows up in
their fingers.'

When all had been sold, Mon Cadet, on foot in the grass,
looked a shade awkward; but only a shade, and his extreme
youth, along with his beauty, was still an astonishing thing
to see. But one thing made Marceau swell with a new joy
so strong it took his breath and speech away. Not only
was it impossible to say that Mon Cadet was taken in by it
all (when the fine folk pressed too close he was given to

certain wild starts much esteemed in the High Hill country,
where pride always has first place), the boy even turned
repeatedly toward Marceau and looked at him lovingly, as
if to say, 'Are you pleased with me? Am I all right? You're
the only one I worry about!'

It was so certain, so good, that Marceau in his delight
relinquished him for a moment disdainfully to the ladies.
Until the sly creatures offered him some tidbits with orange
marmalade. Marceau at once regretted letting the joke go
so far. But only to receive an immediate confirmation of his
joy. Mon Cadet refused, curtly, rudely, more a Jason than
all the Jasons put together, and they finally made their departure, straight as two emperors. Marceau, with great
irony, treated himself to the luxury of bidding the company
farewell with a civil phrase that was, I declare, rather nobly
turned, something that pride in his recent victory had suddenly put in his head. All the same, he was uneasy.
Wouldn't the boy get a taste for it? Perhaps he was already
counting on coming down again?

As they went back up the paths to the High Hills, Marceau said, 'We'll never go there again.' But it was clear that
Mon Cadet had no more regrets than for his first pair of
breeches. He returned coolly to the high lands, happy as a
bullfinch. The fine ladies could bring on cartsful of marmalade—and go peddle it—added Marceau to himself.

In the neighbourhood of Saint-Pierre-de-la-Descente they
were caught in the evening mists. Suddenly Marceau was
worried whether the boy had enough on his back. 'Yes.'
'Wait,' said Marceau, 'don't fib, let me see.' He touched
him. Sure enough: he had nothing but his shirt over his
skin. Marceau took off his smock. 'Put that on,' he said.
'And you?' said Mon Cadet. These two little words held
an extraordinary sweetness. Marceau slipped his great
smock over the boy and tightened it about his waist with a

bit of string. Mon Cadet had a lithe little belly that Marceau could span with finger and thumb. And all the length of his chest, patting him to see if he was well-covered like that, Marceau touched his ribs and the little bird-muscles that bridged his sides, the hot hollows of his armpits and the thin cross-beams of his already quite-broad shoulders. Suddenly it pleased him so much to be touching all this that he began to laugh. Under his hands Mon Cadet made no evasive move. He smiled.

Four days after his return from the war Marceau had married Valérie Galice. She was already something of a giantess when he got her. The only virginal delicacy about her was her ankles. What you could see of her legs above them thickened horridly at once. She had had three children in three years. On the dot. She had grown abundant, and the floor boards had begun complaining softly around her when she moved. Ariane had remained as she was at the time of the adventure that earned her the nickname 'Three Gallons'. Others of her own age easily saw in her the Ariane of Pavon they had known in her blonde and radiant days. 'Not a day older,' they would say. No doubt they meant her strength and courage. In that case, yes. As for the beauty, she had a new kind which was reminiscent of the old one and consisted of a prodigious play of gesture and expression when it came to bossing. She lived in her son's home and shared the housework with Valérie. Sometimes when the women were alone in the house there would be a rumpus in the stable. Strange mules were always frightened by the howling of the wind up here. She would open the door that led from the kitchen to stable and let out a brutal command for silence. The squadron would obey at once. Then she would go on to calm them with a series of moans full of an irresistible tenderness. Her room was partitioned off in the attic just above Marceau's. Often during the night she could

be heard up there pacing interminably, barefoot, up and
down. From his bed Marceau would then call: 'Mother!'
There was the sound if her kneeling as she put her mouth
to the floor and answered: 'My son.' Then, she would go
back to bed.

Valérie lived in the calm of her own fat. Her native farm,
called Cataran, lay back in the wastelands of the region.
It was a great relief for her to live in the village with
Marceau, who had his own way in everything because he
was a Jason, but who had the secret of the Jason gentle-
ness, more dominating, more irresistible than their strength.

The adventure of the two men selling mad mules in the
Rhone valley caused the stir it deserved around these parts.
For us it was a great joke—we have nothing to amuse us
but our pride. A good chance to realize once again what
we're worth; without which there's really nothing in life to
keep you going.

Marceau never lost a chance to tell the story. He'd settle
down in the café of the Hotel of the West (now kept by one
Violette to whom Ariane had sold out) and people never
tired of hearing it and making him go into every last detail
so they wouldn't miss a crumb of it.

He would make Mon Cadet sit down beside him. He
made it very clear that it was Mon Cadet who had done it
all. As he talked and drew everyone's attention to the boy
he would put his arm around his shoulders and draw him
close. He told of the trick they'd played on the baron who
thought he was smart as the Pope's mustard; he told about
all the fuss the fine ladies had made; in short, he took enormous pleasure in the telling, in seeing that everyone was
looking at Mon Cadet, and in drawing Mon Cadet close to
him.

He liked putting his arm around Mon Cadet's shoulders.
It had quickly grown to a habit with him. He had acquired

another habit: on Sundays, when Mon Cadet changed his
clothes before the fireplace, Marceau would come and plant
himself in front of him to watch. That was a world to see!
Arms, legs, chest, hips, everything! Marceau would go and
lock the door so that Valérie couldn't come in. 'And wait
out there,' he would tell her. 'The house isn't afire.' Mon
Cadet was smooth as a spindle. From belly to shoulders he
broadened upwards with just a faint cross-hatching at the
ribs, and here, whenever he moved his arms, shone faint
glimmers of green in the pink skin. Then the Sunday shirt
would cover everything.

In early autumn they brought in the fodder. After that
you had to wash from head to foot. A cauldron of water
was heated. Valérie washed Ariane. Seen from the front,
Ariane admittedly had breasts as withered as bunches of
dried grapes, and she hid them in her crossed arms; but her
back, despite her sixty-two years, was young and smooth.
You could still see those lithe, branching muscles that had
been half the beauty of the girl from Pavon. When she was
clean, Ariane excused herself, as usual, for not being able
to render the same service to her daughter-in-law. 'My son
touches you,' she said, 'and it wouldn't be fitting for me to
go touching you too.' Well and good, but she didn't need
to repeat it every year.

Valérie called Marceau. He came to wash her. He rubbed,
hard. Valérie began to whinny like a mare. He had to
whack her on the buttocks to make her realize it was all
over. 'You might get to like it,' he told her.

Marceau called Mon Cadet. He made him climb in the
tub, took the sponge of birch leaves and said, 'I'm going
to curry your ribs for you, just you wait.' He was astonished
to experience a terrible satisfaction before even touching
his body, just in coming near it with his hand. For some
time now he had wanted to touch this body. It was the first

time he had ever restrained himself from something he
wanted to do. As soon as he began washing his brother
with the sponge of leaves he was aware of an unheard-of
pleasure. His Jason blood, accustomed to indulge its pride,
always took its pleasures violently; but he had never had
this release, this feeling of a victory greater than all the
others. Mon Cadet, when he was clean, proposed helping
him. He refused, and sent him out of the room. He was
drunk from being appeased by a body other than his own.

Before the final winter closing there were still a few fairs
that they called poor fairs, at Lachau and in the communes
of the valley. All they were good for was stocking up on
axes and pruning-hooks. They were strictly fairs for the
edge-tool trade. No livestock was bought or sold. Winter
was coming, and who would be so stupid as to burden himself with useless mouths to feed? For months on end the
stock in the stable would eat without working. Marceau
was never one to put himself out for nothing. As a rule he
stayed quietly at home where it was warm. That year, how-
ever, he hankered to go and have a look. 'Just to have a
look,' he said. 'And what do you expect to see?' demanded
Valérie. 'My own pleasure,' said Marceau.

In reality, the pleasure of seeing Mon Cadet on his mule,
breathing puffs of white into the already frosty morning.
And so they made their way through woods where the mists
tore in shreds on the black branches. They talked of this
and that, perhaps of the sudden flight of a grouse, or a
touch of the cold north wind that suddenly unfurled great,
tumultuous banners of black clouds above their heads. Or
they were silent, glad to be together and, above all, alone.
This solitude was above all else the most important thing.
At home there was always something to be done for this

one or that one, and Marceau for some time now had instinctively found a thousand pleasures every day just in
watching Mon Cadet and thinking that he, Jason, was the
only one to have such a younger brother. In the midst of
that he had to listen to the others. or at least hear them.
Wasn't it better to ride peaceably this way side by side,
and when neither of them spoke to have the time for once
to watch Mon Cadet's body weave gently on his mule like
a prowling serpent? The only noises were the footsteps of
the mules, the rustling of dry leaves on the oak branches,
the whistling of blackbirds, the regular call of the lead-
crows at the head of their black squadrons as they crossed
the sky. Here, of course, these interruptions were welcome;
you could talk about them together. One would shout to the
other to point out the green and blue flash of plovers flying
in tadpole-shaped clusters across the trellis of naked
branches. The slightest thing of the day was a thing in common. This was truly the place it was best to be.

At the insignificant little fair in Saint-Charles-de-la-
Descente—the one they called the dumb-fair, for instead
of being full of shouting barkers like the summer fairs it
huddled mutely in the late November chill—Marceau per-
formed a miracle: he succeeded in selling the mule Gas-
pard. A real prize, that one. The whole summer they'd
dragged him around the countryside with no success. But
here, Marceau sold him to a fellow called Bellini, a Lom-
bard living in these parts for the last thirty years. It took
some finesse. Marceau had said to himself, 'If I sell, it'll be
only natural for us to go out like this in wintertime, Mon
Cadet and I.' That was what made him find the finesse he
required, and even when the sale was made he had some
left over. Not that Marceau needed any excuse to give
Valérie, no, by God, not on your life, that would be the
day. Nor one for Mon Cadet, for that matter. Well, for him,

now, perhaps. . . . In any case, when the mule was sold and
Bellini had shelled out, he felt easier in his mind. This was
better than sitting half-asleep before the fire. The facts
spoke for themselves.

Thus they went through the winter without being separated long from each other. As far as that went, they were
only separated—in a manner of speaking—at home. Mon
Cadet sat at table beside Marceau and slept in his soundless
room beside Marceau's. And they broke through to summer; then, then they were forever underway!—left and
right, north and south, leading their herds through forests
that had put on their heavy leaves and begun to smell of
elders and clematis.

Mon Cadet throve on it as much as Marceau. He was
happy as a dormouse; seeming, amid all these cavalcades,
as indolent as an animal purring in some sheltered, sunny
corner.

Little by little his face took on a tan in which his eyes
shone out with a light that was extraordinarily brilliant. He
grew harder, and began to adopt Marceau's taciturn, con-
temptuous air, disdaining the world. He never laughed
except when he looked at his elder brother, but when he did
—then it was with a fine, wide flash of white teeth.

This went on for three or four years, and there was no
reason why it shouldn't have gone on forever had it not
been for a curséd call-up that arrived one fine morning with
a bang. Really, no one up here ever thinks about these
things until they've snapped over your leg like a fox-trap
and its too late to pull out. It has so little to do with everything we have up here together! So little that conscripts
have been known to do stupid things, very stupid things,
such as once in '21 or thereabouts when the three that were
selected hanged themselves, very tidily, from the same tree:

the oak at the elbow of the road that goes down to Saint-Charles. It's not that they're afraid; what is there to be afraid of? Just that the idea upsets them. Oh, there's a fine, pure air up here, and the land down below when you look at it seems so lush!

As soon as the notice came Marceau thought at once of the oak at the elbow of the road. He went with Mon Cadet to Lachau where the medical was held. On the way back they both, of course, had a skinful of wine, and Marceau found some transparent pretext for avoiding the famous oak tree as they entered the village. Marceau mounted watch during the whole month that followed. Then, one morning, the postman brought marching orders. They stated that the said Ange Jason was to report to Briançon, Hautes Alpes, the barracks of Aurelles, to join the 159th Alpine Infantry Regiment. The said Ange Jason, Marceau repeated. They were a strange lot to be sure, the people that wrote that paper. Wasn't Marat enough for them? If they want another one why don't they take me back? Ange! They could go f . . . themselves! What had this 159th Regiment of Alpine Infantry to do with all the rides the two had still before them, stirrup to stirrup, through the forest?

They left three days early. They had to take the train at Eguiyans-Orpierre. That alone was a three-day ride through the barren mountains. The train came at three; they'd both been pacing the platform since noon, already dizzied by the twelve houses, all new and modern, built on the other side of the tracks, inhabited by people accustomed to the heavy traffic of the national highway which could be heard out there behind, adding its roar of cars and lorries to that of the trains. They had left their two mounts in the garage of the Hotel Moderne. Marcel looked far to the west towards the soaring, blue breastwork behind which the High Hill

country began, where he had lived in peace before they
came along to bother him with their damned nonsense.

But all at once, when the train was announced and the
station burst into a chattering of little bells, the Jason blood
coursed two or three times around at an outlandish rate.
'Come with me,' said Marceau. 'Wait, let this train go, we'll
catch the next one. Come along, you'll see why.' He had
grown clear-headed, solid as a rock, equal to arguing the
case with the president of the Republic—for whom, by the
way, he didn't give a damn. And he was also not impressed
—oh, not at all!—by that row of a dozen modern houses
and the modern railway. About as modern as butter my arse.
Ange would see, indeed : he'd made up his mind at five to
three, he'd got the whole of Orpierre interested in his story;
at the stroke of six he had sold his two saddle-mules for
seven thousand francs apiece, one to the owner of a tile-
works—that was fair enough—but the other (and this was
the Jason miracle) to a green-grocer! What in Gods name
would he do with it? The grocer himself was wondering,
his seven bank-notes of a thousand francs lined up in front
of him, and he wiggling his ears to wake himself up, still not
believing it.

They were both on the ten o'clock train for Briançon.
The carriage they boarded was empty. 'Lie down,' said
Marceau. As for himself, he remained sitting in a corner,
never stirring, and his lap was a pillow for Mon Cadet
the whole night long.

Nothing would have worked out if Mon Cadet himself
had not been up to the mark. Marceau had taken a room
at the Hotel des Alpes near the Pignerol gate. He had not
only brought along his decisive mood from Orpierre, he
had refined it, made it more exact, ready for any circum-
stances at any moment. He had bought a rich new suit, and
stuck out his lower lip in a pout that tolerated no resistance.

Wherever he went, he opened doors with a great sweep of the arm that bent them back against the frame. On the threshold he would pause a tiny fraction of a second too long, six foot four and almost as broad as he was tall, capped at his summit by a fine Bolivar felt that shaded his eyes and turned up on either side above his temples like sliced water curling from the flanks of a ship. He had registered as a mule wholesaler. He immediately pulled off two or three deals, small but spectacular. A week later Savournin Charmasson, an official mule-jobber, very prosperous, who was contractor for the supply of army pack-mules, made a point of encountering him in the Café du Commerce. The following day Marceau went off to the parade-square where Mon Cadet, along with the recruits, was being initiated into the mysteries of the right-turn. During the break Marceau ostentatiously laid his great, corduroy arm about his brother's shoulders. He had him point out and name the little lieutenant who was slapping his leggings with his swagger-stick, as well as the adjutant and two or three sergeants. He was even interested in the corporal. 'It's going to work,' he said, when the whistle called Mon Cadet away. He crossed the parade-square with great dignity, almost cutting through the files, letting himself be seen like the nose in the middle of a face. He had put on his pout. He saluted no one, and went back into town by the Pigernol gate.

At the hotel he asked for pen, paper and ink. He wrote to Valérie; put twenty-four thousand-franc notes on the table near him; called for a candle and sealing-wax; took a brand-new seal from his watch-fob and with great show made a pretty little registered letter which thus, like a good shotgun, fired off two charges: one barrel for Valérie who, touched in one of her soft spots, would say Amen, and the other barrel for the innkeeper of the Hotel des Alpes, who

stood flabbergasted beyond the crack of the door and even
forgot to wipe his hands on his apron.

All this was nothing. And Marceau knew it: he had to
do with a powerful adversary. The handsome face, the stal-
wart carriage and those tender adolescent shoulders that he
had pressed, trembling, on the parade-square were not of
much use now. But Ange was a Jason from head to foot.
Never think that Marceau loved him just for prunes. Ange,
for his part, had instinctively known how to take a leaf
from the monster's own book. And what a monster! From
the very start he had begun at once to navigate among the
sergeants, the adjutants, the lieutenants, with his mule-
tamer's merciless ease. All the more lightly because a
strange thing had happened which neither Ange nor Marceau was in a position to realize, and this was that when
you saw Ange alone like this he gave an impression of irresistible strength. If anyone had told Marceau he would have
been greatly astonished. He himself, at bottom, beneath his
mule-dealer's self assurance and his Bolivar hat, dissembled
a nameless terror at the thought of Mon Cadet, a thing so
gentle and beautiful, lost in that camp where it was impossible—for the moment—to come to his support. It was
this terror that gave Marceau his tactical genius and drove
him to perform the necessary miracles. One morning, at the
hour when the machine-gun and pack mules were groomed,
a flaming new Marceau, decked out with hat, watch-chain,
cane, fob, cigars, with his vast shoulders which he made as
wide as possible at the very summit of his height, as if he
were about to glide like an eagle, Marceau made his entrance into the stable at the barracks of Aurelles, accompanied by the veterinary inspector-major. Ange dropped his
curry-comb at the sight. And whatever the headaches of the
laborious scheming that had got him this far, Marceau was
repaid, more than repaid, by the bewildered look of love

and admiration he at once received from Mon Cadet. But
Marceau didn't allow himself to be thrown by his joy. He
stuck out his lower lip and began inspecting the animals.
He spoke to the veterinary inspector-major as an equal to
a friend. There was no mystery about it, except for the
troopers. The veterinary major had three daughters and a
household to keep up. In the course of buying remounts and
filling out the mule formation he managed to pick up the
odd little payoff with the back of his hand. Marceau bought
outright a dozen mules that were impossible to sell—she-
devils, full of boiling vinegar, a pack of hotheads, which he
managed to quiet on the spot with a roar that almost made
the major himself stand to attention. As they came to rapid
agreement in a corner of the stable over the shady part of
the transaction, the major began to think that this man
might be able to take care of a much bigger operation. That
was the core of the matter. That was what Marceau had had
in mind. Since the previous day, he and Savournin Charmasson (with whom he had more or less gone into business)
knew that the 14th Corps neeeded complete replacements
for pack and mounted machine-gun mules for sixteen battalions. This was what Marceau, after four anisettes con-
sumed over the sergeant-major's files, finally obtained for
himself and his partner. He couldn't go it alone, too big an
advance was needed. But this wasn't what was bothering
Marceau. That could be seen from the reckless way he
dickered. The major and the quill-pusher couldn't get over
it. The point he was trying to reach was the following:

'Have you got a certain Ange Jason here?'

'Could be.'

'Don't bother looking, he's here. He's my brother. He was
in the stable just now.'

'Why didn't you say so?'

'I'm saying it now.'

B

And this was why he was saying it: he was to take charge of finding mules for sixteen battalions, so much had been agreed upon, and they'd be beauties, real little ladies. He would search all through Devoluy, Champsaur, Valgaudemar and Tonnerre de Dieu. But! He'd have liked to take his brother with him. Wasn't there any way of 'detailing' him? He was very pleased with this word which he had been holding carefully in a corner of his mouth since the day before. Remembered from the trenches. Very useful. 'They're enough to make you laugh, these brutes,' thought the major. 'If that's all he wants I'll detail him the Pope.' In the twinkling of an eye twenty great sheets were prepared, there and then, were signed and countersigned, they sent for Mon Cadet who was still standing petrified downstairs beside his grooming bucket, and they hadn't blown the supper-call when Marceau and Mon Cadet left the camp on the heels of the inspector-major, who received a present-arms from the guard-house watch.

The two brothers, the wind knocked out of them, spent a silent day looking at each other.

After that began a year of wandering and riding through the great, blue mountains. A hundred times Savournin Charmasson cursed the day when he went in with this damned, incomprehensible giant. What on earth was he thinking about? You couldn't get it into his head that there was no need to exert himself, the worst kind of carrion would do. Not at all, he chose the mules as if his life depended on it. Did he think he'd get something out of it? Oh, whether he got something or not, Marceau had his own idea, and the mother of a Savournin Charmasson wasn't born yet who could make him give it up. His idea was to be indispensable, irreplaceable, untouchable, unique, and the undisputed master of a remount the like of which had never yet been seen. On condition, of course: Mon Cadet.

They let him keep him, by God, they let him keep him. They would go off free as the air for fifteen, twenty days, a month, two months. They had the whole valley accustomed to the sight of the big man in corduroy and the handsome, little blond soldier who used always to arrive together on their mules, plunging into the depths of the darkest dales, climbing the steepest slopes, visiting the villages and chalets one by one. Peaceable, easy to deal with, gay, and smart about their business; seeming, the two of them, to have a kind of happiness together which was no one else's affair, and which bothered no one else, for that matter. People liked them very much. If they had wanted, they could have made a fortune. 'Who says I'm not making one?' Marceau would say. But their own country was in the High Hills. They wondered if they shouldn't take off on a little excursion in that direction. But what for? To see the dark forests and feel the well-loved chill of their land beneath the wind? It wasn't just a few days' ride. Once there, perhaps they wouldn't have the strength to leave. Let's wait until the thing is finished, and finished properly.

There was only a year to put in, a year that was passing quickly. And Savournin Charmasson, and the inspector-major, and the valleys and the mountains were astounded by the brusque and brutal disappearance of the two men on the very day it ended. Savournin went over his accounts in vain, the major checked over his graft percentages. Everything was in order, more than in order: it was contemptuously generous. The stables of the Aurelles barracks and even at Embrun and Grenoble were full of mules sent by the Good Lord himself. Everything was in order. They didn't leave a hair that could be used against them. They had disappeared.

But not dissolved. The old suit from the High Hills was on again, and the one from Briançon was made into a saddle-roll. Marceau and Mon Cadet, on two choice mules, made their way to their own country by short stages. As they climbed through these strange mountains, not as high as their own but diabolically wild, they began to encounter beech groves and oak and to tread that violently pungent leaf-mould which exalts strong, simple feelings.

Finally, one evening, they glimpsed through the forest grill the see-saw of the great heights where they lived. They arrived at the forest's edge to see before them the whole breadth of the land, from the beeches of Gavary to Silence: the bronze valleys, the bronze forests, and the air like ice. They entered the narrow streets that hemmed the village and dismounted before their threshold just as the first star came out. In the house Valérie was tapping with her wooden spoon against the cauldron where the hogs' mash was boiling. They went inside. There it was: they had won!

Mon Cadet began to have a serious admiration for his brother. Until then he had simply gone along. Suddenly he was all flushed with pleasure when he saw Marceau's look poised on him, unable to tear itself away. This was what had made him want to please with his little accomplishments and feats, whether in breaking mules or in acquiring despite his youth a manner that was so reserved, so knowing and so cool. He had the cunning to observe and learn which gestures more than others won him his brother's look of passionate approval. These were the ones he repeated most often, but being a Jason his instinct was to make this repetition as damaging as possible by performing it with an ever-changing rhythm and fancy. His greatest misfortune would have been for the Elder not to pay him attention. But the Elder paid attention to him; he even paid attention only to him, and Mon Cadet's only care was the preparation of ways in which this grey, pensive and tender look could be drawn to him and held.

In Briançon, now, he had been up against something quite different. Jason and all that he was, during the first days in those barracks he had begun at the start to lose his footing like everyone else. Here the natural values were reversed, and a wool chevron on a sleeve was enough to make nothing of three hundred years of victory over destiny in the High Hills. The first night that he spent on his shaky cot, with the little blankets leaving gaps on every side of him, he never stopped thinking of Jason. He had suffered physically at being separated from him. It was fine that he had come this far; if he had left him at the station in Orpierre, Mon Cadet might well have got up now and gone distraught to hang himself from a branch of the first plane-tree in the courtyard. Yes, Jason was there, on the other side of the walls, in the strange city. But what would he be able to do? There were all these sergeants, and adjutants, and captains, and generals, and then more generals! Mon Cadet couldn't even lie flat on his cot; that pyramid of generals fell on his chest every time to crush him and waken him. What would Jason be able to do? It was no longer a question of the game of catching his eye; Jason was the whole world, and they had separated him from it. Jason became that gentle and terrifying thing that is more than the world, on the day that he appeared, imposing, majestic and omnipotent in the stables of the barracks at Aurelles.

On that day Marceau not only had the joy of regaining what he had lost and easily crushing underfoot this dirt composed of majors and generals which had been robbing him of his sleep for the last month, he also experienced the miracle of shining—his turn for once—before Mon Cadet. And Mon Cadet, paralyzed beside his grooming-bucket, suddenly loved above all else this master of things and of events.

The rides across the Alps for the remount had been one

long paradise. But still they'd had to wear the uniforms of
a mule-wholesaler and a detailed soldier. The High Hills
were paradise and liberty as well.

They went to Lachau, to the Autumn Fair, the biggest of
the year; the fair of the peacocks.

At that fair there are peacocks for sale. Not a hundred
thousand of them; thirty, at the most fifty. But for this sort
of thing that is a great many. It's not a question of buying
fowl; it's a question of buying contentment. All the sellers
of peacocks come from Saint-Hilaire. All the buyers come
from the High Hills. Saint-Hilaire is a land of gentle hills,
a place of caresses, full of flowers: cosmos, hollyhocks,
nasturtiums of every colour, and even sunflowers so bright
in the green of the meadows that we see them and are
dazzled by them from the very verges of the High Hills.
It's easy to see why these people are sellers of peacocks.
Needless to say that they sell them here, in our country.
Bronze-green, black and silent, apart from the roaring of
the wind. It's easy to see why this is the country of buyers
of peacocks. Not only Ariane's father, but all Ariane's
ancestors have had in their blood an irresistible passion for
peacocks. So much so that the farm they cleared and held
is called Pavon. On certain days, back in 1850, and even
now not so long ago, it's been known to happen that at the
end of certain winters that had been particularly uniform
the whole village would leave as if on a word of command
and go straight to Pavon to look at the peacocks. That
would happen at the time of year when in ordinary lands
the first flowers of spring appear. Here, nothing appears.
Very well, we force it to appear, with peacocks. At the same
time a luxury and a gesture of defiance.

And now, by God, something was simmering in Marceau's mind. In fact, he bought a peacock, to commemorate
the heart's springtime. The one he bought was of a small

breed, the ones that stay the size of a cockerel but have a fan with a more vivid sheen than the sheen of rain in sunlight. Nothing less would have been a proper adornment for the greatest happiness he had ever known. It was indescribable to what point everything was new and glowing. He could never have imagined, even at the height of his pride, that Mon Cadet could belong to him alone as he was sure he did; and he was more and more sure of it every moment.

In vain had Ange become a tall, strapping, golden fellow, the heir in his turn to Ariane's great strength and the strength of all his ancestors from Pavon; the blond hair, which he wore long, frothing in curls around his fine temples and his wide, gentian-black eyes, softened his looks so much for his brother that Marceau failed to see how the shoulders he still loved to imprison in his arm were growing hard and square. The love that had overtaken Mon Cadet in the stable of the barracks at Aurelles had never let him go. He no longer allowed himself to be showered with caresses and loving gifts as in the Rhone valley days. But often he was the first to advance and touch his brother's arm or take his hand. Out of his own pocket he had bought him one of those magnificent short-handled whips, where the grip is plaited with a bull's pizzle and the thong, over two yards long and thick at the base as the braid of a Merovingian princess, ends in a goatskin lash as fine as a snake's tail. Marceau carried it proudly in his fist. He was so adept with it that one morning he killed with a single crack a little badger that was trying blindly to make its way out of the morning mist. Marceau had given Mon Cadet a fine plaid blanket of Saint-Chaffray wool, which could easily be worn as a mantle and fell from the shoulders in folds like oil. Neither wind nor rain went through it, and it had a natural gloss that gave full play to its green and red,

even in the midst of a downpour. For Marceau, Mon Cadet
had ordered bridle-ornaments and a bit made of solid
silver from the best saddler in Lachau; and he had asked
them to add two curb-chain plaques as big as crown pieces,
on which he had had stamped in relief the duke's coronet
that surmounts the arches of the city gates. When he received
the gift Marceau made the medals shine by rubbing them on
the thighs of his corduroy trousers. 'Now, that's pretty,' he
said. You could see the coronets three yards away. 'I like
that, I really do,' he said. Mon Cadet continually felt the
gnawing of a furious hunger to be near Marceau, to leave
the least possible room between his brother and himself.
And Marceau, as in the days when he used to lift the
delicious, melting body of the five-year-old child in his
hands, clung to his fraternal passion more and more each
day. They went galloping stirrup to stirrup. At the halts
Mon Cadet would leap from his saddle and come to help
the enormous Marceau dismount. Marceau's first concern
when he was down was to straighten Mon Cadet's necker-
chief or re-settle the plaid blanket on his shoulders. Then
they hooked arms and, never letting go, went into the fairs
to do business. At the inn they never sat face to face but
always beside each other. After meals Marceau would put
his arm about Mon Cadet's shoulders and take his ease thus,
smoking his pipe. They went as equals on the rounds of
ill-famed taverns: drank together, were drunk in the same
way, and in the same way dealt with their drunkenness.
Each could hold as much as the other—another source of
mutual admiration—and they were generally the only ones
to rise from table with some semblance of steadiness. Then
they would go out, saddle their mounts, and make off suddenly together on wild gallops in the pitch dark up hill and
down dale, bellowing like two calves and waking the dogs
for a mile around. They only separated—and then only just

—at the doorways of those widows of easy virtue who sold enchantment for mountaineers in the low alleys of Lachau. On their return from Briançon Marceau had made a point of taking Mon Cadet there. He had given him a lot of good advice and then left him inside for the night without a care, having previously given a lecture to the four or five women among whom he knew Mon Cadet would have to choose. Marceau himself from time to time had the treat of a little change from Valérie in those houses, but in the morning he would come rapping on the windows with his whip; Mon Cadet would drop everything and come down, and off they would go again, the two of them, fresh and carefree, toward the High Hills.

Ariane, like a true daughter of Pavon, admired the peacock; but Mon Cadet found in his heart the proper use of the bird. He trained it to ride the mules. Behind his saddle he fixed a little leather roll to which the bird clung for dear life. In this way they took it everywhere with them on their wanderings. The peacock could stand the wildest gallop. He shared in the frenzy. He screamed for joy when he was carried off in one of the fierce, break-neck races which the two brothers always needed to cool their blood.

And often, as they rushed headlong, side by side, over the rolling, deserted plateau, the bird would spring to Mon Cadet's shoulders and suddenly open its great fan of green feathers behind the handsome, golden head.

Marceau was wild with pride.

The Races at Lachau

Marceau, called Jason the Bull, gets out of bed. It's still black night. The window is barely brighter than the wall. He walks barefoot with his great, padding stride, like a bear; the floorboards cry out one after the other. The stable beneath at once grows silent. The groaning of the floor follows his footsteps. What's there to see outside so early? His enormous shoulders block the window, there's just a slit of light above the grey boar's bristles of his hair. His cheek brushes the pane. It must have rained in the night; down in front the road is black; water glistens in the ruts. The sky looks bad. His head sinks into the enormous shoulders; his eye approaches the pane and looks up past the thick eyebrows. The sky is ugly. His heavy body breathes; the floor creaks at the same time; the little brown eye looks up at the sky.

Jason Mon Cadet lives in the very ramparts of the village. He is right by the great oak trees; their thick, gnarled branches almost touch his wall. A while ago he was wakened by a driving rain that struck at a resonant part of the forest. It was four or five hundred yards away, down in by Pierre Rousse's place. The usual rain. He got up then to start a fire under a great faggot in the chimney. Now he has fallen asleep again. The flames are dying. His bed is high, with its new springs and new mattress. The firelight touches Mon Cadet's long, blond moustache and the folded curve of his mouth; his nose, straight like his mother's; his closed eyelids with their fair, shining lashes; his golden eyebrows that can hardly be seen against the colour of his skin. He is sleeping flat on his back, his mouth closed, his arms out flat, his hands out flat, his legs out flat—he has thrown off the covers—their length pressed into the new sheets. For a month now Mon Cadet has been married to Esther from Jacomets farm. She is stretched beside him all starchily decked out for the occasion in a shift from her wedding trousseau.

The light is spreading over the whole forest. The light descends along the half-naked branches and flows from copse to copse. Birds hop among the topmost twigs of the oaks and then fly off. A dog finds a badger's scent across the road and begins to bark. A light buggy is dancing in the greasy ruts. A voice hauls back on the horse. The lowest oak branches scratch the buggy-top where the driver must be making his turn just under the ramparts to take the wide, forest road to Lachau. The voice spurs the horse. The reins crack. The trot grows swifter and slips in the mud, and the springs squeak as the animal speeds off, then the trot grows distant in the forest and fades to echoes that clatter like trotting shadows in the hidden dales under the great trees. The morning silence creaks in its solitude.

Someone is rattling the door.

'Who is it?' asks Esther.

'Me. Is Mon Cadet there?'

'Yes,' says Mon Cadet.

'Come, open up.'

The Younger Brother gets up and into his corduroy trousers and goes to the door. Esther pulls at the covers and tucks them under her chin. It's the Bull.

'What is it?' says Mon Cadet.

'The fair at Lachau.'

'You're going to the fair?' demands Esther, rigid, her covers tucked under her chin.

'Get dressed, Cadet, we're going to the fair.'

'Are you taking the four greys?'

'No, I'm not taking the four greys. What would you want to go taking mules for, the day of the horse races?'

'Do you need him?' asks Esther.

'Yes.'

'What are you going to do at this fair?'

'Nothing. Where's your wood?' asks the Bull. 'We're going to make a fire for when Esther gets up. You stay in bed, Esther, the weather's enough to make you sick. I'm going to make you a fire.'

The fire is out. Under the cinders a little worm of flame twists and untwists.

'The split wood is in the broken basket,' says the Younger.

'Because,' says Esther, 'my brother was supposed to come today.'

'Who's stopping him?'

'He wanted to see Ange.'

'He can see him another time.'

'He wants to settle about clearing stumps in the glade of the Grands Faillettes. My father's giving it to us.'

'Which brother?'

'Mathurin.'

'Isn't he big enough to clear it himself?'

'You don't expect my father to give it to us and then my brother to work it?'

'Why not! . . . Your famous wood,' says the Bull, 'is willow. You might as well try starting a fire with a wet rag.

Haven't you got a bit of oak in the place?'

'Yes, but it's not split.'

'Give it here and I'll split it.'

He takes the axe and squats in a corner over the chopping-block to pick it up and bring it to the hearth. He has shoulders as broad from one side to the other as the arc of a grain-scythe; they swell up towards the head, and the neck merges into the shoulders, and the nape of the neck is rooted directly in the shoulders by wide roots covered with thick, grey hairs, stiff as a patch of boarskin. Now he carries the block to the hearth. A patch of boarskin that covers his whole head, goes down around his ears, builds at the temples and cuts off in a straight line along two thick furrows in his low forehead. His hair is like that, it doesn't fall out, it doesn't grow, it's exactly like a wild boar's bristles. If you look at it closely the hairs even have the same fork at the tip, which gives the animal its sullen lustre. How often has he said, 'Look at them, close up!'— and you look, and they're boar's bristles. 'Touch them!'— and you touch them, and sure enough! And when the animals shed, his head looks like monk's serge; afterwards, little by little, it regains its grey colour. His eyebrows are of the same stuff. How much space is left between his eyebrows and his hair? Barely two fingers, just room for the two deep furrows—his bull-headedness— which are engraved there and never smooth away. Now he sets the oak log on the chopping-block, stands up, raises the axe (Esther holds her breath, shuts her eyes), swings down with the axe, splits the log with one blow, though he was cutting across the knots, and then, taking the axe near the blade this time with only one hand, splits the halves in halves again with a little tap.

'Are we going on business?' asks the Younger.

'No, we're going to see the races.'

'It would make more sense, after all,' says Esther, 'If Ange saw my brother about the Grands Faillettes.'

'What, you think it doesn't make sense for a mule-dealer to go to the races?'

The Bull is crouched before the hearth, stacking the fire, but he is facing the bed. His broad, flat face, its nose hidden in his boar's moustache, is turned towards Esther.

His eyes are small, and when they stare they burn like acid.

'But,' says Esther, 'Ange here isn't a mule-dealer.'

And she hasn't moved, but you can feel that she is hugging herself under the covers and burrowing out of sight in her hollow in the mattress; the covers are up making a roll before her mouth now.

'What's she saying?' demands the Bull. 'Go ahead, complain,' he says, 'and me making a fire here for you like you've never seen.'

Yes, she had probably seen the like of the fire, but he does build it well. He puts his head down, his mouth comes out from under his moustache, he blows, and the flame crackles and spreads.

'You don't understand,' says the Bull, 'that it's a very important thing to watch the races.'

He stands up, rubs his big hands on his cord trousers, goes over to the bed.

'Are you going to be long, Cadet?'

'No,' says Mon Cadet, 'I'm just looking to see if there's any soup left over.'

'There's soup all ready,' says Esther. 'You don't think you're going to eat leftover soup! I made some fresh for you. In the cupboard, on the right, behind the little jars.'

'A horse . . .' says the Bull.

And he leans on the edge of the bed.

'A horse is not a mule. But the men who watch a horse run, I can tell if they need a mule.'

The Bull's weight is pressing down the mattress. Esther is on a slope, ready to roll to the low side, and she goes stiff as a board to keep from rolling.

'Come on, find me that soup,' says the Bull, straightening up.

'In the red pot,' says Esther. 'I said on the right.'

They've hung the pot over the fire.

'You want some?'

'Yes,' says Esther, 'but then give me that blanket to put over me.'

She's going to sit up in bed. The Bull looks at her with his left eye wide open, half-closing the right, sticking one little shining lip out from beneath his moustache. It's his way of smiling.

'How is the weather?' she asks.

'Not good.'

'Rain?'

'Hard to say.'

'It rained a while ago in the forest. A little tantrum, for about five minutes.'

'It can do that and it can do a lot of other things.'

'It's a strange day.'

'Yes, it's a funny one.'

'Maybe they won't run in Lachau.'

'They always run in Lachau,' says the Bull. 'What did they teach you in school? They've run in snow. They've run in six inches of mud. They've run in the middle of a storm. When you've decided to have fun, you have fun. Did you make this soup?'

'Yes.'

'You're a jewel of a girl.'

'You like it?'

'Yes. Pour me a little more here, Mon Cadet.'

'You don't get soup like that in the inns,' says Esther.

'No, except at the Dame Blanche.'

'How are we going?' says Mon Cadet.

'Well now! I haven't got my buggy, I broke two springs the other night. Over by Pelissière the road is murder. I'm going to see if Bellini will lend me his.'

'I think he's using it. I heard a buggy turning off down below there a while ago.'

'Which way?'

'Why, to Lachau.'

'You don't say! You're sure it was a buggy?'

'Yes, for a minute I thought it was you.'

'I wouldn't go without you.'

'That's what I thought. Besides, it was a horse's trot.'

'The devil you say! So he's left already! And he's going down there!'

'I tell you, it was him for sure. He went off at a trot after the turn.'

'You're right, it could hardly be anyone else. Now, that, Mon Cadet, that's getting interesting.'

'What?'

'Bellini going to Lachau.'

'You're not going to get mixed up with that Italian, now, are you?' says Esther.

She has stretched out again under the covers. She is lying with her lovely, round face in a pillow that throws her ink-black hair curling back against her cheeks.

'Of course we're not going to get mixed up with him,' says the Bull, 'but the fact that he's gone to Lachau, that interests me. Come on, Mon Cadet, let's move.'

'Keep warm, Ange, take your heavy blanket.'

'Come on! If he's left as you say we don't want to get

too far behind. I'd thought of walking if he wouldn't lend me his buggy, but if he's left already we'll ride.'

'Take care,' says Esther.

'Nothing to be careful about, girl, we're not going to do anything. What do you think we'd do? Do you think I'd get Mon Cadet mixed up in anything?'

'I know, Marceau, I'm just saying, take care. Be sensible. Keep warm, Ange, I beg you! Take your blanket. Go slow. Don't cut through the woods. No, really, Ange, listen! Listen to me, Marceau, don't push him into doing anything foolish.'

'Don't fret, Esther,' says the Bull. 'Look, he's with me! What can happen to him?'

'Oh,' says Esther, 'I don't know, it could be anything.'

'No,' says the Bull, 'certainly not anything. We've made you a good fire, Esther. And you go eat at my house. Valérie said to me, "Tell her to come on over." And stay the afternoon there, you won't be lonesome. I think they're going to put up the pork, our mother's expecting Delphine from Lucian farm. You'll have company. So go ahead now, Esther, and don't you worry. I'll let your brother know so he doesn't make the trip from Jacomets for nothing in this weather.'

'Keep warm,' says Esther softly after the door has closed.

Every night now she lets down her thick, black hair: it falls, it slips from her hands, it lies heavy on her shoulders, it hangs there, giving off its odour of dried grass. And in the morning she takes it in her hands again, as she is doing now, and lifts it and knots it again. She loves to fuss with her hair. It is heavy, but so fine that it tangles all the time in her fingers, and just when you think you have it knotted it comes apart everywhere, like water running from a closing hand. She could never do this at Jacomets farm. She had to wear it tight. Here, it needed only two nights of freedom to find its own nature: this heavy suppleness. It's only since then, too, that it has this blue sheen that comes when she turns her head, just above her forehead where she's running her fingers through it, and under her fingers the little highlight gleams like ice; and as she turns her head the blue sheen runs over the whole orb of her hair and slips away to hide at the back of her neck. She could shiver when she thinks that she always wanted to do her hair like this, slowly, down at Jacomets farm. Father could come without a sound in his canvas shoes. He has a blue, shaven face and his cheeks are great, round bones with hollows of tight skin; across them, his mouth, which is a long, thin line of tobacco-juice. When he speaks you have no will left other than his. What she used to hear there, mornings, was father scratching away with the big razor that made so much noise. And there was nothing for it but get out of bed and start saying yes to everything. Everything. Jacomets farm is right in the heart of the forests. After the 'Grand Débat', which is the last farm, there are still six miles of twists and turns through the trees, which stand closer and closer together, sinking in the soil of greenish sand, rising against pale, sandstone cliffs, before coming to Jacomets, which is really the last farm. For, from there to the land of the next commune it's who knows how far before you come, not even to another farmhouse, but just to open fields where you can smell a human being. You hear nothing but foxes or animals clattering over the shale, and suddenly there's a hush when they've heard your footstep on the path; and sometimes the smell of you is enough, without even the rustle of your skirt, when you come back at times from the village where you'd been to fetch—always the same things—salt, sugar and tobacco. And in these parts you think you're alone, but no, even when there's not a sound, even when all is still. Especially when all is still. The

animals are crouching near you, near the place where you
pass. You go by, and they follow your footsteps as they
approach, as they pass, as they grow distant again, with
their green eyes hidden among green leaves, and green ears
pointed at the noise you make, and green nostrils that draw
in your smell and curl back over a few white teeth. So that,
at times, you see them. And then they leap, and you see in
the air a streak of yellow which falls again and cuts through
the shadow of the copses, and afterwards not the whisper
of a sound as they run from where you stand. Nothing.
Sometimes you see them and they stay where they are, not
moving, but you can clearly see their green eyes between
the green leaves. If you can hear an axe chopping, it's one of
my three brothers. If I hear a waggon on the path it's one
of my three brothers. If I hear a tree crashing through the
leaves and falling, it's father clearing new fields.

Jacomets farmhouse is in the middle of the clearing the
farm has hewn for itself in the very thick of the wood. All
around it, at the edge of the fields, the trees press so close
together—and behind them stand so many others just as
close together—that there is no more green nor leaves nor
anything you could call a tree : there is only depth and
darkness. The blocks of the buildings sit sprawling and low
in stone the colour of beeswax; not only do they cling to
the earth, they can be mistaken for it. They form a square
and, just where the road arrives, leave an arched gateway
where a waggon of hay can pass through without touching.
The road, when it leaves the woods, makes its trembling
way between two or three fields, then it goes in the gateway
and stays there in the courtyard. After that, there is no more
road.

Sometimes she used to try—she loves the feel of hair, at
school she used to touch the hair of all the other little girls
—sometimes in the afternoon she was able to try. She was

alone with Mother in all the great gloom of the four wings
of the farm, generally beside the window that was pierced
in the three-foot-thick wall; sewing; and watching the soup;
or putting up pork. Mother cares for all the animals in the
stalls and stables during the day. She is the mistress of the
farm. The ewes know no other step than hers. Alone with her
mother. And Mother goes out to look after the animals.
Then there was a chance to try doing her hair, to touch it a
little, to let it down quickly and quickly knot it up again;
and how nice that was; and towards the end of the afternoon it grows very dark in the room, perhaps you could try
leaving it a little looser, no one will see. And Mother comes
in. She blows on the fire and it's brighter. She says to me,
'Come here.' I don't know how she manages to pull my hair
so flat. She tightens it with her hard fingers.

And now, as she twists her hips into place, tightening
the laces of her skirt, and settles her slightly too-heavy
breasts in her bodice to button it, at the slightest movement
she can feel her hair hanging free behind her head. She has
her father's mouth, it goes from ear to ear, but hers, now,
hers is very full. If you want to laugh you have all you
need to do it with, you just have to find something to laugh
about. The women say, you only have to look at her to see
that she didn't get married for nothing. She'll have a family.
She does everything you have to do to get one, and she
likes doing what you have to do. If only nothing comes between her husband and Mathurin. He's her favourite of the
three brothers. And he likes her pretty well, too. And he's
jealous: that's nice. He mustn't come for nothing today. He
always thinks other people don't work hard enough. If he
suggested helping Ange it was for me that he did it. And
God forbid anything should give my father the right to say
why did you get married, now he's made this sacrifice and
given us the Grands Faillettes. But it's not just worries of

this kind; and it's really not such an awful thing for Ange to leave like that for the fair at Lachau; he was probably thinking about it ever since last night without daring to say so (does he think I don't know how men are?). There, you can hear the sound of trotting down the road. It must be them. Esther goes to the window. The really awful thing is simply these uneasy feelings that come, you don't know where from and you don't know why, in the midst of quiet times when everything's going well. How can you still an anxious feeling when there's no reason for it? Sometimes it's only the weather. Yes, there they are, down in front, turning under the oak to take the forest path to Lachau. Ange is riding the big, grey she-mule; Marceau is on the heavy work-horse; they're on their way. The elder one is waving his arms as if he wanted to massacre everybody; now he's jerking the reins and the horse doesn't know what to do, it stops, he gives it the heels, and there he goes at a trot, still waving fit to take the horns off the cattle. Stop waving your arms if you want the horse to understand anything. Ange holds his mule's reins in one hand, and his left arm hangs gracefully; one hand is all he needs; and even the skittishness, even the sideways leap it just made with all four off the ground—this animal that wasn't out of the stable for a week —even these playful cavortings with her rump sideways across the road—careful!—Ange controls all this with one hand, imperturbable, his left arm still hanging gracefully. Oh, that devil, how well he does it! And lightly with his left hand he has touched her rump, leaning back, pulling up on the reins, stopping his mount to wait for that Marceau who comes up with his everlasting arm-waving. 'Will you stop waving your arms, Marceau!' says Esther close to the window-pane. 'What are you trying to do with your arms?' They've begun trotting normally side by side down this long forest avenue that runs perfectly straight between the oaks. Now they're nothing more than two riders, down, far down.

The sun isn't rising this morning. The sun refuses to rise. What is rising on all sides, is gloom. From one minute to the next it rises higher. There's an enormous pile of it off to the east. The silence is so endless you could just now hear two hoofbeats of the riders' trot—now they're out of sight. The long, straight forest avenue is empty.

Old Delphine arrived at one in the afternoon.

'I'd given you up,' says Ariane.

'The fact is,' says Delphine, 'it takes me to be so stupid.'

'You mean you came from Lucian farm through all that?'

'I had no choice.'

'What's the weather like?'

'No weather at all.'

'When did you leave?'

'Nine o'clock. If I'd waited any longer I'd have heard them tell me to stay home. I said to myself, go while you still can.'

The women have already finished eating. Valérie is picking her teeth with the point of a knife.

'Help yourself to soup,' she says, 'that will warm you up.'

'I'm not even cold,' says Delphine. 'I'm nothing at all. Yes, I'm hungry, that yes, but apart from that I'm not wet, I'm not cold. It's not raining, its not cold out. I'll just edge in to the fire a bit, for I'm sweating more than anything, I walked fast.'

'You're still spry,' says Ariane.

'Yes, but I walked a little too fast just the same, I longed to get here.'

'What's it like outside?'

'Nothing. It's dark. You can't say it's this or that kind of weather, it's not. It's nothing, not rainy, not windy, not cold. But when I'd got past Désirade farm, I don't know, the fear took hold of me.'

'Eat your soup in peace and quiet.'

'Yes, eat. You'll sleep here tonight.'

'To be sure, night won't be long coming. It's night already. It was already night this morning.'

'They know you're here.'

'They know I'm somewhere. What's more, I haven't the legs I had when I was twenty.'

'Or even thirty.'

'Yes, or even forty, you're right.'

'Your children will be worried.'

'Get on with you, they won't worry about an old woman.'

'But they know where you are?'

'Well, and if they don't know, they'll act as if they did.'

'Yes,' says Ariane, 'our time is past.'

'But I declare,' says Delphine—she has taken off her kerchief, she has drunk a little soup juice, she's chewing a potato with the wide movements of her toothless mouth— 'you have the new daughter-in-law here today!'

'Why, yes, good-day, madame,' says Esther.

'Good-day, my girl. So you're alone today?'

'Yes, my husband's away with his brother.'

'She's not alone,' says Valérie, 'she's with us.'

'That's true,' says Delphine, 'when you come right down to it we women have no one but each other. Would you look at that, now, how dark it's getting? I'm glad to be here and not over by the Désirade like a while ago.'

'Valérie,' asks Esther, 'what can I do for you now?'

'What's there to do?' says Valérie. 'One of these minutes we'll clear off this table and put the dead pig on it. Now that Delphine's here we'll not let her waste her time.'

'Work, that's what I came for,' says Delphine. 'Is it all chopped the way I sent word to do?'

'Chopped and salted,' says Ariane.

'Salting and peppering, I'll take care of that,' says Delphine. 'Well, then, we can make the meat sausages and the little tripe ones too.'

'What you could do, Esther,' says Valérie, 'is get these children ready somehow and shove them off to school. If they stay here they'll only stuff themselves with bacon crisp and raw pork fat.'

'You may well say,' says Delphine. 'The fact is, I thought last time your Jules was going to die of it.'

'Well!' says Esther, getting him into his smock, 'and so you like pork fat, do you?'

Jules is the eldest, with his eight years. He has a great double furrow above his eyes.

The next is Maurice, then Rose and Joséphine, and Marie, the last, who is two.

'Give Marie your hands, one on each side,' says Valérie, 'Rose one hand and Maurice one hand, and you Jules, get them out of here and into school. If it's raining at five you're to put your brother and sisters in the covered playground and come and tell me. Don't come back before five.'

'And now, we've a little peace and quiet.'

The fire is blazing. The flames make the shadows shudder right to the other end of the room, as they do in the dark of night. Ariane has disappeared into the rear of the house.

'Quiet!' says Delphine. 'Who has peace and quiet? Some have and some are expecting. Those that are expecting will have, when their time comes.'

Ariane calls for someone to give her a hand. 'Esther,' she calls. Delphine crooks her finger at Valérie as if to say, come here.

'Closer. How long is she married now?' she asks, pointing back to where Esther went out, where the shadow of the flames makes its way through the open door.

'A month,' says Valérie.

'Beginning,' says Delphine.

'Did your sight tell you anything for her?' asks Valérie.

'I saw nothing,' says Delphine, 'I paid no attention to her.'

'Take care,' says Ariane in the hallway, and Esther stumbles over the legs of the kneading-trough.

They come in. They're carrying a heavy pan between them.

'The blood.'

'Come, put it here by me,' says Delphine. 'It's lovely blood.'

She looks at Ariane and winks towards Valérie.

'Valérie,' says Ariane, 'go fetch the uncut meat.'

'Now, then,' says Delphine, 'give me your hand, girl.' She takes Esther's hand. 'Open it, open it wide. Give me the heather, Ariane.' Ariane takes a twig of heather from her apron. Delphine dips it in the blood. She lets a drop of blood fall in Esther's hand. 'Close your hand, grasp your fate. Open the hand, girl, let me see.'

The pressed blood has run in the lines of the hand and makes patterns there.

Delphine turns Esther's hand towards the flames.

'That'll do,' says Delphine, 'wipe it off. No, wipe it on my apron.'

Valérie has come back with a quarter of pork.

'Now,' says Delphine, 'let's get to work. Don't let the fire go down, the fat mustn't harden. And bring the whole shooting-match here to me.'

She clears off the table and the other three go to the storage cupboard to fetch the earthen pots full of chopped meat, and the tup in which the sheep's tripes are soaking. When they return, Delphine is leaning over the pan of blood.

'Flowers?' asks Ariane.

'Flowers,' replies Delphine. Flowers, she says, as if to herself, and she traces in the air with her finger the curls and folds of the line they call flowers, the watered design of minute crystallizations floating in the blood.

She edges over to Ariane.

'Don't touch the tub of tripes,' she says. 'don't let anyone touch it. I have to be the first to lay hands on it.'

'What did you see?'

'Nothing!'

'Now then, the two of you, hands off the tripes,' says Ariane. 'Delphine says they're her affair.'

'Here, take this apron she wiped her hand on and give me another one. No, no, fold it inside so that nothing can touch the stain. Lend me a comb.'

'It's stuck behind the mirror. Help yourself.'

Delphine undoes the string that held her white hair high in a pony-tail.

She untangles her hair.

'A kerchief gets you all mussed up if you do a little walking.'

She combs it, pulls it back, smooths it out well, ties the string tight and winds her hair in a little bun as big as your fist and hard as stone. She has bared a high forehead, big ears and the nape of a neck as nervous and yellow as the neck of a plucked fowl.

'I'll just wash and I'm ready.'

They've moved the long, broad table before the fire, Valérie has covered it with an old sheet freshly washed; Ariane has turned out the earthen moulds of chopped pork. The fire lifts the smell of raw meat into the room. They are all kneading it with their hands; and Delphine comes to join them. At first they don't talk, they knead and carefully crush the fat and the lean between their fingers, then from their pleasure at this the thought of life occurs to them.

'Last Friday in October: Lachau Fair.'

'My two sons have gone there.'

'Did you know Ange was going too?'

'The older one had to go.'

'Had to go, had to go! My husband's never sold a single mule at that fair. He goes there with his hands in his pockets.'

'Ange really should have stayed home today. He was supposed to wait for my brother.'

'Which brother?'

'He doesn't have to sell. All you think about is selling. What do you lack here?'

'My brother Mathurin.'

'I lack nothing, Mama, but there are seven of us to feed, and you're one of them.'

'In his work you make money with the gab. Anybody would think you'd only been with the older one since yesterday. How often have men come here before sunup to do business, and you'd hear them down in the stable, talking and talking away? He doesn't always need the whole herd with him. Just give him a chance to talk about them, and the others will put themselves out to come and see them right here in the stable.'

'Ah yes, and in any case, my dear Valérie, men will be men. At our age, Ariane's and mine, we have to admit that we never once understood them, neither what they were thinking nor what they were doing.'

'As far as Lachau goes, there's nothing to understand. He goes there because he feels like it.'

'That, my daughter, is precisely the best reason in the world.'

'I only know I'd have liked Ange to wait for my brother.'

'The things you'd like, my girl, you have to look for them and find them all by yourself. Nobody's going to do your looking, nobody's going to do your finding.'

'Go on, give her bad advice.'

'I never gave bad advice, Ariane, and you know it.'

'My brother was to come and see Ange any minute now. They'd agreed on it.'

'Maybe he won't have come from Jacomets, with this weather the way it looks. I can't see a thing I'm doing. It seems to be getting even darker. Am I right? Ariane, have them put some kindling on the fire.'

'My brother would come in any weather, because he promised to.'

'You get on pretty well with this brother, eh, child?'

'I get on with them all, but this one's very good to me. He's the nearest. There's too much difference with the others. This one's only two years older than I am.'

'Perhaps he'll have gone to the fair as well.'

'Mother, you seem to think everybody's like my man and can't stay away from the fair.'

'Last Friday in October. Horse races.'

'I'm sure Mathurin isn't going to the races, especially because he promised to come about some work.'

'Every year I have that race dinned into my ears.'

'Your husband sells mules.'

'I know very well my husband sells mules.'

'Mama, there's more than just those that sell mules going there. This morning before Ange left I heard someone else leaving here, very early indeed.'

'Who was that?'

'Even before the peacocks began to sing.'

'The peacocks didn't sing this morning, my girl, at least the ones at Lucian didn't sing.'

'Who?'

'Bellini.'

'Old man Bellini?'

'I heard his buggy take the turn under the oaks.'

'What does that mean, Delphine, when the peacocks don't sing?'

'It means it was dark.'

'That's all it means?'

'Dark means many things.'

'Why don't you listen, Valérie, instead of talking all the time? Do you hear what the girl says? Old Bellini left before them this morning.'

'Is that why they came back to get the horse and the mule?'

'Yes, he said to Ange, in that case let's ride, we don't want to get too far behind.'

'Last night mine said he was going to borrow that same Bellini's buggy. He broke the springs on his a few nights ago.'

'And did you really think, daughter mine, that he'd go borrowing anything from Bellini?'

'I don't know, I thought maybe they'd patched it up.'

'Why? What was there between your son and him?'

'We don't know. Did he ever tell you, Valérie?'

'He never tells me anything. He's your son.'

'Come, you two, that's enough talk about son or not son. A person would think you'd never learned anything. Don't you know men are always close-mouthed?'

'You can't teach me anything, Delphine, I'm just as old as you. And I know one thing as well as you and maybe better : they're never close-mouthed about good news. It's always bad, what they keep to themselves.'

'Oh, Mama, don't tell me you're afraid of something!'

'It's not a question of being afraid, girl. I know what you're going to say, Valérie.'

'Yes, I was going to say, when she's been married ten years she'll know what she doesn't know now.'

'What she doesn't know now she'll never know. For there's no question of learning. If she has a heart now she'll have it in ten years' time.'

'I know you say I've no heart. She'll get to know the Jasons.'

'What have you got against them?'

'Nothing.'

'Just watch, the two of you, if you keep rubbing away at each other you'll start to burn.'

'Nothing, because I could tell you about it till tomorrow . . . and for you it would still be nothing.'

'Because I know my place. In my time we were taught it, once and for all. On this side are the ones who are out and about in life, and on the other side there's us, the women. You can talk all you like, but I always say, who knows what they're up against that makes them so bad-tempered? Who knows what stands in their road and makes them take all those roundabout ways, when it seems to us they're doing everything backwards? It's always easy to speak *against,* daughter. And to speak against the one who touches you nearest, the one you live with, is easiest of all. In my time, in Delphines time, we were taught to speak *for.* We were forced to speak *for.* And all our lives we made ourselves useful.'

'A Jason can only love a Jason.'

'You love whoever's worth it.'

'It's the same in every family.'

'No, Delphine!'

'Yes, Valérie, in every family there's something, and they think it's the greatest misfortune on earth. But it's only that family's misfortune.'

'What do you mean?'

'I mean, when it's real misfortune, then we fall down and die.'

'Let her be, Delphine. Isn't he good to you, Esther?'

'Yes, mother.'

'It's all very well to ask her, she's only starting. What do you expect her to say? Ask me, I've lived with it and have to go on.'

'I mean, Valérie, that real misfortune doesn't belong to a family; it doesn't belong to anyone. Nobody can claim the glory of it. If it fell on you, just to feel the wind of its coming would set you screaming so, you wouldn't know if it was yourself screaming or a wild beast. And here you are talking at your ease. Ah, that's how it is with the young and their everlasting misfortune! Wait till you know what it is.'

'Please, I beg you, don't talk any more about misfortune on a day when my Ange is off in the forest and this weather fit to stop the roads.'

'She's right, and it's only this weather that got us talking gloomy things. You know, when the weather's like this I. . . .'

'You can't have seen weather like this very often. In sixty years I've never seen the like. Look, it's like a wall outside the window. Just listen! Stop for a minute! If only the fire would be quiet too! The village is dead, you can't hear a sound; not a dog, not a goat. They must all be in the back of the houses by their fires.'

'Yes, just as I said, it's the weather, mother will tell you, if we argue it's only when the weather's bad. It's true, it must be extra gloomy today, for the work we're doing is pleasant enough. Look at those piles of meat and tripes and these pails of blood. Is there anything prettier than that? What could be nicer for us? For the four of us here?'

'Yes, it's nice to patty-cake around in meat, preparing things.'

'Yes, with spices, and salt and pepper.'

'Yes, look, you crush a pepper-corn like this and when they come to it they eat it never suspecting, and then it takes their breath away and their mouth hangs open. It makes their eyes water a good long minute before they can say a word.'

'Then they make up for it and say all the words they know.'

'Yes, but they got what we wanted them to get.'

'Preparing things for them.'

'There, put a pinch of nutmeg and a juniper-seed in the middle of it, if you want them to pay attention to you.'

'Or a clove. Sometimes that will make up their minds for them.'

'What you can't do with meat and blood!'

'Even just kneading it, nothing else!'

'I like kneading meat.'

'It was the weather, after all, that made us talk about gloomy things.'

'Perhaps there was another reason, too, that I know of.'

'What reason, Delphine?'

'You can read the future in animals' stomachs.'

'What do you mean?'

'I mean, people's future.'

'Whose, ours?'

'We haven't one of our own. Ours is with everybody else's.'

'Don't talk about the future like that; it's a frightening thing when you talk that way.'

'Fright or no fright, it's the future.'

'The whole future? Anything you like?'

'Oh, no! The whole future is there, sure enough. Once it

starts there's no call for it to stop, but if you wanted to see
it all of a piece you'd have to open every belly in the world.
There's a little in each one. When you open a rabbit's belly
you look at its bowels: you watch them steam; you see
them move. You see them, how they were knotted together
when the belly was living, and you see them move now that
death slips its hand in softly to undo the knots. All that
tells you something. But how could the future of the world
be in a rabbit's belly? And why a rabbit, you might well
ask. Yes and no. A rabbit's belly has its share of the future,
that's all. You're seeing that much at least. At least you
have that.'

'You make me afraid!'

'Hush, Esther, let her talk. What then?'

'Why, then, there's no then, that's all there is to it.'

'Yes, but if it doesn't tell you what you want to know?'

'Why, you just start wanting what it tells you.'

'How?'

'Dear girl, how can I explain? The future, just think, it's
everything. And you, what you want to know in this everything, is perhaps nothing at all, just a speck, look, like
this grain of nutmeg here. But then there's another thing
you're not thinking about—and the future's just that: the
things you dont think about—and that's what you'll see,
all written out in the rabbit's belly. Do you suppose you're
going to go on thinking about your grain of nutmeg?'

'You make me afraid, madame!'

'Here's what I mean, Valérie, perhaps you were looking
for a certain thing, but what you find makes you lose all
desire for the thing you were looking for; you mustn't ever
think you can see your way in all this the way you do on
a road at high noon. You go into it as you'd go into a cellar.
An animal's belly is like a cellar. And the very minute you
open it—just when its most important, for all of a sudden

c

you surprise death undoing the writing—that very minute the blood spreads a great darkness over the liver and the bowels.'

'Don't tell any more, you're frightening me!'

'Let her talk! What then?'

'You and your what then! Then nothing. A little bit of the future. Sometimes enough to tell more or less what's coming for you. Sometimes not enough, but enough to know that something's coming. Did you think you could read it like a newspaper? There's the smell of the belly, there's the steam. There are those knots in the guts that untie themselves as if someone were softly undoing them and you couldn't see it. But not everything is there. If you wanted to know everything you'd have to open all the bellies at once. You'd be drowned in all the bowels in the world: they'd be higher than the mountains, the smell of the future would stifle you, and how would you go finding yourself, now, in all the steam it would make?'

'You make me afraid. I'd have been better off staying alone in my house.'

'Listen, my daughters, listen to a woman that knows more than you.'

'I don't want to know, mother. I want quiet in my own mind.'

'Men's stomachs too?'

'Of course men's stomachs! Ah, what you couldn't learn if you could look in the stomachs of men! I should think you'd learn something! I think you'd learn too much.'

The door opens.

A man is on the threshold. Behind him the weather is darker than his body; his cord jacket is almost light against the forest thick with clouds.

'Is my sister here?' he says.

'Here I am!' cries Esther.

'I just came from your place. Where's your husband?'

'Come in, Mathurin, my house isn't burning.'

'I haven't time to come in.'

'He went away with his brother.'

'Went away? He said he'd wait for me.'

'Come in, Mathurin. He went away because he had something more pressing to do.'

'He broke his word to me.'

'Listen, no! Come in!'

'I don't need to come in. I need to know why he pays no more heed to me than he would to a dog.'

'He told me he'd let you know.'

'He didn't let me know.'

'He must have had no time.'

'I suppose I have lots of time!'

'We don't have to know if the men at Jacomets have time or not.'

'You talk pretty high and mighty.'

'I talk from where I am.'

'I want your son.'

'Well, make him appear.'

'I came through all this weather.'

'He went off about his work through the same weather.'

'What work?'

'I wouldn't be bothered telling you.'

'Because it wouldn't be easy.'

'Because I don't answer impudence.'

'Because the kind of work your clan. . .'

'Because I am in my own house. And I'm the mistress here. And I don't have to answer. And our clan is as good as yours. And I don't owe explanations to anybody. And we don't need anybody.'

'Then I'd like to know what my sister's doing here.'

'She's at home.'

'Then I'll leave her at home.'

He takes a step backwards.

He has already blended into the darkness as he slams the door shut violently.

'Always thinking they're stronger than the next one! Always wanting to boss each other around. Like billy-goats. Whoever put two men on this earth made a mistake. There's always one of them feels the others aren't needed. But if they think I'm an old woman, they have a think coming.'

'He's not a bad boy, mother.'

'Are you crying?'

'No, I'm not crying, maybe my eyes are watering a little, I think it's the onions.'

'There was nothing meant for you in what I said.'

'Forget the whole thing, the two of you.'

'What did he want, anyway?'

'He wanted to arrange with Ange to tear out the stumps in the clearing of the Grands Faillettes. Father's given it to us.'

'And so the master of Jacomets has wakened up to the fact that the world exists.'

'Have you something against him too, madame Delphine?'

'Nothing against him, my girl, on the contrary. We've been friends for a long time, you must have heard of it. And we're still friends, for nobody's seen or heard of him for more than thirty years. If he's given you the Grands Faillettes it means he's heaved a sigh at last, he's tired at last.'

'Tired of what?'

'Of collecting all that deserted land. Of burying himself in his desert.'

'He did it for the best.'

'Everybody acts for the best; but there's not much of the

best. But if you had to load all the worst on one waggon. . .'

'Well, all I can say is, if he's given them the Faillettes. . . the whole Faillettes?'

'Yes, the whole clearing, from Cotte-Longue to Descharmes.'

'Then Ange should have waited. It's a handsome present.'

'I must say, Valérie has never surprised me. All she'd have to do is not think about money, just once in her life. That would surprise me. Don't be angry, I'm not saying this to make you angry. It's the way you are, daughter. I'm just telling you.'

'I'm not angry, all I say is, that piece of land, cleaned up and worked, would make the biggest rye-field in the whole countryside.'

'Don't tell me about rye-fields today. Come and look out the window; it seems to me the weather's getting horrid. What worries me is, there's not a sound; and yet something's moving in and growing thicker.'

'Wipe the pane.'

'It's not steam; it's all the darkness outside.'

'Can it be the sky, now, that's hid the forest all around us? There's not a tree to be seen. Not a single tree!'

'Except the great chestnut-tree, there in the square. All by itself.'

'What's that red you can see, there, between the three branches where the leaves are gone?'

'It must be the fire from the chimney of one of the houses in front.'

'I felt it coming, on the way here this morning. Just as I reached the heights of Aurifeuille I looked and you couldn't see the wide fields at Silence, and a hundred yards farther on you could see nothing at all, right nor left.'

'It's unbelievable.'

'In all the years I've been looking out this window, it's

the first time I can't see the forest above Pinto's house. There, straight ahead of us.'

'You can hardly even see the house.'

'But look, you can see something red.'

'It's not cold, but they've all lit big fires.'

'If only my brother hasn't left alone for Jacomets!'

'The houses have turned grey, you wouldn't even know they had people in them.'

'Listen! The neighbours, now, can you hear them going up the stairs or down?'

'No.'

'Wait, listen, can't you just hear them faintly, stirring the pot?'

'No, no, not a sound. As if not a soul was there.'

'He'll be all alone in the forest if he's gone off now in a rage.'

'You can't hear them. And the animals down in the stable, you can't hear them either.'

'And nothing's moving on the square. The village is dead.'

'Let's go back to the fire.'

'He won't be able to find his way.'

'Who?'

'My brother.'

'Perhaps he didn't leave. Maybe since he was coming anyway he's taken advantage to buy salt and sugar; and tobacco.'

'It would be just like him to come for nothing but me.'

'He'll find his way all right. He's a man.'

'It's easy for you to talk, he's not one of yours.'

'Mine are at Lucian, they're no better off. Where is Lucian in all that blackness out there?'

'They have a house.'

'He has his anger. It's better than a house.'

'Never mind looking. Come and work.'

'Put some dry wood on the fire.'

'I'm thinking what you just said, Delphine.'

'What?'

'You feel too, don't you, that something's moving in and growing thicker.'

'You can see it.'

'I'm not talking about what you can see.'

'I can tell you one thing: the peacocks didn't sing this morning. Today's light had no herald.'

'Perhaps because it was dark.'

'Maybe it wasn't quite as dark as we'd like to think, my girl. Our peacocks were up and about as usual. I was out in the yard before them. They went straight to the front gate to look at what they usually start calling-to at once. Go to it, little fellows, I said, when I'd waited a moment. And they had no more colour to them than a guinea-hen. And afterwards, what do you think they did? As a rule that's the time when they show off. It's the time when they open out, and you say to yourself, just wait, they'll blow up like soap bubbles. And what do you think they did? They jumped on a saw-horse leaning by the wall and all grey and colourless, like rats, they slithered through the window of the sheep-pen and hopped down inside with the sheep. And yet the morning was there, outside.'

'I am coming nearer to something that frightens me.'

'Death, like the rest of us. But the world isn't going to stop going around just for that.'

'No, I feel something coming that's not everyone's lot.'

'To be sure, there are people like that.'

'Even if the sun had shone today, even if there'd been the brightest sunshine on earth, I'd have holed up in the back of my house. I have the feeling as if any minute I'd open my mouth to curse the day I was born.'

'Mother, you don't mean something is going to happen?'

'I don't need to know if the peacocks sang as usual or if they went in with the sheep. I've shut myself up in here and till this moment I've been able to go through the motions, getting more nervous every minute. But the more it goes on the less I dare to move or speak, even in here, for it seems as if whatever it is were coming at me as easily as if I were all alone in the middle of open fields.'

'Until now you've only had what was coming to you.'

'Until now! Let's hope what's still to come is no worse.'

'Whatever comes, you have it coming.'

'I've always been able to hear the village creak about me, against my walls, and now I hear nothing more, as if the others were afraid what might happen to me. And yet it's not often people are afraid of what might happen to others. Or if they are, it must be some trouble they're not accustomed to.'

'Don't worry, there's no trouble we're not accustomed to.'

'Just now, this minute, I saw some violent thing that made my fear swell inside me suddenly, bigger than a cat, and it leapt for my throat.'

'If you mean my brother, I can tell you, for I know him, he could hold a fearful spite for years. That he could do. But he could never do a person harm.'

'Indeed, it was your brother I meant. But to tell the truth it has nothing to do with him. It was just at the moment when we were at loggerheads. But he's not what frightened me. Though perhaps he's more of a sign than the peacock's cry. Yes, it was then, when he and I had our backs up. There are dark reasons of some kind behind my fear that began just then to burn like ice.'

'I wish I could ease you mind, mother.'

'Now she wants to ease my mind. And you were afraid just now. Because it was your brother.'

'Yes, because he's my brother, and I know him.'

'Better for me if it really had only to do with your brother, even though I knew he was the meanest man on earth. But listen: this is a thing that calls for quiet.'

'Oh, Ariane, you can listen all you like, there's no more to hear than there is in the grave. Unless it's the noise of the fire that stops us from hearing.'

'If it didn't stop us, you'd hear a real fire. I can tell you that. The one I heard just now. I'm listening hard to see if something doesn't reassure me after all. But nothing will. Not even the sound of the fire here beside us. For this one will go out, little by little, but the other one I heard, all it will do is crouch over its own embers, watching itself go out in one house after the other in the whole village, watching itself finally go out here, and there'll be no sound anywhere; everyone will be in front of his own hearth watching it. Because I'm the one it's coming at.'

'You're always the same. You think there's no one but you in the world. You always think you *are* the world.'

'So far as the thing that's coming goes, yes, I think I am the world.'

'Maybe it's a war you feel coming.'

'This is the worst day of my life. Why did I have to come here today? I'd have done better to stay home all alone in my own house.'

'Would you listen to this lamb! I do believe she's in for a share of what's waiting for me.'

'It would have been a funny thing if you didn't try to drag someone else into it with you.'

'Do I do that?'

'Everybody does it.'

'And haven't I showed you a hundred times that I can

make my own way without help, even when big things are at stake? You know my life.'

'There's a time comes when we lose our pride.'

'Nobody's talking about pride.'

'Yes, yes, when you want to bear everything alone it's always out of pride.'

'It was my nature.'

'It was your nature to be proud.'

'I really think, Delphine, that you're saying things to her that you shouldn't say.'

'No, Valérie, that's not why I left your side, that's not why I'm walking. Let her talk. I'd give ten years of my life to see clear.'

'Night has closed in completely, mother. Isn't it growing late? What time is it?'

'You think it was my nature to be proud?'

'What I thought was, that you knew it.'

'I know nothing.'

'No one ever spoke ill of you, Ariane, but what they often said about you was, that you were the very image of pride.'

'Who said that?'

'Everybody. And for a long time now nobody's said it, for it's news to no one any more.'

'Was it so plain to see?'

'I'm surprised you ask. Don't you remember your life?'

'What did I do?'

'It's true, of course you'd be the last one to realize it.'

'Come back here, mother. Stop walking up and down like that.'

'Let me be. Let me alone for a little, just so I can still hear what you have to say.'

'It's not that you did wrong, Ariane, not that.'

'I did what I did.'

'There speaks your pride again.'

'Where?'

'In what you just said.'

'No, no, what I meant was, what's done is done and there's no going back on it.'

'If it's only a question of me, I'll gladly give you my quittance, but I know what you'll say.'

'What?'

'That you don't give a fig for my quittance.'

'No.'

'Mother, don't pace back and forth as if you were in a cage.'

'You say no, but you think yes. You let that be understood.'

'No.'

'Go ahead, say what you have to say.'

'I don't think I've committed any crimes. I didn't know I was to be judged apart. It's the first I've heard of that. If we're all to be weighed and tried and sold to one side or the other when our day of judgement comes, fine, for that's what must come to everyone. But I don't see why I should be judged alive, I alone. If that's to be done, let it be done to the great sinners. But to me?'

'You ran a big house all alone.'

'That charge was given to me. I didn't ask for it.'

'But you didn't refuse.'

'How should I?'

'Like anyone else, crying, suffering, being afraid.'

'Would the burden have been taken from me?'

'No, for it was yours in any case, but you'd have been less pleased with yourself.'

'I don't like what's easy.'

'It isn't easy to put our fate to sleep. Our fate is a fearsomely jealous thing.'

'There's nothing to be jealous of.'

'It doesn't like us to put ourselves in its place.'

'But who can go against his fate?'

'No one. But the will to do it counts.'

'Very well, now say what you have to. It's as if your mouth had turned to a knife. Until now you've been cutting off little bits, too small for the cure I need. And at heart you want to talk as much as I want to listen. Come, out with it.'

'You always wanted to have the better of everybody.'

'Who else can you get the better of?'

'Never mind, I'm just saying what you did.'

'And I'm telling you what I had to do.'

'You'd have been drawn and quartered rather than be in the wrong, and that's a fact.'

'Because I was right.'

'You always had to be the strongest.'

'Because I was the strongest.'

'Oh, Ariane, no, you have to boss. You're bossiness from head to foot. Every time in your life you were mixed up in something you were always the first, the one giving orders, the owner. Do you hear, Ariane? The owner, for you did what you wanted, with everything. Can you remember any other thing but yourself, Ariane? Then, remember, think back a little, you'll see what you were owning the whole time. Do you hear, Ariane, do you hear, baby of the family, last born, owner of nothing, one girl too many, the girl who barely had the right to yawn and drop dead. Think back, count, count on your fingers; if you have fingers enough. Don't think I'm jealous. You know me: Delphine, jealous? Everybody would laugh. And you know it. I don't say this in anger, you know that too. We're alike in too many ways and we've known it too long for you to misunderstand if I sometimes use a hard word because I want a clear one.

And anyway, acre for acre, if it's a question of land we can easily look each other in the eye.'

'I know it has nothing to do with land. I'd give all the land in the world to tear loose the thing that's here and won't let me live.'

'Stop beating your breast. You haven't all the land in the world to give, and you'd be getting off too easy in any case.'

'That's just what I'm saying, but in the state I'm in you can't stop me wishing.'

'I know you'd gladly give the whole world to save yourself, yourself alone. That's what I say is wrong with you.'

'It comes down to this, you're reproaching me for doing what you all do, because I do it better. Come now, you haven't shown me anything new. Except that I may have to pay a terrible price for a life as simple as my own hand.'

'What a long day, mother! What a long day it's been! And what a long time we've been here! What time is it? It's been pitch dark for a good while now. Won't they come soon? Mother, don't stay back there not saying a word, it's all shadows now.'

'Yes, come back here, do. This came over you all of a sudden. You weren't talking about it a little while ago. I've never seen you like this. You'll end up making even me afraid. There now, come on back here by the table. There's still work to be done. Don't stay hidden there in the dark saying nothing. What are you doing there?'

'I didn't mean to hurt you, Ariane.'

'Be quiet, Delphine, hold your tongues, both of you, I've just this moment begun to understand the worst.'

'Tell us, what's wrong? Tell us!'

'Mother, come here, I beg you.'

'Leave me here alone. What can fate do to me? I'm an old woman. Make me suffer? So little flesh is not worth the trouble any more. The anvil will break with the first

hammer-blow. I wonder what I've been thinking until now.
Worrying about something that would threaten me alone?
No, I'm in no danger. It's not over my head that it's hanging. Oh, I've a deathly fear, I don't dare to speak. It seems
to me that if what I'm thinking now slipped out. . .'

'Say it. . .'

'I tell you, no. If I once let out what's stuck in my throat
I'll know the name of our misfortune.'

'Say it, then.'

'Mother!'

'Don't urge me, oh, the two of you, don't urge me to it,
above all you two. It's there. I'd only have to say one word,
no, I won't say it—oh! It almost came up in my mouth. No,
I'll not say it! Our misfortune would stand before us like a
child.'

'Tell!'

'Didn't I just speak of a child?'

'Yes, you just did. Now, then, at last you've come out of
your shadows there at the back. Come ahead, now. Come.
Why do you stop? I've never seen you like this. Why are you
looking at us like that, at Esther and me? What's wrong
with us? What is it? Tell us, don't stand there now saying
nothing. Yes, you spoke of a child. Where are mine? Where
are my babies? Esther, Delphine!'

'They're at school.'

'But it's past the time, it's pitch-dark out. What time is
it, anyway? And where are they?'

Valérie runs to the door; Esther watches her lean out.

Delphine, with a jerk of her head, questions the motionless Ariane, and Ariane replies in a low voice:

'No, not these, the others.'

The door is open, the five little children are there, sitting
on the doorstep.

'What are you doing there?'

'Nothing.'

'Why don't you come in?'

'We heard granny talking. She scared us.'

'Come now, I don't usually frighten you, and it's not the first time you've heard me talk. Come, Marie, I have a lump of sugar in my pocket.'

'You've frightened them, look at that, they won't go to you. Here, let go my skirt. Let me get the door shut. It's not nice outside. Isn't that better, now, in the house? Why don't you say something? They're afraid to stay inside. You see what you've done?'

'All I'm good for any more is to frighten them.'

'You should know that children need a peaceful house. I mean, you shouldn't talk about everything in front of them.'

'Valérie, just look how these two are rubbing against my cheek. Your little heads are all cold. Wipe your nose, Joséphine, no, not on my hair. Let me up, now, so I can take you. Valérie, now that they're on my knees give me the soup for the three girls. Come here, Rose. I'll feed them.'

'You can't open your mouth in your own family without being told to hold your tongue. Old age is good for nothing.'

'These little ones were freezing. Don't sniffle, Joséphine. Haven't you got a handkerchief?'

'I have no pocket.'

'You have no pocket. Here's my hanky, blow, don't hold your nose. One side at a time. Now the other one. Now wipe. Marie's looking at me as if she didn't know I was her aunt. You two, you know it. Now, the biggest one gets the first mouthful. Open, Rose.'

'What kind of soup is it?'

'It's split-pea soup.'

'With bread?'

'Marie gets the first bread because she's the littlest, there, and she wants to grow up like Rose. Even bigger. Is your nose at it again? Valérie, this one's caught a cold.'

'Don't worry, one of the five always has one. Now, you two, don't climb right into the fire. Were you out there long?'

'Yes.'

'Well, Jules, you're the biggest, you should have made them come in.'

'He's the one told us to sit down. He said, you're not to go in, you're to stay here.'

'I said, "Wait a little while." '

'Maurice, this time you're going to eat all your pea soup, never mind making excuses and don't wait till it gets cold. That's all you get to eat, and if it gets cold you eat it cold, understand?'

'What are you after in there with your hand, Marie? What's your mouth looking for there in my bodice? No, I haven't any milk! Look, Valérie, how she's after me!'

'She'd rather nurse than eat soup.'

'I haven't any milk, little one, it's no use looking.'

'Why have you no milk?'

'Only mamas have milk.'

'Show her.'

'What do you want me to show her, Rose?'

'Show her your titties, to see if you have any milk.'

'Take care, Esther, if you give her the end and she gets angry she could bite.'

'Oh, no, don't bite, Marie. You see, there isn't any. Oh! She's pumping for all she's worth. Now, that's enough. I'm going to put it away now. No, there's none. I have no milk.

I haven't any now, when I have I'll give you some.'

'Put it away, Esther, the boys are looking.'

'Oh, they have no eyes for that yet.'

'Before you're old you imagine you'll have one or two joys left in life. There's not a one, not a single one. All your life you do what you have to do to grow old, and when you're there you realize you did all you had to do to get like that—to become nothing at all. If a person dies at forty everyone's sorry for him; if he goes on to seventy they think that's fine. And he's unhappier than if he were dead. When you're dead at least you no longer see, or know, or speak. You mind your own business, you've no call to mind other people's. What must be must be; you don't have to worry about it. But if you grow old among a family you have to go on doing everything; you're like a jackass trying to knit socks. Oh, and youth is every bit as stupid. Is it all worth the trouble to be born?'

'What's that you're saying, mother?'

'And you, Delphine, you should rest now while they feed the children.'

'I'd rather work. But one thing, now it's night we don't have to worry if it's getting darker than it should be. There now, things aren't as bad as they seem.'

'Yes, perhaps it's all a kind of play, like lambs trying to stamp on each other's toes.'

'You know, Valérie, what I'd really like is a little something to drink.'

'What would you like, Delphine?'

'If you have any white brandy give me some in a big glass.'

'Help yourself.'

'Pour it for me, my hands are all meat. Pour away. Go on, so there's something in the glass.'

'Why, you drink it like a man. It seems to do you good. You're all perked up.'

'Yes, it's good for the old. It kills this kernel of chill that sits all the time in your body like an almond. Ariane, come, have a little drop with me.'

'Oh, you know, I mostly drink when I go out in the cold.'

'Well! It seems to me, after all you've said, we might as well just be outside. Have a drop.'

'Oh, very well, on second thoughts. At our age it's surely better than eating.'

'And what's for these little ones here, after their pea-soup?'

'Go to the cupboard and get some butter and make them a piece of bread each. And have one yourself, Esther.'

'I'm not hungry, my stomach's all nerves, I'd rather cry than laugh if it weren't for these three, here. Would you look at them eat!'

'You know, you're right, Delphine, this is our bottled bread. Give me another drop. For old women like us this bottle takes the place of a heart.'

'Well, don't go using your heart as if it was your hand or your arm or something else you use all the time. It's not the same thing, mama, so watch your step. If you want to live long don't go too heavy on the heart. That looks to me like another good glassful.'

'You mind your own business. I've told you before, you'll never strangle on a heart the size of yours. Women like you go to sleep on this stuff. And women like us, it wakes us up, so never you mind.'

'Not so loud, Marie's just fallen asleep on me, and I think the others are going to drop with their mouths full.'

'It's not my place to begrudge you your own son's liquor.'

'Yes, let him give me this much more than he does, if it's only this. Let him give me heart with this drink that he made himself. Let him give me something to help me put up with him.'

'I do believe, Delphine, it wasn't such a good idea of yours, asking for a drink.'

'It may not seem good to you, but it was just what I needed. You're well packed with fat to cover your chest. What we have there is thin as paper, and when the wind blows wrong there's no warmth beneath.'

'You young ones have no idea.'

'We know more than you think. It's always the same. You think you're the only ones in the world. It's easy to say that other people have no troubles.'

'Then take a drink yourself.'

'The thing is, we have to go on making the soup, whatever happens. And we have to make the beds for everybody. And we haven't time to howl with one paw in the air like a dog that's been caught in a trap. We haven't time for that. And what's more, we know all your fussing and nagging as well as we know you.'

'Shh! Valérie, look at your three daughters. They've run themselves dead-tired! Come and help.'

'Just a minute, I'll be there. Hold the little one's head. If she chokes she'll cough and wake up. We'll put these three to bed. Look out that Joséphine doesn't slip out of your arms. She sleeps like a log right from the start. I'll take her. Let her down on my knees, now. Shove that Rosette over this way, I'll take her too, I can carry them both. Hold up Marie's head. If the bigger ones wake up they go to sleep again at once. But that little one, if she opens her eyes she won't shut them again all night.'

'You can't manage the two together.'

'I can manage very well, just watch, with them lying like this in my arms. Your own children are never heavy. Now look at this, you two, will you tell me how we could be bothered with outlandish notions, and the children in our arms? We're going to take them upstairs. Open the door for us without making a racket, if you can still do a simple thing like that.'

'You make quite a fuss yourself.'

'She has a big mouth.'

'One thing she doesn't lack.'

'And now tell me what you're afraid of.'

'I don't dare. The two boys are still here.'

'You don't have to shout. Come over beside me. Work and talk.'

'I'd like to scream it out for the world to hear.'

'Tell me, quietly. Is it some misfortune?'

'A great misfortune.'

'You mentioned children just now, but not these. Which ones, then?'

'Mine.'

'Your men?'

'Yes. The Bull and Ange.'

'If the Bull is part of it, then it could be really bad, as you say.'

'What I feel coming will make us curse life itself.'

'Has it something to do with the Italian?'

'No.'

'You're very sure of yourself.'

'What could there be with the Italian? I don't even know if there's anything between them that could lead to killing. And what if there was! It would take more than that to make me freeze the way I'm freezing now. Feel my hands.'

'You're enough to frighten one! Here in this house you talk about killing as if it happened every day. You're a strange clan, I must say. Don't be too surprised if misfortune comes looking for you.'

'Don't be so proud. Misfortune is looking for me, but in the end it finds us all.'

'Shush, here they are.'

'And if Ange spends the night away—I don't say this so that he'll do it, but if by some bad luck he had to—you must give me little Marie. She can sleep with me.'

'The minute she's in bed her little hands curl up like shells.'

'She rubbed her hair against my mouth. You'd think it was pigeon-down.'

'Now then, you boys, in just a minute you're going to high-tail it off to the bedroom.'

'I should think! It seems so late!'

'The day passed so quickly.'

'I never saw one so long.'

'Wait. It's not finished yet.'

'Doesn't anyone know what time it is? There's no way of telling.'

'All I know is, Ange should be back by now. He knows he's left me all alone. Any anyway, it's night in Lachau, too.'

'It's never night in Lachau.'

'It's night everywhere.'

'Oh, no. It's never night in Lachau. In '05, when my youngest broke his leg, we took him by night to Cosmes to see Monsieur Gallician. We leave here: it's dark. In the forest: dark; nothing but our cart. On the peak of Mévouillon: dark. At Saint-Charles-de-la-Descente: dark. In the plain: dark. On the flat fields: dark; nothing but us, plodding away. My youngest has his leg broken in two places, and he's screaming. Albéric is leading the horse by the bridle. I'm behind the cart, crying. Dark. Everywhere we go it's dark. But just after the fork that leads to Cosmes we

come into Lachau. At that time of day not a thing is moving here. It might have been past midnight. We cross the
bridge. There were lights on in the square. Under the
arcades the Pernod Bar was open. When they hear my
youngest screaming they all come out. There were at least
fifteen waggoners, and their carts had the horses all hitched
up and wide awake under the plane-trees, at the wide place
where the roads go off in all directions. It was the time of
night when here not a soul is moving, when the horses are
asleep. Our horse was walking in his sleep. There, they were
all wide awake with their big collars and little bells on
them, and they kept making their collars ring when they
stamped or shook their heads, for there were as many flies
as there are here in broad daylight. There were lights among
the leaves of the plane-trees. The birds were all awake.
They came pecking at the horses' dirt and even the oats in
their nose-bags. Albéric almost stepped on some pigeons.
It was after midnight. It was night-time. It was the time
when nothing's moving here. Not here, nor in the forest, nor
at Mévouillon, nor at Saint-Charles-de-la-Descente. The
keeper of the Pernod Bar came out with his blue apron.
They made us stop. They asked us what had happened.
They told my youngest not to scream. They brought us
three coffees, all ready, all steaming; boiling; after midnight; without having to wait to heat it up. It was boiling
hot, all ready, after midnight. Three cups, one each. The
fire never goes out. The birds were fighting in the plane-
trees. The horses were all ready to go, all wide awake.
Everybody was wide awake. The waggoners went from one
of us to the other, from Albéric, to me, to my youngest.
They went from one to the other. They talked to me, they
talked to him, they talked to my man, to me, to my youngest. They asked my man if there was much pain, they said
Monsieur Gallician would fix that up. They told me I

should drink a good shot of white brandy, for a woman—
and the mother at that—would need a pick-me-up because
of all the fretting. They walked, they talked, they did all you
can think of for me, for Albéric, for the horse, all three
of us—and the whole time we were half asleep in spite
of everything, because we're from up here, and at that hour
not a soul's moving. Though the youngest had broken his
leg in two places and all, I tell you they forced me to take
a drink. They told us it was time to go now. That we had
only four miles to go, that the road was smooth, there'd
be no more jolting in the ruts to hurt the child. People were
coming and going the whole time in the square, tying their
horses up at the arcades, going into the Pernod Bar and
three others that were full of lights and wide open as well,
coming to look, talking to us, telling Albéric to fold a big
sack under the youngest's leg, helping to do it with their
wide-awake hands, very gently. They had said, we won't
hurt you. They didn't hurt him, not one little bit. Three of
them untied their horses and said they were coming with us.
And they went with us about their business, to keep us company as far as Cosmes. It was on their way. So that we
wouldn't be alone any more. One of them up front with his
waggon and his big lantern, and he shouted, 'Daizé!' to
warn us when the road was bad. The two others followed
us, and they came up to keep me company and talk to the
youngest, who wasn't screaming any more. We went like
that through the whole of Lachau, from top to bottom, from
the bridge to the Square of the Arcades, and then down the
street with all the stores. Some of them were still open,
harness makers selling whip thongs and straps, and rope
makers with coils of rope. It was well past the stroke of
midnight. We passed in front of a shoemaker's, and he was
hammering away under his lamp. We went on into the
street where the hotels are. Everything was open, from the

big, black carriage-door that opened into the great stables
and there at the back two or three lanterns swinging gently
from side to side and piles of hay in the lantern-light, to
the front entrance of the inn at the top of the steps, opening
into the corridor with a green plant in it. The windows all
lit up, with the dining room away inside. You could hear
the sound of spoons and forks. You could smell the beef
stew the whole length of the street. I was hungry. There was
more cooking going on than here at noon. And it was long
past midnight. There were more kitchen stoves burning that
night than there are here on a feast-day morning. I was
hungry. I was hungrier there in the night than here by daylight after a hard day's work. All along the street you could
hear the sound of plates. In the doorway of the Maltese
Cross stood the woman who kept it at the time. A big, fat
woman, getting a breath of air. Nothing would do but we'd
stop again. The waggoner keeping me company asked for a
rabbit's leg for me. The woman brought it out piping hot
with a bit of bread. Afterwards I gave the bone to my
youngest to suck. It was long after midnight. At that hour
everybody here is asleep, and nothing is moving. All the
waggoners had started rolling along behind us in this street.
They were the ones that go up-country. The carts were starting to move out of the great stable-yards, with their little
lanterns swinging high on their light-rails. There we were,
with my Albéric. We'd stopped thinking about our youngest
who had his leg broken in two places. We couldn't believe
it was night time. We couldn't imagine that it had been
night when we left up here, and everybody shut up in their
houses, no light, no nothing; then the trees of the forest and
the dark of the forest and the two of us, Albéric and I, walking alone on the road with our youngest and him with his
leg broken in two places, over those rutty roads in the dark,
alone, not seeing a thing: with me afraid and my child

screaming; the dark; and then of a sudden all these people, these carts, lights everywhere, the hotels, the kitchens, hot coffee, stew, a rabbit's leg with steam coming from it, as many men as you want to help you do whatever you like. As we were leaving the town we could hear the wheels of all the waggons rolling down. They were going along Maraîchère Street. And in that street there were more lights and more hotels lit up, stables open, shops still lighted. Well, by now it was long after the stroke of midnight. We started up the little slope to Cosmes. When I looked back I saw all Lachau below me, with all its streets and crossings as full of light as a grill on coals.

'It's never night in Lachau, my girl.'

'Yes, but that was in '05.'

'All the more so now. I've been back there maybe four times. The third time I didn't recognize anything I'd seen before. Everything had changed. I'd be going down a street saying to myself: now, it seems to me it wasn't as long as this. I got lost. Everything was growing. It used to be a place where all roads pass; and it's still a place where all roads pass. It's built just for that, there are fireplaces inside made just for that, and big kitchen stoves; and kitchens all fitted out with great copper pots. And the hotel stables, there aren't enough notaries to fill them all. It can never be night in Lachau. There can never be anything but those lights, as I say, and those doors, wide open, those people, wide awake and coming from all sides, eating, smoking, going, coming, sleeping, waking, selling at all hours; for what they have to do doesn't start in the morning and finish at night as it does for us, they're always busy at something or other that keeps them going at all hours, whether it's daytime or long after midnight. We here in our forests, we don't know anything, we're not up to much. What do we know? Wood, and land, and raising trees. What's that?

Nothing. It's only normal, that all goes on from morning to
evening, and then in the evening you go to bed and sleep.
The whole village sleeps. What do you expect it to do?
The woods, the land, the trees won't run away. They stay
where they are. You leave them tonight, you find them
again in the morning. You keep your household alive. But
man is full of works of all sorts. Down there, now, you see
them up to all kinds of things. Even if they had a house,
what would they do with it? They don't need one. They
have to fill the hours of the day, this way and that way.
Lachau is a house, it lends itself like a house as you go
through. They all come there together and rent it for the
time they're going to stay, with kitchens, stables, women,
maids, workers, clerks, servants, tables, chairs and beds.
They make use of everything. Then they go, and others
come. They go on their way. And wherever they're going
they'll find other houses to rent for a few hours, and there
again they'll have all they need: women, maids and all,
kitchens, boiling coffee at midday, at midnight, whenever
you like, it's always open. It's never night in Lachau.'

'The brandy's surely loosened your tongue.'

'Yes, and you can give me another glass of your blessed
white brandy. It has an edge that wakes you up for fair.
And so you've never been to Lachau?'

'No, I never left Jacomets farm. And none of the rest of
us ever left there. We're not the kind. And I only left the
farm to get married.'

'Your husband will take you there one day. The men here
always end up taking their wives there.'

'I'm in no hurry.'

'You will be. You'll want to go with him rather than let
him go alone.'

'Maybe he won't want to go there either. Why do you
think it will be one way with me just because it was that

way with you? You don't know how we are together, he
and I. He'd never have thought of going this morning if his
brother hadn't come to get him.'

'Lachau is the scarlet city.'

'Mother, don't you say that. I've never been out of the
High Hills, but I know that country well, for I often went
right to the peak of Buc mountain. I spent whole days there
keeping the sheep. Down below I could see Saint-Charles-
de-la-Descente, and along the whole road across the plain,
through the fields and the birch woods. I know that road as
if I'd built it myself. And I know when it passes close to the
farmhouses hidden in the elms, and I know too that at one
place it goes into a long avenue of plane-trees, and right
afterwards it's Lachau. You can see Lachau in the green of
the trees. With its ramparts and its great gate, and its steeple
and its towers. It's true, it looks all red above the green of
the trees. But it's red because the mortar is red and the
clay in that country is red, and that's the only reason.'

'If you've seen it from the top of Buc it's just as if you'd
seen beneath its skirts. It's a whore all crowned in scarlet.
Nothing more. No need to go there to know it. You can
find out as much from far as from near.'

'Oh you, you're always against everything. It's still a
lovely town. I enjoyed the few times Marceau took me with
him. He had us follow the little path that leads under the
aqueduct. The mules walked in single file through the high
reeds. You come up to the ramparts near the big city gate.
There you turn up the main road and into the town. The
streets are cool.'

'He didn't take you to the big café on the Market-Place?'

'The Thousand Pillars? Yes! One day it was cold. We
went in for a coffee in the morning, but it made my head
whirl, all those glass posts and mirrors. Marceau wanted me
to sit down. And then I said, "Who's that one, over there?"

I saw a woman. There was nobody when we came in. Marceau said to me, "Sit down, you great goose, don't you see it's yourself you're looking at? It's you, in the mirror." '

'When my second had his hernia we went a few times to Lachau. We went to Monsieur Verrier who used to come every Wednesday to the parlour of the Maltese Cross. He had made him a truss to his measure. But my second has big hips. He has two big bones. There was a spring that hurt him all the time. We were stupid to have paid a hundred and twenty francs. Oh, and once I heard the choir singing on the Square of the Arcades. It was black with people. I saw one there in the middle, thin, he was, with a little black beard. He opened his mouth, he closed it, he opened it again. They all sang together. It would grow loud enough to break your heart, then fall like the wind. A man up on the platform would make a sign with his hand and bang, it was all the women going it together; then the men, then the little voices; then the big voices, then all at once, and the arcades echoed like hallways. Then he'd make a little sign, and it grew small like a soft breeze. You could hardly hear a thing. You could hear the wind in the plane-trees. Oh, it was lovely! I was standing there against the wall. If I'd moved I would have wept. I wanted never to leave.'

'Why aren't the men back yet? It's late.'

'Well now, I really have to tell you what happened to me once. It wasn't long after we were married. I was that way with Jules, but I didn't know it yet. Marceau tells me, "Go ahead and do your shopping, I've enough to keep me busy the whole day." I hadn't much to do. Afterwards I go for a walk, but a person gets tired. I look in the store windows, but that only makes me want things. I go up and down the streets—what can you do all day? Walk up and down, stay on your feet. I was getting tired. The time was long. Finally

I go into that very same Maraîchère Street you mentioned just now, and I see a sign that says "Dancing" and I hear music. I had no notion of stopping, either. It was in the big stables of the Two Worlds Hotel. The round-topped doors were open and out front in the street there was a whole crowd of men looking inside. I'm trying to see as well. You couldn't see a thing. It was dark in there. You could hear them dancing with their feet. All you could see was a cloud of dust coming out the door. I feel somebody take me by the waist. I turn around. It was a blond man with big eyes. He makes a sign: come let's dance. He was dancing there already with his shoulders, standing still, without moving his feet, holding me, and he was laughing. I thought we were going to dance outside. I turn around and take hold of him. Oh, when you're young! Then he holds me tight, puts me in front of him, we dance, but he pushes, he pushes me, the crowd divides and little by little we move inside. I tell him, "No, let's stay out here, I have no time." He says to me, "There's always time, and besides you have to hear the music. You can't hear it out there." Oh, he was a one, not a hope of getting loose. I hardly knew what was happening. I'd no sooner grabbed him, out in the street, than he'd grabbed me and we were inside. It was full of people. We danced close together, pushed from all sides. You were hooked on arms and legs and everything that was rubbing against you, everywhere. It was black as ink until you grew used to it and I saw the big door down at the end getting farther and farther away, with the light it let in from the street. Every time I turned around I was buried deeper, with the big door far away down there growing smaller, as if I'd been carried off at high speed. But what could I do, you couldn't move in the place. I had this big blond man glued so hard to the front of me that I could feel the smallest bones in his body move, and I began to see all around me now, there wasn't room to drop a pin. I could hear the music. There was a drum that seemed to be beating on my stomach and a great box of a thing that seemed to hit me on the belly, I swear, that's exactly what I felt. And then, I don't know, some kind of cornet that tore into my ears. It was like a pointed knife that cut my ear along by the neck, all the way along. I was cold, I was hot, you couldn't breathe, I had the blond's moustache over my nose and I could see his big eye like the eye of an ox against my eye, and there far down at the back of all the darkness. . . a circle of light, no bigger than a penny: the door. (Don't forget I was at least two months gone, oh yes! for it was springtime, on towards the end of May, and I had my Jules a month before Christmas that same year.)

'Well, then my blond starts taking liberties, he starts try- ing this and that, he starts touching me. And what could I do? What could I do? I couldn't move my arms. It was no use twisting, I couldn't hide from his fingers. Believe me, he knew what he was about, that one! Oh, he'd got me into a corner, no doubt about it. I said no to him, and managed after all to make him understand that it was no, but with the music and all, what could I do? There he was, working away at me, puffing like an ox. Unless I screamed, but there were women screaming all around and I said to myself, "It's not helping them, is it?" There really are times when strange things happen to a person! And how it might all have ended, who knows, that dirty swine! But suddenly there's something going on, I don't know what. People are pushing, and I get the blond's elbow in the breast and it hurts. I shout at him, "You're hurting me." He shouts back, "I can't help that." The pushing gets rougher, the music stops. I hear men talking to each other, shouting. Then everybody's shouting and running. I didn't care a damn what it was all about, I only wanted to breathe. The blond had let me go. The blond wasn't there any more, the crowd was thinner. I was beside a woman and she was crying. And suddenly I'm in front of a clear space and I see two men fighting and rolling on the floor. You couldn't tell what they were doing. You could hear blows hitting something soft. He must have been hitting him in the face. The one on the bottom was screaming for all he was worth. He was moving his legs, then he stopped moving. The top one gets up. The other one stays stretched out. The one that's standing starts kicking him in the head with his shoe. And the woman hides her face in my belly. And I, I can still hear myself, I said to her, "It's nothing, don't worry." I felt white as a sheet. I hear something go crack. And then I see, oh yes, I see it, a police club whirling against the light of the door. I hear it strike the head of the man who was standing. He goes, "Ah!" as if he were going to sleep, and he falls. Then everybody crowds around. I say to the woman, "Let go of me." I felt sick. Everyone starts pushing for the door, and if it hadn't been for that I'd have dropped on the spot. My legs couldn't carry me any more. They pushed me right outside that way, at the same time as the one on the ground who's being carried. When we come out in the street where it's light, I see that he has no nose, no eyes, no anything left on his head, and it bobbing around like a melon of blood. I just have time to rush off to one side and I start vomiting. It wrung me out, but I vomited. I could still see that melon of blood. It made my stomach heave as if there was a hand under it.'

'Tell me, why aren't the men back yet? It's late, it's very late!'

'Oh, the fights! There's lots of those. Yes, I can tell you, Lachau is the town for fights. Whether it's the lavender growers—they're almost all Piedmontese—or the mountaineers that go down to hire out—except the shepherds—or

even our own from the High Hills—no flies on them either
—well, all that lot, if they've a chance to dust each other
off, believe me, they don't let it pass. When my oldest stuck
the scythe in his thigh we went down in the middle of summer, at three in the afternoon, and we were able to make
good time. He'd already lost at least two quarts of blood.
We'd tied it off, here, with a twisted wet rag and a cord,
with a stick put through and turned between the two. I was
in the cart, holding the stick for all I was worth. And you
didn't dare let go. You'd think the flies knew it. My hands
were black with flies. If I even made to let go for a second
to chase them the blood spurted again, quickly, stiff and
straight as a plant. Like that all the way to Lachau. You
can just see me. Finally everything was all right. At the hospital they told me, "Don't worry, madame, the worst is
over, all's well; leave him here for two days, you can take
him away the day after tomorrow." What could we do?
We were relieved, but what could we do? We had to stay
the two days. We'd left everything up in the air, all the
doors open, we'd gone just as we were. I say to Albéric:
"You go on back up." "Oh," says he, "no, I won't leave
him, I won't leave you, oh no!" You can see how right you
were when you said funny things happen to a person. It's
then that one of the little doctors dressed in white says to
me, "Send a telegram to someone to look after your
children and whatever you've left up there." And that's
what we did. We sent a telegram to my brother. Of course,
there's no trick to that.

'We stayed the two days. We had no idea. We went to the
Hotel of the Universe, in the rue de l'Ours. You can see the
two of us, we'd come away with nothing, I just had on an
old bodice and Albéric had no jacket. They said, "Do you
have any luggage?" Now I ask you, did we have any luggage! "You sleep, now," says Albéric once we're in bed,

but just try sleeping with your worries. The strange bed would have been enough, I might as well have been lying on the harrows. I heard every hour strike. I heard people come and go in the hallway. I heard people passing in the street. I heard them going to bed under our floor and over our ceiling, and right and left of me and at my head and at my feet. Servants came with jugs of water and knocked at doors. Women said, it's not hot enough, go fetch me some hot. Women threw their little shoes on the floor. Men had their shoes shined. They laughed, they shouted, they were all quiet. They were listening, I could hear them saying, "Listen, listen now!" They walked barefoot; they went to listen at the wall; they all kept quiet. There was a bed squeaking and somebody whimpering like a little dog. Laughing, and then low voices. Then the beds behind my head and on my right and my left, and men's low voices and women's low voices. And then the squeaking and knock it all apart and cry and groan, behind my head, just the other side of the wall! Now what on earth are they up to with all this groaning? You'd think it was little pups going crazy over empty teats. I was thinking about my oldest. I thought he was still under my hands and I had no more strength to hold on, and that he was going away groaning with his plant of blood growing out of his thigh, that he was emptying himself, that he was lost, that he was twisting under my hands with his blood pissing out. I was covered with it, between my fingers, all over my face, hot, sticking to everything, and me whining like a little dog; I couldn't hold on! Oh, would they shut their mouths!'

'It's late.'

'And all the night hearing and waiting and waiting. And then the morning, which finally manages to wear them out, one after the other. And one last servant went all alone down the hall and up the stairs, one, two, three flights. She

D

opened her door and closed her door. Morning. But even at
the height of summer it doesn't come quickly. Down in the
street I heard men dressed in iron going by. I thought I was
dreaming. But the next day we go out and Albéric says to
me, "Take care, don't go out alone, the harvesters are here."
Harvest was over in the plains, all the crews were going
back up to the mountains. They were in gangs of four:
three men and one woman or three men and a child. But
the woman, you'd have thought it was a she-wolf, and the
child, just meet him alone in a corner of the woods! They'd
been paid off, and this was where they divided up before
separating to go their own ways. They were in every café.
There were long tables put out beneath the plane-trees,
under the arcades, on the squares, even along the streets.
They sat around by crews from early morning on, quiet as
yet. The big bag of coins was on the table between them and
one was putting his hand in and splitting up four ways.
They had full quarts of wine before them, still corked, and
glasses that were still empty; bread that was unbroken, ham
still uncut and cheeses with the string still on. All along the
streets they were dividing up the money: under the plane-
trees, under the arcades, on the squares, even along the
streets where we passed, Albéric and I. Not too noisy, covered with scythes, reaping hooks, sickles, knives, blades
and whetstones hanging from their belts, making just that
iron noise that I'd heard when they arrived in the morning,
pulling their shares in front of them, one coin after the
other. "Wait a little, you'll see," says Albéric. They even
put tables in front of shops that were not cafés but had wine
to sell. And as soon as the tables were out the harvesters
would straddle the benches and sit down and order the
wine, the bread, the ham, and pull out the purse and start
dividing, leaning over the table with their faces like old
wolves, their straggly hair, their shifty eyes, their skinny

hands, their noise of iron. And there was nothing else the whole morning—they wouldn't let us into the hospital—nothing else but what I've just said. And I couldn't understand why Albéric didn't want me going out alone; except for the two on the Place aux Oeufs, who were squabbling more in words than anything, apart from one good blow that each of them managed to land, but they pulled them apart at once; and two others who may have gone a little farther, one with an arm torn by the slash of a knife and the blood dripping down from his fingers like five little fountains; and a few of them who were all brawling together on the corner of Maraîchère Street, and came out of it with noses like crushed mulberries; and except, I must say, for two wilder ones who went off all alone, saying not a word to a soul, to rip each others guts out with sickles in the reeds under the aqueduct where they found them towards evening, dead as you may imagine, and everything around splattered with blood and their insides strewn on the grass. At the fork of the road to Cosmes a trombone was starting to play rigadoons.

'But in the afternoon! The lady of the hotel says to me, "I hope, madame, that you're not going out." "Oh," I say to her, "certainly not, madame, and yet. . . I have my child in the hospital." "What's wrong with him?" "He stuck the scythe in his leg." "But you don't belong with that lot?" "Oh, no! We're from the High Hills, we came last night." She says, "I know, but you say he stuck a scythe-blade in his. . ." "Oh," I say to her, "we're farmers, we don't belong to these people." "It's just as well," she said, "there, listen to them!" You'd have sworn there were savages outside. She shouted to close the doors. And you should have seen them shut in a hurry. I tell you, there'd been some drinking going on! The storekeepers pulled in their displays and let down their great shutters. They have big windows that cost two arms and a leg if they're broken. They'd stayed open until the last minute to do business, but now they closed as fast as they could, except for a few that were caught with one or two gangs in the store buying cord trousers, taking their breeches off in front of everybody, or buying melons—they'd bite through the rind and spit it all out again; or the ones buying watches in the jewellers', rapping them in the flat of their hands to make them start. Then it was too late to close. "Hurry up, hurry up!" but it was no use saying it, they took their time, they laughed, they said a hundred thousand scurrilous things to Jesus Christ and his family, a hundred thousand home-truths to the storekeepers and their daughters, and a hundred thousand filthy words; and then at last they'd say, "You want us to hurry? we'll show you!" Then everything started to fly, the baskets of vegetables, the rolls of cloth, the watches and clocks and the whole shooting-match. And your grocer's wife, it didn't take long to turn her up on the counter and raise her skirts and build a cheese-wedge of crushed tomatoes between her legs and paddle her arse with dried codfish, yes, I swear it. And it was no use shouting what about my cloth, my scales, my boxes of ribbons, and all, and my windows, and my daughter—all except the money. They never touched the money, unless in special cases they threw it in your face; they'd wreck the room at the back of your shop, tear up your curtains, your carpets; they'd crack the faces of your clocks like egg-shells. They're people who have no houses, except little dark ones at the back of the mountains.

'But the sun goes down and then they start looking for trouble on all sides like so many he-goats. Albéric, who'd had the sense to stay inside, says to me, "I'm going out now." I say to him, "I'm going with you." He says to me, "You stay here. I'm bound I'll find out how the oldest's getting on, I can't stand it." "Ah," says I, "but he's my oldest too, and I can't stand it either, and anyway, what do you think I am? I can look after myself." Then he said, "All right, come along, so much the worse." As we're going out I say to him, "What do you mean by your so much the worse, do you think I'm a woman to let myself be pushed around? No!" And he says to me, "Nor I," and I see that he's taken along the big brake-handle from the cart, a club like my arm bound in iron. I'd got my back up at his "so much the worse" but I didn't have far to go to regret it. Not that they laid a hand on me, no, that would have been easier. If something happens to you, you're so excited you don't see, anger covers your eyes. But as it was, what we saw, we saw cold; it was seen from outside anger. Talk about blood! Pitiful. You said war a while ago, Ariane. This was war they were making on each other, without any reason, each one as wretched as the others. Lord, how stupid men are! You didn't see any storekeepers now, not a one, they were all hiding, closed tight, locked up. Not a soul was out, excepting only the parish constable, an old fellow, and they'd taken off his hat and dunked him two or three times in the fountain and then go dry yourself. And he'd run off to do just that. There was nobody out, but rather than not fight at all they fought with each other. You'd have thought if they couldn't fight they'd have died of hunger. Now, what misery in the world could make them tear each other apart like that, battling together like madmen over nothing at all? Especially now that their work was finished, their toiling was over, their money earned, and they had only to go back to the peace of their own houses. As you or I would have done. Unless their houses aren't worth going back to.

'I think it's the power of the blood. And yet the blood that was lying in great pools on the pavements or running deep in places between the paving stones, that blood hadn't much power in it, except for the evening flies. I think above all it was the town that was behind the fighting: all this orderly storekeeping, all the fussing about weighing things in scales and putting money in cash drawers, in front of these men who always risk everything on one throw. And then, my God, all the stink of those hotels that made my head turn the whole night with their shameless bitches, it's too much for people who in their own country do everything for a reason, as we do here. Oh, you can see, I'm making excuses for them. But there we went, and Albéric as well, through streets that we longed to be shut of. I hadn't gone thirty steps from the hotel and I started to vomit, like you, but without stopping to do it, and I wasn't even pregnant. You said a scarlet city, Ariane? Well, it was red, sure enough! What I saw was, one man sitting on the ground against a wall, his feet turned out, his arms hanging down, his mouth twice as big as a real man's mouth, all stopped with a clump of clotted blood, his eyes wide open, white as chalk. And I saw another, wounded I don't know where, doubled in two, his hands on his belly, jumping from side to side like a spring, hitting his head against the walls, falling, getting up, jumping, all alone in a corner near the town hall, spraying blood around him like a wet dog shaking himself. Then we ran, Albéric and I. And at last we were there.'

'Why aren't the men back yet? It's late! Why isn't my husband back? If the older one wants to stay in that town he could leave him, he could come back alone. Here I am waiting for him. He could come by himself. It's late already.'

'Do you think my sons would come home without each other? Do you think the elder would let his younger brother go, even to go home? Do you think the younger would leave the elder all alone, even to come home? When you're old, girl, you'll know what a family is. Of course I don't expect you to know it now, and it's only right that you think of just one man, it's natural, for he's the one that's going to give you all your own family, and all your cares. Call him, but don't expect him to answer just because you need him and because you call him. That's not the way things happen. You talked about red clay a while ago. Did you hear what they said, these two? You see the funny kind of red clay it is? You see the strange kind of red mortar? You see how your town is, now, that you saw from your mountain top, with its red ramparts above the trees? And what does it amount to, the harvesters' fight once a year? There's better than that. It would be easy if the fights were marked on the calendar. Try to count all the grudges, when you don't even know how they start, when they're small as flea-bites at the beginning: and afterwards, if they grow, it's inside, in the dark. I, now, I could smile to your face for a hundred years and want to kill you right up to the day when I can smile no more. Who can tell when the moment is to come? You? Not even I myself. Who can mark it on the calendar for me, with the day, the hour? What is that town down there? Don't ever think it's something wonderful, or anything else but what I'm going to tell you now: what it is, is a meeting place. It's the place where people look for each other and find each other. How many are looking? How many are finding? Tell me if you can whether this one is going to town to drink his coffee or for something else again? Does he know it himself? Ask him. Maybe he'll tell you he's going there to drink his coffee. And it's true. But what does he meet there? Who is this that he meets, suddenly, not expecting it? If there was no more to it than brawls in a dance hall or gangs of harvesters, you'd only have to go away when you heard the music,

or spit in the man's face when he pulled you in. You didn't
think of spitting in his face, Valérie, but you could have,
easily, and there's no mistaking what you mean by that—
if you want to be understood, eh! And blood only makes
those vomit that have a full belly. But the blood of your
son, Delphine, that blood closed your mouth instead of
opening it. How well you held that blood in! I'm sure you
held tight with all your strength. I'm sure that plant of
blood didn't grow often nor even sprout between here and
Lachau while you were holding tight with your fly-bitten
hands. It's one thing to turn away and vomit. Your own
family's blood is another thing. You haven't enough hands
to cherish it. At those times, even if you want to vomit, you
have no stomach and no mouth. Everything's busy stopping
the hole where your family's blood is running out. Your
stomach stops the hole, your mouth covers the hole, your
hands, your head, everything. You feel that something far
inside yourself is calling to every last particle of you to
come and harden over the mouth of that fountain. Blood,
my girl, oh, I tell you, all of you, blood is something! Yes,
you see them there, the blood leaving them, the life going
out of all that life is for you—that's what it is. You have
nothing else in your life: this son, these sons, one of them,
more than one, what do I know, bleeding away. You have
nothing but that in your life. If they weren't there you'd
have nothing left. And there they are in front of you, pour-
ing out their lives. There are their lives, running out in the
dust of the street. A little keg. Stop the flow, now, or all at
once it will be empty and nothing can fill it again. Ah, the
good blood! Ah, the good wine! Stop it, turn the spigot!
There they are, dying like a leaking keg; hear the hollow
groaning of the cask as it empties. Two, three times more it
gurgles, and that will be the last.

'Oh, yes, that's a strange sort of clay! Now you see a

strange, red mortar on the ground! Go try to build with
that! Try to build it together again, start over. I'm too old
now to be any good with the trowel.'

'Tell me, why don't the men come back? Is there something you're not telling me? It's not the first time they've
gone, is it? You've seen them go before? Did they always
stay so late?'

'Ariane, I know what my family's blood is, you don't
have to tell me.'

'Delphine, I know the blood of mine as well.'

'Ariane, you can't tell me anything about that. Remember how Albéric died.'

'Delphine, Albéric died in a day. I lived twenty years with
Jason. And I remember once Bellini came and told me. . .'

'I'm sorry, mother, but don't talk any more, don't say
another word, don't talk any more, any of you. It's less
than a month I've been married. My husband never left
me before today. It's hardly a month since the wedding. I
never came to your house, mother. I didn't know your
house, Valérie, I don't know your husband, Valérie, I only
know he can't live a day without my husband. And I only
know him because he danced with me the day of the wedding. I don't know any of you, don't you see? I hardly
know you at all, it's the truth—by "know" I mean live
together for a long time, please understand me, mother. I
want to do what's right, I'd like to please you. I'd like to be
your daughter as Ange is your son. I come from the forest,
I'm all alone. I've no one but my husband, I've no one but
you. And look at the first day I spend with you! Be kind,
don't frighten me. I'm afraid. Please forgive me, but I'm
worried. It's late. They've gone out. They haven't come
back. They're still not coming. It's very late. You were
talking, you didn't notice. It's very late. They should be

here. Please forgive me. I'm afraid. Excuse me, but I'm anxious for them.'

'She's right.'

'You're right. It's true. We didn't notice. The time passed as we were talking. I'm beginning to worry too. It's true, Marceau never comes back so late when he's without his mules. Jules, run over and see if there's a light at Bellini's place. If there's a light, go upstairs, rap at the door and ask him if he saw your father at the fair. And you, Maurice, go to bed.'

'Forgive me, Valérie, my fear was too much for me.'

'You did well, Esther. It's time to think about it now. I don't know if it's this strange weather, but it seems very late. There's no reason they shouldn't be here by now.'

'I know I oughtn't to worry like this. I know men have their own things to do. Oh, I know very well it's because I'm young and not used to it like you, but I do ask your pardon, really.'

'No, Esther, there's no reason why they shouldn't be here by now. They should be here.'

'I know your husband is the elder, Valérie, I know he loves his brother. I know there's no danger to Ange while he's with him.'

'Just the same, you can't say that Marceau is careful. For him the main thing is to do what he wants. When he's taken a thing into his head there's no risk would keep him from going through with it.'

'He's used to going out, Valérie, he's used to being alone on the roads at night, and it's not the first time he's been to Lachau. He's used to it.'

'Yes, it might be better if he wasn't so used to it. There are things that seem like nothing to him, but they're something after all.'

'When you're waiting you always have strange ideas.'

'A person can be here quiet, and they're out there in trouble.'

'Don't go imagining things, you two.'

'But there must be a reason why they're not back at this hour.'

'There may be a very simple reason.'

'It's not a simple reason would ease my mind, and I'm not looking for complicated reasons. Indeed, there's one very simple reason, but it wouldn't be the prettiest one.'

'You always go looking for the worst. Here's Jules!'

'Come along, quick, come in. Don't fall asleep now, there was time for that before if you'd wanted. Well, tell us. Did you see him?'

'Yes.'

'He's back, is he, already!'

'Yes.'

'What did he say to you?'

'He said I was a son of a pig.'

'What had you said to him, then?'

'I asked him if he'd seen my father.'

'What! He said that to you!'

'He picked up his shoe from the floor and threw it at me.'

'Come now, what devilry were you up to? Didn't you ask politely?'

'Yes. There was a light. I went up. I knocked at the door and went in. It was full of people. Bellini is lying in his bed. He has a cloth around his head. He has one arm all wrapped up. Marianne is washing his shoulder. They've washed a whole basin of blood from it. I asked him, "You didn't see my father?" and he shouted, "Get out of here, you son of a pig," and he threw his shoe at me.'

'Well, get off to bed with you.'
'Be quiet, I hear a horse coming.'

You have to listen closely, but perhaps in fact you can
hear it. Valérie walks softly to the door. The four women
have opened their mouths so that they can breathe without
making a sound. Softly Valérie lifts the latch and softly
opens the door. It's the footsteps of a horse. In the upper
night where the wide dome of the forest must be hidden, the
little echo of the hooves comes closer, striking from branch
to branch. There is more truth in a sound that comes
through the trees than in one that travels on the ground.
Esther has also gone silently to the door, not breathing; she
cocks her head towards the night; she looks up, she listens.
At the other side of the doorway Valérie too looks up and
listens. The horse is walking step by step up there in the
vaults of the forest, at the tips of the branches.
    'Just one.'
    'The other must be walking in the dead leaves.'
    'No, it's one horse, alone.'
    'Yes. And there's no one on its back.'
    'Or Ange is riding it. He's light as a feather.'
    The horse comes nearer. He has come down from the
treetops. He enters the village. He's gone at a walk. It's
true, it's the pace of a riderless horse. The night is swollen
with an incredible darkness. You can see nothing. You see
a wall of soot. The more you look, the more you see the
soot, the flatter the night lies against your eye. But there's
an endless silence and nothing but the horse's footsteps.
He's in the village. He's coming to the square. He's in it. He
goes past. No, he's cut across in front of the great chestnut
tree. He's going in the other street. He goes into the street.
He walks on.
    'Come here,' says Ariane. 'Close the door and listen.'

She stands with one finger in the air. Her voice was
hushed. The other two have left the doorway. Ariane makes
a sign to listen. Through the house, far back, through the
thickness of all the walls, you can hear the footsteps of
the horse, walking down there in the back.

'It's going to the stable,' says Ariane.

'But they'd have come here first.'

'If the horse is alone he'll go straight to the stable.'

The footsteps halt.

'It's there.'

Esther is about to scream.

At the rear of the house you can hear a great door opening.

'It's not alone! Somebody's opening the door.'

Esther swallows her scream: a loud scream with a deep
breath behind it, hard to swallow in silence. Her lips are
trembling.

'Somebody's with the horse. Someone opened the door.'

'Ange, he's light as a feather. He was on the horse.'

'Someone's talking. Listen! It's the elder. It's the elder's
voice.'

'He's talking to Ange.'

'No, he's talking to the horse.'

'Listen, he's not talking to the horse now. Listen what
he's saying.'

'He's talking to himself. He must have been drinking.'

You can hear a voice. It's asking questions. You can
hardly hear it; but you sense that it's asking questions in
the air. Now you hear it a little better; maybe you'll be able
to make out what it's saying down there behind all those
walls. Suddenly it's loud, you could almost make out a
word. It's interrogating the air, it's asking questions. Its
asking. It has grown soft; it goes on asking questions all

around, waiting for an answer. There's silence. Then it
starts asking again.

'He must be talking to Ange and Ange doesn't answer.'

'He's talking to his animals. He's going from one to the
other in the stable and asking them what they did the day
long without him.'

'Look, the three of you, Ariane and you two girls, if
you're worried don't stand there like sticks. Call him. Good
and loud, once and for all.'

'Hold your tongue! It's one of my sons. Listen how the
stable obeys him. The mules sang just now. He's telling
them to be quiet. They are quiet. It's my eldest. But what
has he done with his brother?'

'His brother doesn't belong to him.'

'Hold your tongue. He's coming. Hold your tongue. He's
coming here. Say nothing. Don't talk. Listen to him. Hold
your tongue.'

The footsteps approach slowly up the stairs that come
from the stable through the long interior of the house. It
is a narrow, tortuous passage that climbs through the walls.
It pierces the extraordinarily thick walls of this old house
which is a former peasant castle. The footsteps approach
through the stone walls six feet thick, built in those days
in such a way that the peasant could be sheltered from life.
The footsteps climb through the walls. The feet search for
the stair steps, go more slowly in the darkness, come nearer.
He's coming from below. All is silence. There are only the
footsteps climbing through the walls of this peasant castle.
The sound of a big hand feeling its way, rubbing against
the wall. He's there behind the door. He's breathing hard.
He feels for the slide-bolt. He opens the door. Nothing but
shadows. He comes in. He himself is a shadow.

'What have you done with Ange?'

'What's this, now, these four women here? Do I have to

start talking before I'm inside? A fine way to say good evening. You're barely in the door and they want to know this and that. What is this, a courtroom? What do you think I'm doing? What do you think I am? Do you think you can go doing whatever you like and still have people pay attention to you? Am I made of iron? And even if I am! You'd like to see everybody dance to your step.'

You can see him now in the shadows with a long burden on his shoulder. A heavy weight. Something in a long sack, something soft and heavy that hangs down on either side of his shoulder and humps his back as he carries it.

'Do you know where you are, when all's said? You're here below! That's the truth. Here below, and don't forget it with your big eyes that see nothing. And what does that mean, here below? It means that nobody's the best of the basket.'

He throws the thing to the floor where it falls full length like a sack of wet linen.

'Here, come and look: look what I've brought you. Light your lamp and look. Come along, come and scream now. What I've done with Ange, madame? I sent Mon Cadet on an errand, madame. I sent him on an errand on my behalf, madame. He's gone to the old devil. He's gone to invite the old swine. He's gone to tell him from me that I had a few words to say to him. There's the truth, he's gone to play the messenger. He's gone to represent the family in the old devil's house. We've been at war with him long enough. He's gone to tell him, let's make peace, put it there, I've had enough. You're an old bastard and so are we. We, the Jasons, we're bastards too. Come, the whole business is finished, come to our house tonight, right now, just as you are. Come and eat a good slice of roast horse.

'Here, mother, come take a look at this, will you? I see

you there at the back lighting the lamp. This is something for old Ariane.'

'I'm coming, son, I'm coming to see what you've brought. What can there still be on this earth, I wonder, for old Ariane?'

'Oh, there must be one or two feats of strength left for you on this earth. Take a look at this for a feat of strength. Have a care, you women, don't come too close, the rest of you. Don't walk in what's running. It's blood, and you'll go tracking blood all over the house.

'What did I do with Mon Cadet? Here, come and look, mother, let her come closer with her lamp.

'Mon Cadet, I sent him to Bellini's. I've made peace with Bellini. I've made peace with the world. I want no more war with anyone. That's finished. From now on I want only friends. There's nothing finer than friendship. Friendship rules the world. It's clear that what makes the best part of a man happy, is what will rule him. That's the truth. What gets obedience out of every man? Pleasure. And what's in a man? There's the head and the body. Cut off your head : see how small it is! Put your body beside it : see how big it is! How many bits of machinery it has! And how they all mesh inside there every which way, each part making the next one go. It's easy to see, if something pleases your body, what a pleasure it is for all that machinery. What's your head? Nobody knows. And what kind of machine is inside it? A brain. And what's this brain? It's a kind of white coal : it heats up. And what pleases coal? Fire. That's what pleasure is for coal : burning. Now take bossing. What does bossing do? It pleases the head. There's the pleasure of knocking down and winning. There's the pleasure of destroying and overturning. There's the pleasure of killing, and it's the same pleasure as bossing. But if you're boss once or a thousand times it's always the same. You can have fun killing fifty things, it's the same every time. You can destroy all you like, all you're doing is destroying. The effect is always the same, it never changes. And apart from bossing, what's the other thing that never changes? Fire is the other thing that never changes, apart from bossing. Once it's lit, fire is always the same. There's not an oak fire, a chestnut fire, a walnut fire, a fire for brush and a fire for coal. There's fire, one and only one. And it always does the same thing: it burns, and bossing always does the same thing: it bosses, nothing more. And fire is what gladdens the head. Why? Because fire makes light. That's the sad truth. But what is there to a man? There's the head and there's the body. And what gladdens the body? Friendship. And what does friendship do? It goes from the heart to the bowels, from the bowels to the belly, from the belly to the hands, and from the hands to the feet. And what does it bring to all those things? Fun. And what is fun? It's gladness. It's dancing. And what happens then? What happens is that friends are glad of their friendship. And what happens after that? Finally? Why, it happens that the friends go together like that through the world.

'Stand back, now, here's my old Ariane with her lamp, coming in like a wolf. Careful there, don't you step in the blood yourself. Now look at that.

'There's the four of them leaning over it like ferrets with their pointed noses. Wait now, my tabbies, my bitches, my flesh-eaters, stay where you are and keep your paws off. Let the wife of the wolf do it. She'll manage, you'll see. If anyone knows how to handle what's in there it's my old mother. Open the sack and take a look at the fine feat of strength inside. Wait, I'll help you. Hold the lamp and give me some light. And you young thing, stop wriggling around like a weasel. Is she starving, or what? You've lots of time to see what's in the sack. Keep your paws off. Look at the owl's

eyes she's making. Wait your turn. Let me do what I have
to do. You'll see when the others see.'

And there they are, glued above this thing all smeared
with blood, like hoopoes in birdlime. They can't tear themselves away. If I'd told them it was a sack of sponges with
water running out of it they'd have been chattering and
fussing around me like magpies. But it's blood, and they
hold their tongues, they wait, they look, they listen, they
don't move, they stay where they are, their heads are so
close you could put them all in one hat. It's blood: and
already they're away ahead of themselves. This is none of
their old wives' tales, it's blood. What a tale that is! The
greatest in the world! It's even the only one. Lower your
lamp, mother, give me a little light to undo the knot. There's
money to be made. No need to work. All you'd want is a
man who bleeds, and you'd show him at the fairs. Blood is
the best sideshow in the world. You could charge to see it
and they'd borrow money to come. Is it sickening? No, it's
not that. Or perhaps it is, when it starts to flow, but why?
It's because you see that life running out into the countryside, running wild in all directions. There, now, there's a
tale for you! But wait. At the start you're white as a sheet,
then all at once your eyes are as big as your face, you've
opened them that wide so as not to miss a thing. You can
see strange things in blood. Make yourself a well-spring
of blood and watch them all come running. They'll pay
whatever you ask. They'd take the bread from their own
mouths to come. Why, all I'd have to do is go shout outside,
'Come see the blood!' In five minutes the whole village will
be in here. At first they'll be timid, but they'll get over that
right away: this is something interesting. They look.
They're not timid any more. They feel better. They take
hold of their life again, they hold it tight, they tie it up, they
put a collar on it, they hold it on a leash. They hold it with

their hands, chained up like a dog. They've made it listen
to reason. There's no cause now why they shouldn't feel
easy about watching that other life, unchained, running off
into the countryside. I tell you, that's a show. Stupendous!
Blood is a real performer.

'It wasn't a one-armed man tied this knot. He tied it wet
with blood and now it's caked together. It's a good piece of
cord. Don't worry, I'm not going to cut it. I'll untie it if it
takes a hundred and seven years. Hold the lamp down. Ah!
I do believe it's starting to give.'

And you could do even better than that. Take your man
that's a bleeder and bring him up on a mountain. Make him
sit down on the rocks. Let him bleed, let his blood run till
it makes streams on all sides. Let the streams run till they
trickle down through the forests and out into the world.
Then, you'll own the world. And that's the truth. They
could see a hundred thousand good streams of drinking
water, they wouldn't move. Then comes the blood. It won't
take them five minutes to start following it back. They
won't pack a bundle, they won't leave a note, they'll just
take the time to slip a collar on their life and hold it firm
on the leash, and off they go, this one pulling the other
along, holding their lives chained to their hands like dogs.
You, up on your mountain, you'll soon see them coming.
And what will they do? They'll stand around you there,
never moving, with their dog's life on a leash beside them.
They'll look at the blood-show. Without stirring, like sleep-
ers. They're yours, all of them. Just see that enough blood
flows at first, and then that it doesn't stop flowing. You
might say, there's not enough in one man alone. That's for
you to arrange. You'll be rich enough right from the start.
Call your servants, have them bring you men and more
men. One after the other. When one has finished bleeding
you open the next. And so on.

'There, it's loose, I'll unwrap. Raise the lamp high, now. You're going to see something.'

It's not exactly a sack, it's a length of sacking wrapped around the thing that bleeds. It's heavy, but the Bull leans over, lifts up the weight and unwraps the thick covering. He discloses an enormous cut of meat from some animal. There must be at least a hundred pounds of it, and the whole animal must have weighed at least five times that much. On one side of it there is still hide. The hide is fine and smooth, glossy. It must have been brushed and washed and caressed by hand. It is still beautiful to see in the parts not smeared with blood. At the very moment when the thing is uncovered, Mon Cadet, the fair-haired, comes in. In the moment it takes him to open the door and close it again he is so blond and fair that he stands out against the night. And inside the flickering of the fire leaps towards him, surrounds and envelops him as if he were the only living creature in the house.

'Did you see Bellini?'

'Yes. He's coming. He's going to come. He's up out of bed. He's just trying to pull a jacket over his bandages and he'll be here. He's had enough too. He said to me, "Tell your brother it's basta, finished." '

'Little Ange! You're here?'

'Yes, Esther, where should I be?'

'Here, Lord save us, where I can see you!'

'Well, have a look.'

'Your hair's all wet.'

'No.'

'It wet my hand.'

'It's the mist.'

'Where were you so long?'

'And you, what were you up to?'

'Nothing.'

'Just under your eye your cheek's turned red, and that's when you tell lies.'

'No, we didn't do a thing. We stayed here waiting.'

'But that didn't stop you from talking about all the things women talk about when they're alone. That's why you turn all red now when you look at me.'

'We didn't talk about anything.'

'Four women, and they didn't say a word!'

'They talked about whatever they liked.'

'And you, of course, you're above all that, you didn't open your mouth.'

'No, Sir! Hardly once. And it's not because I'm above it, it's because I'm stupid: it's because I was thinking about you.'

'My pet said almost nothing. I wonder what it was, that almost.'

'I tell you no, idiot! I'm still not so well used to this house.'

'Perhaps we're still not so well-married, who knows?'

'I know very well we are.'

'Ah, you know, do you? And how do you know?'

'Don't play the fool, I'll scratch your eyes out.'

'Gently, now! What would I do without my eyes?'

'You'd stay with me, you'd stop running around.'

'Run around? With my own brother?'

'Running around is when you're with anybody, except me.'

'In that case, I'll soon be quite a runner.'

'Why? Are you thinking of going away again?'

'Not now, but it seems to me in my lifetime I may just have to go away with a few people other than you. In the next hundred years, by the time I'm a hundred and twenty.'

'A hundred and twenty!'

'Yes, a hundred and twenty. It seems to me by then I'll have had to do quite a little running around.'

'Then you can go this minute.'

'Wait. Just now I'd rather go to bed with you.'

'Well, I wouldn't. You can leave at once, since you say you'll have to. Go ahead, I'll sleep by myself. Go on, I'm going home to bed. Go, I know what I'm keeping with me.'

'Oh? And who are you keeping it for.'

'That's my affair.'

'It'll be lonely all by itself.'

'I'll find it playmates.'

'Oh, come now, my pet. . .'

'Aha! Pet, now I'm your pet!'

'Yes, I thought about you this afternoon, I'd sooner have been with you. If I'd done what I wanted to do this morning I'd have stayed. But I couldn't because he came to get me. I spent the whole day with you. And I wished I was here. I spent the whole afternoon longing to be with you. You say we're well-married. If I'd stayed with you this afternoon we'd have been better married still. But you lost nothing by waiting, my pet. Wait for tonight.'

'Let me go. . . not yet. Let's speak louder now or they'll wonder what we're saying. Let's go where the others are.'

'Come along over here, you two, you've time all night to talk.'

'My brother came this afternoon. And I told you he would be, he was angry.'

'We saw your brother. Marceau, didn't you tell her we'd just seen her brother?'

'I haven't said a single word since I came here. They jumped down my neck right away. Look here, my tabbies, look at that hide, would you? Isn't it pretty? Feel how soft it is to touch. Look, Valérie, here's a hide that's had more petting than mine.'

'Stay home, you pig, instead of running around, and you'll get your hide caressed as well. I haven't a hand that goes from here to Lachau and I haven't a wire arm to follow all the turns wherever you ride and then go caressing you at the other end. If you want to be treated like others, do what they do.'

'Now, wait, it was only a manner of speaking. Good Lord, if you mention petting to that one she has her skirts over her head so fast you'd think it was raining. A little modesty, Valérie, if you please.'

'But did you really see my brother?'

'Yes, I saw your brother.'

'When?'

'Now.'

'What was he doing?'

'Buying nails.'

'Ange, did you speak to him?'

'Of course I did. Marceau did the talking.'

'What did you tell him?'

'I told him everything. But above all I told him we didn't see him often enough and he should come over here for a bit and eat some roast horsemeat, that we'd all be pleased.'

'When?'

'Tonight, now, right away.'

'And what did he say?'

'He said yes. He's on his way. He's coming.'

'Is he in good humour?'

'You're damned right he's in good humour! Why shouldn't he be in good humour? He's coming here. Happy as a bullfinch. And Bellini's coming too, like another bullfinch. This is the night for bullfinches.

'We'll pull the table over to the middle and light the big lamp. We'll get a great fire going. It has to roar and it has to be big. We'll open a carboy of wine.

'And you, Valérie, with the bottom like a wheat-bin, instead of thinking about caresses you're going to take a pan a yard wide and fry this horsemeat for us. Good, thick slices. So it's tender, with all the blood in it. We have to be the masters of what happens. We have to steer our lives. And when all's said, we have to see to it that we have peace and quiet. If we don't do it ourselves, who will? As soon as you admit you have enemies, you admit that somebody can stand up to you. And where's your power then?

'Your brother's coming, with his bull neck and his square head and his jaw as big as his forehead. And Bellini, with his old hide like oak-bark, he's coming too. And we'll all eat together: the big blond there, and me, like four little finches.'

'Next time you go to Lachau drink another wine, Marceau. Whatever it is, it seems to bother your stomach. What is this horsemeat you keep talking about? And whose horse?'

'This horsemeat here, at the foot of my legs. What did you think it was? Wild boar, maybe, or wolf? A nice, sweet little boar, just gone over with the clippers, or one of those tame wolves that weigh seven or eight hundred pounds, that all the fine ladies of Lachau keep in their rooms and take on their knees to pet? That's why the hide is so soft, touch it. What do you think that hide is, anyway? You can still see where the hands touched it. Its wolf-hide, of course. Everybody knows Lachau is full of wolves. If you want wolf you go to Lachau. You say, give me a hundred pounds of wolf, and they give you a hundred pounds of wolf. Aha! But then you say, give me some wolf with a hide that's been well caressed, and then they'll pick it out for you and sometimes they'll even put perfume on it. Look at that. Look, with your big eyes. What does it tell you, this hide that's had maybe a hundred francs worth of brushes used on it?

It says, friendship; it says, kindness; it says, oh! but it's
fine to have you; it says, I'll take care of you like the apple
of my eye; it says, you're the most beautiful animal in the
world; it says, horse. There's the horse.'

'You bought horsemeat?'

'No, I slaughtered horsemeat.'

'My son, you may have started something that will lead
to a strange end.'

'No, mother, it leads nowhere, it leads us here where
we're going to have four friends around a table just now.
But I know what you mean. You've seen that it was a fine
horse. It may well have been the finest in all the valleys
down back. And I killed it. I was the one who killed it. In
the middle of the street. Everybody saw it.'

'It's true, my brother killed it. And all the tongues in
Lachau must be wagging over it now; and they won't stop
for a while.'

'Yes, I killed it. And if his owner was still alive he'd
thank me for it. But he's dead. We waited in Lachau until
he was dead. You think I've been drinking. Well, I have, a
little. But if I'm talking it's because I was stirred up by
something else. Now I can be friends with everybody. It's
finished. Bellini can go to see my customers if he wants to.
He can make the rounds under cover of night. He can go
to it in broad daylight. I won't say another word to him. I'll
tell him, "Make your place in the sun, Marceau Jason won't
stop you." If you have anything against me, whoever you
are, say it right out, don't be afraid, I'm listening. I'm peace
itself, in person. I killed a horse in the rue Maraîchère.
Almost in front of the hotel. It happened there in the crowd.
He jumped over some women he'd knocked down and I
could see him coming at me. I can still see him. He had
great, black eyes full of tears and a little steam in his nostrils. Between his rearing forefeet he had a pointed breast

like a plucked bird. I saw that he was mad. I saw that he was bare, without a bridle or bit. I said to myself, what can I do? I don't know. All in a flash. Just imagine, there he is, up in the air, and I feel as if I'd turned to lead right in front of him. I push Mon Cadet away. He falls.'

'I slipped.'

'Then, I really feel like lead. That was my rage. I hear nothing more. Silence. It seems to me that the horse is coming down again, softly, like a horse made of feathers. He's bucking. I see his arse go up behind him like a sheet in the wind. All of a sudden his great head is all I can see before my eyes. Then, I hit him. With all my strength.'

'What's the matter? You're crying.'

'Nerves. No. It's when I see myself. When I think about it. My nerves are still cramped across my chest. I turned to lead. I didn't move a step. I hit him, I stayed where I was. It was afterwards that I tried to lift one of my legs. I felt as if I was planted in the earth up to my knees. What did I do then?'

'You called to me.'

'I called to you, yes.'

'And the horse?'

'Yes, I called to you. I'd lost track of where you were.'

'I was standing behind you. I shouted, "Here I am." '

'Yes. By then I'd begin to hear noises again. They were pounding into my ears. Women screaming, and the screams of one woman. I had started hearing just as I tried to clear my leg of that weight of lead that was sucking me down into the pavement. The horse? I couldn't see a thing. The crowd was milling around. And there was no more horse. He wasn't up in the air any more. And I heard you behind me saying, "Here I am." And what did I do then?'

'Nothing. You stayed put.'

'Yes. Stayed put. A funny thing, that lead that changed

my blood just as I felt this rage explode and almost throw
me down. My arm weighed two thousand pounds.'

'I saw you hit him. I was down on the ground. When you
pushed me, I slipped. I fell to one side. I saw where you
hit. Your arm hardly moved. You hit just beside the ear;
between the ear and the forehead. I heard a scream. I said
to myself, it's trampled a child. It was the horse that had
screamed. He tossed his head as if he were balking. In that
second his feet touched the ground. For when you hit him
they were still in the air. I don't know how you did it, I
don't know if you jumped. I know I didn't see you move,
but when you hit him the horse was still in the air. His
hooves weren't touching ground. The blow pushed him to
one side. And as his hooves touched ground his legs folded
and I saw him roll. I heard his head strike the pavement.
I scrambled up, for he was about to roll on me. I heard his
belly lie down. In the second when I saw him all in a knot
in the air he was already untying himself on the ground. He
died when you hit him.'

'I only hit him once.'

'There wasn't another sound out of him. He didn't even
rattle. He stretched out. There was a minute when nobody
said a word, not even the woman.'

'And then what did we do?'

'You started bawling at the crowd like a bull-calf.'

'Yes, who had let his horse loose with no bridle? What
idiot had let this mad horse loose in the middle of the
fair? If he'd had a bridle or bit I'd have tried to stop him,
but I saw right away there was nothing to grab. He was
smooth as a drop of water all over. Just try to hang on to a
thing like that, try hanging on to oil for dear life. There
was nothing to do but what I did.'

'And that you did in a hurry.'

'But it still seems to me that I did it very slowly. It seems

to me you could have played ten games of cards. And I'd
rather have done that. What a stupid business. The horse
belonged to a man called Mornas, one of the Mornas from
the valleys. His brother-in-law runs the mill at Villefranche.
He kept this horse as if it was a holy relic. He'd coddled it
along and trained it. He'd taken it to Lachau and it won the
three races. All three. And well, with a big lead. Then they
start saying he'd come to Lachau two days early and doped
the horse's oats. He was at the Hotel de France. Of course,
at the Hotel de France they say he didn't dope the oats.
Well, whatever they say, one way or the other. . . the truth
is, he won. Mornas brings him back to the stable. And
there you had it: jealousy. Before the race the favourite
was a horse belonging to Pierrisnard. Pierrisnard comes in
the stable at the Hotel de France. "Well, I showed you,"
says Mornas. "Yes." Pierrisnard puts his hand in the manger, takes a handful of oats, smells it and says to the
others, "Here, smell this." "What?" "Go ahead, smell,"
says Mornas, "tell me what it smells of." "It smells of
brandy. You sprinkled your oats." It went on with one
word and the other word, sprinkled and not sprinkled, until
Pierrisnard says to him, "You wouldn't ride that horse now.
You wouldn't ride him bareback. You wouldn't ride him
without a saddle or bridle, nothing, with your hands in your
pockets, to show us if he's really quiet as a lamb." He goes
and says that to a man who's won three races in a row,
even if he did dope the oats. The stupidest part is that the
other one says yes. Yes. And they bring him out. Bare. And
the other one gets on his back. And away he goes. On the
fairgrounds. You can imagine, the grounds full of people.
And this silly bugger riding bareback through the crowd,
as if he were doing something great. Well, of course nobody's going to come out now it's all over and say "I did
it." There was a whole gang of them following along behind.

I know animals, and I think there were two things: first, a barker selling blankets, shouting into a loudspeaker. And second, at least two hundred bullocks that had been penned up there since morning and now felt evening coming on. The hawker was playing the fool to make people buy. That's his job. On purpose or not on purpose, it's hard to tell with a man like that. He snorts like a bull into his horn. The horse rears. What could the other silly bugger do? Without a bridle? The steers answer. Mornas throws his two arms around the horse's neck. The horse was afraid, and now he feels strangled. What does he do? He goes like this, he shakes himself. Mornas hangs on, but he's slipping, he falls on an iron picket. It goes through his belly. The horse jumps into a display booth, a red apron falls over his head. He goes mad. Everybody's shouting and upsetting each other. He gallops over them. He gallops into them. He falls in the crowd, he gets up again. By now he's a thousand times crazy with that apron hung on his head. All of a sudden the smell of blood. Two or three had been badly trampled. Then it's the steers that start bellowing all together on every side, and there's our drunken horse in the open, going raging straight ahead of him. Nine went to the hospital. One man tries to catch him. Just try it without a bit! A kick in the stomach. Next. Another tries to catch his muzzle. What are you going to hang on to? His head? And what then? A mad horse has a head like grease. You'd need steel grappling irons! He drags him. He breaks his hip. Another one. They were out of their minds! They didn't see that he was bare. The next one no more than touched him. He went flying like a cannon ball. And then, the stupidest ones of all. He'd got as far as the road to Cosmes. He was heading for the fields. There, he'd have had room. No. There were three or four of them. They stand across the road. What did they think they could do? The

horse is blocked like a jet of water in front of them. One of
the four took a front shoe in the jaw. He'll be a sight, that
one. As the horse jumped he left the paving stones full of
sparks, like coals when the poker hits.'

'And did you see all this?'

'No. I know it. And then he goes into the rue Maraîchère
galloping full speed. The street, at two in the afternoon,
with men, women and children, pressed in there like water
in a siphon!

'I struck just one blow. My hand? I don't feel a thing.
Supple as ever. I could thread a needle at one try. My arm?
Nothing. As if it had been telling bedtime stories. The
horse? With one blow he was down. I still have just a little
of that leaden feeling left. I'm quiet now. But it seems I
can't hear very well. No, not that, it's a kind of silence, and
like the sound of a stick of green wood whistling in the
fire. When you speak, it comes through that whistling.

'And what did we do then? We went back up the street,
Mon Cadet and I. From time to time I asked him, "Are
you there?" He answered, "I'm here." The crowd was
following us. There in the street was a woman with her
shoulder broken. Mon Cadet said, "You're not hurt?" I
said, "No, I'm not hurt." In the fairgrounds we saw all he'd
done. Mornas is dead. The third one that tried to stop the
horse, the one before me, he's going to die. His head's
crushed. They say a woman's going to die as well, without
counting the ones that don't count, Bellini for example,
who was trampled by the crowd as he ran along with them.
I said to Mon Cadet, "Well, what do we do now, Mon
Cadet? Come on, let's go and see him." I wanted to know
how I'd managed to kill him. We come to the place where
he'd been. He was gone. The constable was there. They
told him, "Look, that's the one." He asks me, "Was it you
killed him?" I tell him yes. He says to me, "You did a

damned good thing." Well, of course, I had. He didn't need to tell me that. I say to him, "What did you do with him?" He says to me, "I told Charlot to take him away." "Which Charlot?" "The butcher." "Aha! You aren't so slow, are you now?" "And what would you have done with him? He was healthy, wasn't he?" "By God, you can believe he was healthy. Not a speck of mould on him, that I can swear. He surely didn't smell of the sickbed." "It's all right," he says, "you've a right to joke, but the rest of you here that find it so funny, you weren't so cocky a while ago. What's more, a man is dead, it's no laughing matter." I say to him, "Don't get mad, tell me where this Charlot is, I'd like to have a look." "Charlot is over there, just across the street. Thank you very much for your good work." This Charlot let me look. He took his little knife, he cut the skin between the ear and the eye. He tried to bare the bone. He was wasting his time. The bone was in splinters. What I couldn't help looking at was the open eye of the horse. Still wet with tears, you saw it, Mon Cadet?—as if to say those things that are only in a horse's head; I know I've never been able to understand them: when they look far away, past anything you're saying to them, soothing words or whatever. Speaking of horses, another thing: this morning I sold the mule, almost against my will. For cash. That's what held me up. The money's in my jacket, Valérie.'

'Come,' says Ariane softly to Delphine, and she calls Valérie over too. 'Let's not make a fuss, but I'm not set on seeing Bellini. I'm going up to bed. Come along, Delphine. Don't say anything, Valérie. Give us some cheese and bread, we'll eat upstairs in our bed. It's better that way. What do you say, Delphine? I'll get the candle.'

And in the stairway she has stopped and leaned towards Delphine who is coming up behind her.

'You don't mind?'

'I have nothing to say, I'm not in my own house.'

'What did you mean before, when you told me, "You won't run things in heaven?" '

'I meant, pray the Good Lord the day won't come when you'll wish you were older than you are.'

'I didn't want to hurt your feelings, we're both the same age.'

'I didn't want to hurt you either. Now then, we're not hurt, neither of us.'

'You saw, it's all right about Esther's brother. The older one's going to give him a few pounds of meat. With those people from Jacomets, when you give, you're friends. And he's right about Bellini. Peace is the only thing. It's not because I don't agree that I'm going away now. But we've been fighting too long. I don't want Bellini to think everything's patched up as easily as that. Well, well, this day proves that sometimes you fear the worst and nothing happens.'

'And other times you fear nothing and everything happens.'

'No more bad humour, come along. Which side do you sleep on, by the wall?'

'No, the side where there's nothing.'

'Well, then, up we go. The old women are going to lie down and sleep.'

'Oh, you flatter yourself, Ariane! Sleep! Try is the word!'

Key-of-Hearts

Just before the snow and the coming of winter, the season
brings the gift of a few sudden days that are astonishingly
limpid. They are preceded by a week of hard frost at night.
This frost brings the silence with it. The forest loses all its
leaves. From one morning to the next you can see the bones
of the trees lose their flesh. The forest skeleton appears little
by little, as if out of the silt of troubled waters, slowly
settling to earth. Farther and farther down through the
branches the sky shows bright, and soon it surrounds the
trunks of the oak trees. In the deserted cantons, where the
trees grow thicker, you will see daylight back behind the
forest, as through a grating.

Nothing inhabits the open plateau except four beech-
trees: the beeches of Gavary. They are all in the same
place. It's said that a shepherd planted them there. This is
possible, for they stand in line, ten yards apart; and if the
wind had brought them it would have brought more than
these four. They are the only beeches in all the High Hills.
The land doesn't suit them. But just in that spot, it suited.
It takes three men with their arms outstretched to reach
around the trunk of one of them; and their branches are a
tangle of fantastic ladders that climb from the level of this
naked land into the very terror of the sky.

Marceau has hitched up his long, blue cart, put on a tilt-cover and left for the beeches of Gavary to gather leaves for stable bedding. There's always a tremendous lake of them at that place.

The weather is clear. Already a white stain is beginning to creep upwards within the deepest gorges. Winter is here. The strong sunlight today is powerless. There is another will that is stronger. It's cold.

The horse is puffing white smoke. He walks quickly, energetically, to keep warm. The empty cart dances behind him. Marceau urges him along, faster still. They are already in open country. The track was made by sheep. It winds for a long time through the gorges, then takes off to one side and goes up the knoll. From there it follows the crests.

The young morning sun is dusty as ripe wheat, it lights up the frost on the grasses. The herd of naked hills stands all around, stock-still, back to back. What remains of the wind blows across the hoar-frost as across white coals. From time to time the four beeches find another word or two to say. The cart's tarpaulin lifts and flaps like a half-filled sail. The body of the dead leaves, stretched out on the ground, swells and falls like the panting of a gigantic, wearied fox. The silence comes. Nothing moves. All is quiet, except the cart. From the depths of the sky an old lark falls like a stone.

In front of the four beeches lies a hollow. As a rule the leaves pile up there. Thicker than in the other hollows. They make good bedding; they're even drier than straw. And you have only to come and get them.

Towards noon, Marceau arrives at the beeches. He had been the first to see them rising ahead of him, and had begun at once to talk to the horse. The animal had heard the sound of the trees and pricked up his ears. As they come closer he shakes his head and snorts. He looks ahead and makes a move to leave the path. Marceau puts him on it again by pulling at the rear of the cart. Who's giving the orders here? The horse stops, Marceau takes it by the bridle.

'Come along, now, they're only trees.'

The horse follows, step by step, but it sniffs, it snorts, it begins to whinny. Crows rise from the grass, climb and fly off in the direction of the village. Trees that grow alone are bulkier than forest trees. They smell strong, they can stretch all the muscles in their bodies.

As you come to them—by this pathway over rolling land that hides them, then reveals them little by little—you see them not thrusting out of the earth but descending from the sky, as if they were gathering all their thin branches together to spear the earth, like a shaft of lightning. And at the place where they enter it their trunks are full of the distortions of cruelty.

You can't come here with mules. You'd have to fight them. You can take a chance on coming with a horse: a horse's nerves can be soothed.

Under the beeches there is a little fieldstone shelter that is sometimes used by shepherds.

Marceau turns his rig on the rim of the hollow. It's full of magnificent leaves. He'll soon have his load. He holds the horse by the bridle. And he goes with him right up to the trees:

'Yes, go ahead, smell my hand. Yes, it's me. If I go here you can do it too. What do you think it is? It's a tree.'

And he even ties it to a little, low branch, near the trunk.

The horse shivers.

'Don't try to tell me you're cold. You're not cold.'

But he covers it with an old coat. Then he sits down nearby. It's a fact, when you look up in the air you'd swear those trees were going to fall on you, they're so tall. That comes from having to tip your head so far back. He sits and eats a chunk of bread and a piece of salted pork belly.

At three o'clock he had finished loading, and he unfolded the tarpaulin to pull it over the top. As he climbed on the rack to fasten the cover he saw a man passing by along the pathway. He was coming from the direction of the valley, heading for the village. He must have come by the Richaud Pass, which no one uses any more this long time. It's hardly even fit for travellers afoot. Anyone who wants to come here does better to follow the road and ask for a lift from someone with a rig. Nobody refuses. This one was striding along the path at a good rate, his hands in his pockets. He seemed heavy-built. He musn't have seen the cart. The horse shook its collar.

The man looked over. He stopped. He left the path and came down into the hollow. He was indeed heavy-built, now that Marceau had a good look at him. He shouted, made a little gesture, and approached Marceau.

He was a funny creature, with a well-shaven, broad face the colour of pigskin, and at his neck at least four chins in folds that went up on each side to suspend themselves from his ears. And curled moustaches, black, plastered flat, waxed as if by a polishing brush. He lifted his hat, not to say good-day, but as an affectation; he had a splendid parting in the middle of his sleek hair in which you could count every tooth of the comb. He asked if it was far to the village.

Marceau said it was seven good miles. He had on fine shoes with buttons. Marceau tossed the rope across his load and went to get down and go to the other side.

'Stay where you are,' the other said.

He took the rope, pulled it good and tight, and made a

first-class knot. His fingers were thick as blood sausages.

'If you're not in a hurry,' said Marceau, 'you can wait for me. As soon as I have the load ready I'll be slowly on my way, taking my time.'

'If that's how it is, then I'll wait, friend.'

He had the loud, metallic accent of the valleys. Marceau doesn't like to be anyone's friend right away. He says to him, with great and caustic politeness:

'That way my horse can carry you. You'll save your little shoes. Up here the top side of the stones is always sharp.'

'It's not the first time I've been up here,' said the man. 'But I'm glad you mentioned it. They've been bothering me long enough. I'm an idiot not to have done it before.'

He sat down. His belly fell between his legs. He leaned forward to get at his shoes, and despite his jacket you could see inside his waist-coat what looked like the swell of two great breasts. He sighed. He was really forced to pinch his belly as if between pliers in order to touch his shoes. But, puffing, he succeeded and took them off one after the other, then pulled off his socks.

'Barefoot,' he said, 'I can go a hundred miles over razor blades.'

It was a fact, his feet were the colour of an old pair of boots. He stuffed the socks inside his shoes.

'Here,' he said, 'put them in your tool-box, will you? I don't like carrying packages.'

He wiggled his toes.

'I thank you,' he said. 'That feels better. We've time to roll a cigarette.'

'If you have tobacco.'

'I've all the makings.'

'Then roll me one too,' said Marceau. 'My hands are black.'

'Should I lick it for you?'

'Lick it,' said Marceau. 'You don't look too sick. If I catch it, I catch it.'

The cart was ready. There was nothing more to do but take the old coat off the horse. The evening began to lay over the ground about them a violet light that smelled of cold. But here, at the bottom of the hollow, there was still a good warmth. Marceau lit his cigarette from the other's and sat down to smoke. The man had a fancy way of smoking, sticking out his little finger. All his nails were broken in the middle.

'You're a wool-carder?' said Marceau.

'Yes,' said the man. 'Is that so plain to see?'

'You're late,' said Marceau. 'We shear earlier here than they do in the plains.'

'That's not why I'm here,' said the other. 'In any case, this isn't my district, and I don't compete with anybody. You've got a man up here by name of Bournette who comes from Buis-les-Baronnies.'

'Yes,' said Marceau, 'but he's getting old.'

'All the more reason not to take the bread from his mouth.'

'Well, well,' said Marceau, 'I don't know anything else about you, but at least what you say sounds good.'

'The fact is,' said the man, 'my real job, you see, would be more in the line of inspecting the finished product.'

He began to laugh.

'Have you any relations up here?'

'No, though I believe, now you mention it, that I have a forty-second cousin at la Colle. That is, a man who's married to a cousin of mine. But who's going to walk fifteen miles to go and see the people that marry his cousins?'

'Well,' said Marceau. 'I see. You're just going to the village. On your way through.'

'Sly dog,' said the other, both eyes blinking out of cheeks

as fat as tomatoes. 'Why don't you come right out and ask?'

Marceau laughed. 'Up here,' he said, 'we don't see many people, and so we're interested in strangers.'

'It so happens that what I'm doing here is no mystery. So you don't need to go roundabout. I'll tell you. Do you know a man called Jason, Marceau?'

Marceau was nonplussed.

'And you,' he said after a moment, 'do you know him?'

'No, not at all. But he's the man I've come to see.'

Perhaps this was a customer. Unlikely, though, with that waxed moustache and the rest of his looks, like a barkeeper. And coming on foot like this by the Richaud pass and all. On the other hand, now, there was a horse-shoe tie-pin to be seen in the cravat under that bandoleer of chins.

'And what,' said Marceau, 'do you want with him?'

'That,' said the other, 'is my affair. . . and his,' he said after a moment.

'Then it's mine too. Marceau Jason, that happens to be me.'

The other shut his mouth tight among the many folds of his lips, his chins and his fat. He had opened his eyes so wide there was hardly room for his forehead. He looked Marceau over, up and down and right and left, his shoulders and his arms.

'Ho,' he said. 'They say nothing's impossible. But that would be a joke.'

'Let's have a laugh, then,' said Marceau, 'for my mother can't go back on it now.'

'Go on,' said the other, 'you're not serious.'

'Indeed I am.'

'Then put it here!' said the other. 'Shake my hand. Good day, and very pleased to see you.'

'So am I,' said Marceau. 'And how are things?'

'Fine, and you?'

'Me too. Just fine. Well?'

'Well, here it is: you've never heard tell of a man called Galissian?'

'No.'

'You must have heard tell of him.'

'I don't think so.'

'Galissian, called Key-of-Hearts.'

'Now, wait. . .'

'You see!'

'Yes, wait now, Key-of-Hearts, yes—the wrestler?'

'Exactly.'

'Key-of-Hearts. Of course I've heard of him. Everybody's heard of him.'

'That's me.'

'How do you do,' said Marceau.

'How do you do,' said the other.

'Well, now,' said Marceau, 'is there something I can do for you?'

',You can do a lot,' said the other. 'You can satisfy me.'

'Indeed, if I can do that, it's a lot.'

'I'll tell you what I mean. I heard about you at the fair at Sorgues.'

'I've never been to it.'

'You didn't have to. Your reputation went for you.'

'That's funny,' said Marceau. 'What do they care about mules down in there? It's in the plain.'

'They don't care about mules. They care about a horse.'

Marceau began to laugh.

'Then you must be mistaken,' he said. All the horses I have is that one there. And he's a long way from being a purebred.'

The other said nothing for a moment. He had lowered his big head, he wrinkled his whole forehead to widen his eyes, he folded in two extra chins, he was nothing but folds everywhere, except for his wide eyes which held—what is so must be said, and it's very odd—a kind of tenderness. He looked at Marceau.

'It's the truth,' said Marceau.

'Listen to me,' said the other. 'You're a funny bunch up this way. Let's speak frankly. Don't tell me you've forgotten that you killed a horse in Lachau?'

'Oh that!' said Marceau. 'The horse that belonged to Mornas. Yes, true enough.'

'With a blow of your fist.'

'Yes, with a blow of my fist.'

'Well,' said the man, 'do you know, even if I'd come up here for nothing but what you said just now, I wouldn't have wasted my time. You're really a funny lot up this way. You did that, and you don't find anything out of the ordinary about it?'

'I should say I do find it out of the ordinary!'

'But you don't think about it all the time?'

'Why, no. How could I? There's too many things to be done.'

'A man would have to hear that to believe it.'

'What do you expect? I tell you, we have to make a living.'

'And what more do you need, if you can't live off that?'

'It won't keep the soup-pot boiling.'

'Maybe it would,' said the other. 'And then some. But doesn't it give you satisfaction?'

'In one way.'

'Ah! You see?'

'Of course, I'm glad I did it.'

'Look here, you are a flock of funny jays in these parts. Are they all like you up here?'

'For sure they're not.'

'I don't mean the blow with the fist. I mean, do they all
not care a damn, like you?'

'It's not that I don't care a damn. I killed a horse. What
then?'

'Holy thunder of God!' said the other. 'What then? What
then? What then? I've come up here for you to fight me.'

'Why?' said Marceau. 'You've done nothing to me.'

The other remained for a long moment puffing in every
possible way. He even had a way of puffing up into his own
nostrils, which made a curious noise.

'You'd send a saint to perdition,' he said. 'It's the first
time I've ever seen a man like you. I've never done anything
to you. You're right. Now what do you say? And I wouldn't
do anything to you for all the gold in the world. That's not
the question. I've said it already: are you going to satisfy
me, yes or no?'

'If I can,' said Marceau, 'I don't see why I shouldn't.
There's no need to lose your temper.'

'I'm not losing it, I'm not losing my temper at you, I'm
losing my temper because I can't get around to what I want
to say.'

'At times like that,' said Marceau, 'the simplest thing is
to say it.'

'You've heard tell of me. You know who I am?'

'Yes.'

'You know my life?'

'Well, I've heard them talk about it.'

'But you know that nobody's ever been able to beat me?'

'Everybody knows that!'

'You see, we're getting somewhere.'

'Go on.'

'Now, I'm not like you. I get satisfaction from what I do.
To meet some fellow, glue yourself to his belly, lift him off
his roots, give him the scissors, the pincers, lay him flat,

tie him in knots, and beat him : that's my life!'

'You mean, the ring.'

'Yes. It's my life. I love it.'

'I can understand that,' said Marceau. 'You haven't another man on earth that can understand you better than I can.'

'And yet you thought just now that I'd come to buy a horse off you!'

'Because I,' said Marceau, 'I have a passion for more things than you have. They're mixed. I can make a choice.'

'Well, then,' said the man, 'if you want to satisfy me, it's easy : just for once choose the one that interests me.'

The evening was growing red over the lip of the hollow.

'When I heard about what you did in Lachau,' said the man, 'I thought it was a joke. Now just a minute, I know it's true! It's a tremendous feat. Can you wrestle?'

'No. I know how to hit when I'm cornered. At any rate, I knew it that time. And cornered I was, more than you might think.'

'What interests me,' said the man, 'is strength. Whether you did it for this reason or that doesn't matter, you did it. Suppose you hadn't gone to Lachau that day. The strength you have, you'd have it anyway. But I wouldn't know about it, and it wouldn't bother me. But now I know you're strong. So it's only natural : I come and say, wrestle with me and we'll find out who's stronger, you or I. You see, it's simple.'

'What have you got to gain?'

'A lot. To know that I'm stronger than you.'

'And if you're not?'

The man began to laugh noiselessly, his whole mouth an expanse of white. In his eyes was still that strange tenderness.

'There's a good carpet of leaves here,' he said. 'No danger of hurting ourselves if we fall. I usually wrestle on straw.'

'Yes, but just what is it we're going to do?' said Marceau.

'We're going to take off our coats, our waistcoats and our shirts.'

'I've no taste for it.'

'That will come.'

He was undoing his tie. I have time, said Marceau to himself. I have no tie. He watched him undress. This man had a collar that was held to his shirt with little iron buttons.

'These we'll put away,' he said. He caught them with his thick fingers and stuck them in his waistcoat pocket. 'Well, what about you?' he said.

'Go ahead,' said Marceau. 'I won't take long.'

'And have a care with the watch,' said the man. 'When I threw that Poitevin I won fifty francs, but the swine had stepped on a watch worth a hundred.'

He went to deposit his waistcoat a little farther off.

'Hang it on the tree,' said Marceau, and that made him think about his load and about his horse.

As usual, it had grown very little colder. The light wind had died at sundown. The flat stones breathed warmth. Evening had already taken several steps into the sky. It won't last long anyway, said Marceau to himself, for it'll soon be dark. After all, he too was beginning to want to know. Strange! The man wasn't as big as all that. He was flexing his biceps effortlessly. With the collar off, the four or five chins that went up to his ears had melted into a neck that wasn't bad at all, and solid to say the least.

'How much do you weigh?' said the man.

'Right now, two hundred and thirty-five.'

'That'll do,' said the man. 'I'm two fifty-one.'

He had no belly, that is, no paunch like some you see that look like pounds and pounds of rising yeast. No. But from shoulders to hips he was round, straight down, like a barrel. He took off his shirt: he was white, clean, with muscled teats. He was like a great block of frozen oil.

'Hurry up!' he said. 'They forgot to light the stove.'

Marceau took off his jacket and pulled his shirt over his head. He appeared with his pads of hair, his breasts black as coal, big as two soup plates, and the long hair hanging on all sides of his body.

'You were born in the nick,' said the other. 'Ten minutes more and your mother would have made a monkey.'

'It's the honest truth,' said Marceau, 'I've no taste for this at all.'

'That'll come,' said the other. 'Now, let's do this by the rules. Listen! There's to be no fist-fighting. We have to upset each other, make the other's two shoulders touch the ground.'

'I know,' said Marceau.

The other put his heels together and stood to attention.

'We are,' said he, 'soldiers of the noble art.'

He gave a military salute, then held out his hand.

'We swear that there is no private strife between us, and no question of gain.'

'Very well,' said Marceau.

'. . . and that we will fight fair before you for the love of the ring. There's nobody watching, but that doesn't matter. It's what you always say. And rules are rules. Now, shake hands. There. Oh, one thing! It's forbidden to pull moustaches. I just mention this, for a man did that to me once.'

They remained a moment facing each other.

'No taste for it at all,' said Marceau.

But the man, almost without moving, made a little feint, and Marceau reacted, bending his knees slightly. A kind of will-power in the other's fat which until now had been immobile made tiny ripples run from one shoulder to the other; at the place where the ribs join a hollow began to leave its shadow on the white skin; the big hands hanging at the ends of his arms had opened; his eye was searching.

Marceau wanted to stay exactly in front of that eye. He understood at once where it was looking; he had only to sway a little to put himself there: he bent his knees again. He too had opened his hands. The man slowly spread his arms. 'Run away?' said Marceau to himself. 'No, I'm not afraid, I don't want to run away, anything but. Spread them as wide as you like.' He felt himself hardening. In spite of the little swaying motion that he was obliged to keep up so that the other couldn't attack him at the 'place where he wasn't.'

He became like a block before the outspread arms of the other, who came no closer. He bent down, his head leading.

'Not with the head,' said the other sharply, 'that's against the rules.'

'I'll beat you,' said Marceau to himself.

He felt a great force against his gullet, and there was no air in his mouth. He saw the man's thick neck lean over him, swiftly, very swiftly, he saw it clearly: no fat, but two enormous pillars of strength, one on either side. The black earth and its burden of red sky rolled like a cartwheel. He saw the open mouth and smelled the raw inside of the man.

He tried to breathe. He fell. All at once the earth was flat against his back.

He could breathe now. The man was on his feet again. Marceau stood up.

Now, as he saw again the black rim of the hollow and the red sky motionless and level, one atop the other where they belonged, he realized that he must, in fact, have been turned about and flipped over.

'Just a second, get your breath. Wait,' said the man.

Yes, it seemed to him that he still had the ground glued to both his shoulders.

'That's what I would have done if we'd fought before a crowd. And now I'd be saluting and I'd be the winner. But I didn't win. There was no test of strength there. I pulled a Trafalgar on you.'

'But you threw me.'

'The way I did it,' said the other, 'anybody could throw the Pope himself. Yes, if you'd come to challenge me on some fairgrounds, that would have been fine.'

He scratched his ears.

'Listen. The hold was regulation. But what wasn't regulation was the way you were going to butt me just now.'

'I don't know,' said Marceau, 'it came naturally.'

'Of course it did,' said the man. 'And then I said, "Not with the head," and you straightened up. And I was able to get my arm under your chin. That's how it happened. Every time I fight with a beginner it's the same. I know it's natural. I had it myself, this same instinct, at one time. You see a big man in front of you and you say to yourself, "Let's have a go." And—what do you know!—that's just where you make your mistake. Look, I'll tell you, with a fellow a tenth as strong as you, but who didn't do that, I'd still be rolling around on the ground. He wouldn't be beaten.'

'In that case,' said Marceau, 'strength has nothing to do with it.'

'Strength,' said the man, 'is the prettiest part. And I'll tell you why! See here: say I go away now, if anybody mentions you to me I can say, "Jason? The horse-killer? It took me just," wait . . .'—he went to his vest and took out the watch—' "it took me half a minute to put both his shoulders down." And it's the truth. Nobody can tell me different. Not even you. But deep down in myself, when I

wonder, "Are you stronger than he is?" I'll have to say,
"No, you don't know one way or the other. Maybe he's
stronger than you." Strength? Now we'll see. Are you
rested?'

'Yes.'

'But tell me,' said the man, 'still no taste for it?'

'That's coming along,' said Marceau.

'I knew it. Come a little nearer,' said the man. 'We don't
have to jump at each other like bears. No, gently. Here, take
my hand. Now, easy does it, and there you are. . .'

They were in a clinch. It had been quicker this time.

'Name of God!' Marceau had said to himself. 'Shite,
now, wait a minute!' He had gripped the other roundly,
like a sack. 'Two hundred and fifty-one,' he said to himself,
'why I'll. . .' Yes, but it wasn't so easy.

He had had to stoop to girdle the other, who still had his
arms free. He had stretched them out and grasped Marceau
at the hips. Marceau could easily lift his weight, but not
when somebody was squeezing the sides of his belly where
there was no protecting bone. He felt how the other went
in there with his thumb as if it were butter. Lifting was
easy. You did it with a hoist from the loins; but you
needed support from spread thighs and the inside of those
hips, just where the other was hurting more and more
deeply with his knifing thumbs.

He tried it anyway. Nothing doing. He felt a pain like
fire there. It was almost enough to make him cry out, what
with the straining, and the pain made him loosen his grip.
And there, as soon as you gave, the other took advantage
at once. He realized this quickly, but he could still feel with
anger how the other slipped his arms under his stomach.
Now he was the sack. Oh, if this went on he was going to
be lifted up in no time. He had put himself in a bad position. It wasn't hard to do.

The other had all the advantages. He was holding him in his arms as if in a belly-band of hard webbing. He had only to stand up straight, which he did. Marceau lost touch, first one foot off the ground, then the other. It was no use waving his legs in empty air, he was lifted bodily like a sack. But then he really used his strength, and everything changed.

'Stop!' screamed the other.

It was a terrible scream, which had to be obeyed at once. When you stopped fighting it was easy to stand straight again. Evening had come in the midst of a wide-spreading silence, softly. The wings of a great, dark sky beat softly, softly bringing the night.

'What's wrong?' said Marceau.

'Nothing,' said the other. (He was getting to his feet.) 'That's against the rules,' he said, puffing.

'What's against the rules?'

The knees he'd given him in the belly.

He? Marceau had given him knees in the belly?

'Yes.'

Never on your life. He was sure of it.

'Yes, yes, yes.'

'I tell you, no,' said Marceau.

He was saying it to himself. He was trying, honestly, to tell himself, 'No.' He remembered perfectly well: 'Certainly not. No, not a bit of it.' He had drawn his thighs up like a frog, very slowly, a little at a time.

'Not at all. I never gave you the knee.'

'You gave me the knee between the legs. I suppose you're going to say that's only natural. If this natural business goes on I'll end up losing my temper! And that'll be natural too. This isn't murder, it's wrestling.'

Come, come, now! What was all this about? He had a
good enough memory to know exactly what had gone on,
after all! Well, fair enough, let's take him up on it if he
insists.

'First you caught me below the belly and then you lifted
me in the air, head down. Now just tell me how I could
have given you the knee in the gut then.'

'You did, you did.'

'What do you mean, you did you did?'

He'd be better off listening to what a person says than
puffing around right and left paying no attention and saying
you did, you did.

'My head was down and my legs were in the air, and my
head was right against your belly? How could I have given
you the knee?'

'Maybe so. But afterwards.'

'Afterwards? All right, let's see about that. No danger
of the knee. I was far too afraid to move my legs. I was
holding your arm with one of them, and—yes, now I know!
My other leg . . .'

'I don't like arguments when I've said a thing. Who's
the professional, you or me? Do I know what I'm talking
about or am I a half-wit? Do I show you how to load your
waggon? No? Well, don't try to teach me wrestling. I know
my job better than you do. And I know your type, and you
too. And I know what you do when you feel cornered, when
you find a man that's too much for you: you'd rather kill
him than lose.'

What, lose! Oh, now, that was a good one! Something
suspicious was going on here.

'I was cornered? I was?'

'Yes, when you're cornered you hit like hypocrites. You
people think nothing of killing a man! Fair play goes by

the board, you only want his hide. I know your sort.'

'That's enough,' said Marceau.

The silence really was profound.

Black night fluttered suddenly down beside them.

'Do you mean to say I was cornered?' said Marceau. 'And that I used foul blows on purpose because I was cornered? Come on, answer me!

'And what does your heart of hearts tell you now? You started bawling like a calf for me to stop, just when you knew I was going to win. There's the truth.'

It really was night, dark as pitch. Where was he, the other one? You could no longer see him. It was uncanny.

'Go on, move, you over there,' he said to himself. 'Say something, so I'll know where you are. Up to now he's tried to diddle me. Have a care! What's he up to? A proper key of villains, he is, key-of-hearts my eye.'

He saw through the trickery now. But he would have been very much surprised if this was the end of it. Now, in the silence and the dark, the thing seemed to be assuming its true form. The underhandedness of it all was so obvious that it became a kind of candour. Instinctively he moved a little to one side. Just in that moment the other leapt at him.

This time, it was a real battle.

Oh, yes! And a good thing he'd made that little sideways move as the other attacked, or he'd have taken the blow square in the belly. As it was it had knocked the wind out of him, but most of all he was choked with rage. At the same time he was clasped as if by a bandoleer by the two arms, which were gripped about his chest from the side. The pressure of the other's shoulders dug into his right upper arm. On this side all his strength was penned-in. He couldn't even move his fingers, and at the same time this pig of a man was pressing with his joined hands into the tender left side of his stomach. Only his left arm was free. But there was nothing in front of him. He couldn't strike a blow. The other had come at him from the side, and was trying to break him in two from left to right.

He must turn. He felt for better footing in the leaves. The other too. And he seemed to have spread his legs.

'Aha! You don't want me to turn!'

He must undo those two hands that were crushing his spleen. He couldn't do it with one hand. And he was obliged to take his share of blows as well. They didn't hurt too much, but as he tried to separate the locked fists he felt them jump and heard the blows sink into his belly. The other one must be jerking there to hurt him internally. He heard a great rustling in the leaves. Without realizing he must have continued trying to turn and succeeded; but he had taken the other, with his spread legs, along and nothing was changed. Except that he had been strong enough to take him along bodily just by turning his hips.

He shouted aloud. The bruising fists had just found a really tender spot, and a red arrow had flown past his eyes like light. He tried to strike a blow to the right, but he hit himself, and striking sideways he had not much strength. He swelled out his chest. His right arm felt like cotton-wool, but he finally managed to swell it as well against the shoulders that held it fast. The other's head, with its hard chin that bored into the bone of his arm, slid a little to one side. He struck another blow with his left. This time he connected. He had felt something at the end of it. And the chin trying to move back where it had been.

But that had let some life back into his right arm. He swelled the muscles again as much as he could to prevent the head from leaving this spot that he could reach with his left, and he struck again. This time, right on the swine's ear. He had felt it crack. And again. This was getting somewhere! And again. He heard a groan.

'Are you going to let loose? Are you? You want to stave in my gut, do you?'

He went on hitting that ear. What now? He had felt a burn like red-hot iron in the fat of his right arm.

'What's this? Now we're biting, eh?'

Yes, he was biting. He struck at what this time must be the eye of the head that was turned to bite. The other began whimpering as if he were weeping. That big body, and crying like this! But he himself let out a bellow like a cow. He had just taken a first-class blow in the side of his belly that had already been worked-over. A chestnut of light before his eyes, with a burr of very sharp, red prickles.

But the other had loosened his grip and he was able to turn and face him. He still had pulses of luminous blood shooting before his eyes. He waved his arms around like a blind man and he touched a piece of the other who was moving away, rustling among the leaves. It must have been a piece of cross-buttocks as the other was turning, perhaps to take him in the rear.

Marceau whirled in this direction and tried at the same time to clutch the flesh he had touched, with no more thought of fair play or anything else, but only of grabbing as hard as possible to hold him no matter how and strike no matter where. He sank his fingernails into the flesh, which came away.

'Son of a slut,' said the other.

Marceau struck with all his might at the voice, at empty air. He stumbled forward. He let fly another blow and again the inside of his eyes lit up. He struck again, a sweeping blow of the right with all his strength behind it, and this time he hit something.

As if through a quilt he heard vaguely how the other squealed like a stuck pig; heard him running in the leaves. He dashed after him: he thought he was farther away, he was there, nearby, bent double with his hands over the place where the blow had landed. He ran into him at top speed, tipped him over and fell on top of him. He rolled on him, lost him, fell in the leaves. He got up again, and felt a blow that splashed his eyes with light.

He sought for the man, found him, tumbled him, lost him, struck at the air, felt a blow to the belly: his head began to ring like a bell struck by handfuls of earth. He rose, turned around, leaned over, grasped the other's shoulder, pulled, made him fall, hurled himself on him, lost him, ran on his knees, found him again, straddled him, held him fast between his knees. His left hand felt its way up the man's long chest. He touched the neck, the chin, the head. With his other hand he struck one good blow at that head. It was all over. The other gave in at once; his arms and legs stretched out to the full length.

'There it is,' said Marceau after a moment.

He had waited to get his breath. He began to get up.

'I said, there it is!' he said, shaking the other.

'Yes,' said the other.

On his feet again, he called to his horse. The animal shook its collar. He walked towards the cart, looking for his shirt and jacket. He found them at once. There was no wind, there were no stars. The night, completely soundless on all sides, must have covered and huddled down. There was the very peculiar odour of low cloud, the heaviness that smells like red sulphur matches.

He turned the cart around. He looked for the path, feeling with his foot. The earth seemed soft; it gave under his steps like the belly of a dead cow, as if he had drunk too much. But the path was there just the same. He pulled the horse along.

From the very first paces he felt as if he were walking with the steps of a bird. Despite the slow bouncing of the wheels in the ruts and the jerking of the horse's head, it seemed as if he were going along holding a falcon by the bridle. A stone whistled past his ears. He stopped, turned his head.

'Will you shut your mouth?' he shouted.

He heard the other down behind, weeping with little sharp sobs. And he started down the hillock. Two or three times the horse pulled on the hand holding his bridle, to put them back on the path. Marceau let himself be led.

He went up the other side of the coomb. The cart moved along peacefully, the horse walked slowly. The path was almost straight along the crests. The horse had understood that this hand was not holding the bit, but clinging to the bridle. He sniffed to get the smell of the path, and from time to time he sneezed to keep his nostrils clear. Finally he struck out at his normal pace. He had got the feel of the whole length of the roadway unrolling before him. The load was not heavy.

Marceau followed his lead. He still had little flames flickering in his eyes, and his blood had not yet grown quiet, it still sent high waves crashing into his ears. He could do no more than obey the horse and cling to the bridle.

The night was like a wall on every side, but he heard the wheel turning behind him, forcing him along, and every step lit up his eyes with his own stars. He would have to wait for his blood to be silent and retire to its normal stream-beds. For the moment it was a tremendous flood that rolled in frightful waves this way and that. It was good to walk while all this was going on.

The horse kept bringing him back to the path with little

tugs at the bridle. Once he thought he saw a star. It was a little red speck, motionless in the dark: but he looked down, and the red speck was there as well. It was in his eye. Like a faintly veiled star. It was to the right, it was to the left, there was no getting rid of it. He took a few steps, clattering into the wide, flat shale. The horse, with a small jerk of his head, drew him back to the path. Straight ahead of him was this star in his eye. He tried to go around it. The wheel touched his arm. And on the other side the horse was tugging at the bridle to pull him to the path again.

The red speck persisted. He said to himself:

'That bastard has hurt my stomach!'

It was beginning to be painful. Three steps later the pain suddenly grew so acute that he stopped the horse and stood a moment, suffering.

'That bastard has killed me,' he said. 'Let's just see if I don't piss blood.'

He put his arm through the bridle so as not to lose it, and looked by the flame of his lighter.

'By, God, no!' he said, delighted. 'It's clear as a rock spring.'

He went on his way more lightly. He felt well, the red star was no longer planted in his eye. Two or three times something like flames flickered before him, and then he was walking beside the horse again in inky blackness. He knew that his blood had cooled completely when he was able to hear a fox make its getaway. A moment later, above the noise of the cart, he heard a nervous yelping which must have been addressed to a vixen.

Long afterwards, he saw far ahead of him the lights of the village. He was no longer clinging to the bridle for support. From time to time the horse went to sleep, and he woke it with a jerk at the bit. He thought of the other man, and said to himself:

'If he's still crying, his moustache will be in a fine state. . . .'

It was only when he came to the last slope below the village that he remembered the tool-box and the shoes. He stopped.

He recalled now that as he was leaving the place the other had started roaring, as if he wanted something of him. That must have been it. He stayed there undecided for a long second or two. Then he said to himself:

'After all, I'm not going back the six miles—or twelve, the round trip—to bring him these! . . . And since he has feet of iron,' he finally thought, 'let him at least have the fun of using them!'

He took the shoes from the box and threw them in the direction of the village dung-heaps.

The Croup

'Winter or no winter,' said Valérie, who was bringing in the pails, 'I can't get near the billy-goat. Go and see what's wrong with him.'

Marceau went down to the stables.

The goat was a big, black animal with splendid, mad eyes. He was standing up like a man, with his front hooves on the manger. He was watching the door where Valérie had gone out.

'What's wrong with him,' said Marceau to himself, 'isn't hard to see. He's not hiding it.'

'You've got big eyes yourself,' he said to the animal, 'but you can't see for looking. Don't you know what it's like outside?'

He opened the door to the street. It revealed a pallid daylight, snow and silence. With all your being you felt the desire to do something to come alive. The goat turned his head and looked at this chilly desert with immobile tenderness.

The long weeks of snow had set in.

When the thick of winter comes like this, the son, Basile, carries his father to the Hotel of the West. Six years ago the father was suddenly paralyzed in his lower parts, from his belly to his feet. From belly to head he's still more or less in order.

154

The son gets on his knees before the father, turning away from him, and says,

'Up you go, on my back.'

There are five or six steps that lead to a roofed-in terrace. At the back of the terrace, two yards above the snow, is the glass door of the Hotel of the West. The woman who keeps this great barn of a place now is a widow: the Jasons have sold out. She comes from some valley or other. She is attractive, to those who admire a certain girth. Her face is round, completely round, and in it are three little ruled lines: two eyes and a mouth. And the mouth never moves—not when she talks, and not when she laughs. She talks a lot, she laughs often, but nothing moves, neither the three little lines nor the circle. You see her breasts jumping with laughter, but her face is elsewhere. Some like her very much. She is the woman no one talks about in the village: one word louder than the next could start trouble. Her name is Violette.

'What will it be?' says Violette.

'A carafe of white wine,' says the father.

There was no one else in the café. The stove was roaring. Father sat there in the warmth, with one chair on his right and another on his left so that he couldn't fall one way or the other. Violette had gone back to her kitchen. You could hear the fire crackling in her hearth, and wood that was a little green sputtering in the coals.

'What are you cooking back there?' says the son.

'My bite of dinner. Come and see.'

Big Cather arrived. He stamped his feet outside on the ground of the terrace. He said there was going to be snow, that the weather was piling up by Saint-Charles, that there was already a great, black wall. And it was a fact, you

could see the sky growing darker. Cather rubbed at his
large eyes, blinded by the snow. When he could see again
inside, big Cather spotted the son at once. He said to him :

'What! You're here already, are you?'

And he changed direction to go and sit beside him. He
reported that over in the barn they were flailing the wheat
for fair. In this weather you could do that, or come here,
one or the other.

'Then why don't they come?' said Violette.

'They haven't much more to do,' said Cather.

And sure enough, through the steamed-over windows
you could see them coming over from the other side of the
square. There were five or six of them.

Marceau Jason came in behind them. He had come out
by a little side-street and met them as they were stamping
their great snowy feet on the terrace.

And they wanted coffee.

'But what time is it?' said Violette.

'Oh, almost one.'

'I'll have to make some,' she said. 'You can wait a minute,
can't you?'

'We can wait as many minutes as you like.'

Marceau's face was small and gaunt within its broad
outline. Only a little was left of it, starting with the eyes,
and under the eyes where you could see that it was hanging
on bone, then the nose, because it was a bone; and the
mouth and the chin; but all around, all the rest where the
fat had melted away, there was nothing but sagging, grey
skin with an ugly fortnight's beard.

'How is he?' asked Fauques.

'Better,' said Marceau.

'Will he live?'

'Yes, he'll live.'

They had stayed by the door and both were looking outside.

'It's starting to come down again,' said Fauques.

In addition to old man Basile and his son, there were Cather, Tallien, Granon, Voltaire, Arcadius and Dragon. Fauques took a chair as well. They were sitting around the fire.

Falling snow hung before the doorpanes like a great curtain of lambskin.

Marceau stretched his legs towards the fire and laid his hands on his knees.

'How's the Cadet?' asked Basile.

'He's going to live,' said Marceau.

Violette arrived with a handful of glasses, heavy ones, and the coffee filter in the other hand.

'Here,' said Marceau.

She opened her thumb and he took the glass. She lined the others up on the table.

'I've got little chills all over,' said Marceau.

Violette served him first. With her eyelids lowered her face was nothing but the little line of her mouth.

'Well, is it all over then?' she said.

'It must be,' said Marceau, 'if I'm here.'

'How is he?'

'Completely cured.'

'Who says?'

'I do!'

He drank the boiling coffee at a gulp.

'No sugar,' said Violette.

He made a gesture: 'No matter.'

'Ah!' he said, 'Good. Good and hot. Here, give me another drop. Yes, I can tell you this much, if he wasn't better I wouldn't be here.'

'Oh, I know that,' she said.

'Well,' said Voltaire, 'how about serving us now?'

'I was cold inside,' said Marceau. 'You hold yourself in like that for weeks on end, and then when it's finished everything lets go at once and you feel it. Up all night, not moving, that's what tired me out. And then the worry. And then the whole business. And then because it really is cold.'

He set his glass on the enamelled top of the round stove.

'I'm going to give you a cognac,' said Violette.

'Not just yet,' he said.

He rubbed at his lighter to get his pipe going.

'Yes,' he said, 'at night you huddle yourself together. There you are on a chair. No use lighting a fire, if it flames up you'll think, "The light's going to wake him." And just then you'd give anything to see him sleep sound. You stay put, you don't move. You're cold. But you hug yourself. All the same you feel a little cold under the arms, on the backs of your legs and just below the arse. But every time you get up to have a look you freeze again all over. And that for scores of nights and days. I don't care what you say or do, night was meant for lying in your bed and sleeping.'

'When you get the chance,' said Violette.

'And what did he turn out to have, your Cadet?'

'The croup.'

'That's a children's sickness.'

'Yes, but for a child or for you death is all the same. I realized that. What surprises me now is how a kid can stay alive through that for even four or five days.'

'Do you mean the strangling croup?'

'Look here, isn't that catching?'

'Yes.'

'And what if you've got it now?'

'What,' said Marceau, 'are you afraid I'll give it to you? Don't worry. Look, I've put my glass on the stove. It's not going to be mixed up with yours. You can drink in peace. Anyway, it's not leprosy. And what if it was? . . .'

'Yes,' said Violette, 'what difference would it make?'

She laid her hand on Marceau's shoulder. She let it be seen for a moment, she withdrew it very slowly.

'Where do you think he picked it up?' said Tallien.

'I don't know,' said Marceau. 'He'd been down at Fongates two days before. Some land he got from his wife. There's still as much land to clear as you can plough in three days. That afternoon he started in at the brambles. He hardly did a stroke of work. He just took two or three whacks at them, didn't even take his coat off. Then he came home, very quiet.'

'What makes you think he caught it in Fongates?'

'I don't say it came from Fongates, I'm only telling you what he did.'

'It's healthy in the forest.'

'I'm not saying it isn't healthy. And anyway I had other things to worry about. I come along to his place. I say to him,

"You look funny to me."

He says:

"I don't feel so well."

I say to him:

"I didn't see you the last two days, what have you been up to?"

He tells me he's been to Fongates and since then he's stayed in the house. I say to him:

"It's from staying penned up here. Come on with me, I have to go to Saint-Charles. Get out from under those skirts for a change."

He says to me:

"No."

"What's the trouble?" I say.

He was by the fire: How I realized finally was from his eyes. I say to him:

"What are you looking for?"

He answers:

"I'm not looking for anything."

I say to him:

"Yes, you're looking for something, you're looking all over the place as if you needed something."

He was only looking because he felt sick. He says to me:

"I'm not looking for anything, I feel sick."

'I'd seen it now, and I say to him:

"Give me your hand. It's cool. You've no fever."

He says to me:

"No, it's not that."

"What is it, then?"

"Nothing."

"What do you mean, nothing?" I say to him, "there must be something wrong if you're sitting there like that."

He says to me:

"It's my throat hurts when I swallow."

I say to myself, "Hurts when he swallows? He has a sore throat, that's all. It's a cold, he's caught cold, he has a chill, that's all."

"Go to bed."

Right away he says:

"Yes, I'm going to bed."

I tell Esther:

"Warm his bed for him."

He says:

"No, don't warm it, I'm not cold."

I say to myself:

"A funny cold if he's not chilly."

I tell him:

"Come, take a drink of brandy."

The Croup   161

He puts his hand to his throat and says:

"Oh, no! No, I don't want brandy. No, no."

"Why, what's so bad about brandy? When you have a chill it warms you up."

"I haven't got a chill."

"Come along, into bed with you."

When he's in bed he says to me:

"It's better now. Go away. No don't tuck me in, that's too tight, I can't breathe. Good, that's better."

I say to him:

"I'm going."

But I say to Esther:

"What's the matter with him? Look at him. The way he is! Look, he's shut his eyes. He has to fight to breathe."

She says to me:

"I don't know, he's worse than he was this morning."

His cheeks were red as fire. She touches them and says to me:

"They're cold."

He didn't move, he seemed to have asthma. I say to Esther:

"He's caught a good cold. I'm going, because he wants me to go, but you come and get me if he's worse."

That was at three o'clock. At nine she comes. She says to me:

"Come, quick!"

I say:

"Why, what's the matter?"

Valérie says:

"You two make an awful fuss over a cold."

I say to her:

"Shut your mouth, you, and don't bother us. Get a move on, Esther, I'm coming." '

'It shows up so soon, does it?'

F

'Talk about showing, it doesn't take long, I can tell you
that. When a murderer goes for your throat what do you
expect him to show? He murders you, that's all. I wasn't
even in the door and I could hear him breathing. I'd been
thinking about that noise all afternoon. Now it was terrible.
I say to him:
    "Is it worse?"
His eyes were like eggs, sticking out of his head. He
looked first right, then left, never stopping, right and left,
right and left. I say:
    "Mon Cadet! Oh! Mon Cadet!"
No answer.
    "Oh, Mon Cadet, my poor Cadet! Look at me, Cadet."
Nothing.
Those eyes, still turning right and left. And the noise of
his breathing. A terrible noise. I'd rather hear anything than
that. Anything, you understand, anything!
    "Oh!" says Esther, "run quick and get the doctor."
    "I'll run," I say to her, "I'll run!"
At the door I meet Valérie, who'd decided to have a look
after all. She says to me:
    "Where are you off to like a madman?"
    "To the doctor."
    "In this weather?"
    "The weather, shit on the weather!"
It was that famous Friday.
    "Your children," says Valérie, "think about your
children!"
    "My children? What about my children!"' '

'Oh, was that the famous Friday when the snow started!'
'Yes, it was that Friday night, when there was more than

three feet of snow. I hadn't noticed a thing. I start off running. I go up to my knees. Snow, Snow. I hadn't noticed the weather. I go back to my house anyway. Then I say to myself, no, it's no use. No horse. What could you do with the horse? I call my mother, I tell her :

"Quick, go to Mon Cadet."

And I start off on foot.'

'Alone,' said Fauques. 'Why didn't you come and tell me?'

'Too proud,' said Tallien.

'No, not too proud. I was alone. And anyway, what could you have done? What did I do? Got lost in five minutes. Ran into trees. Snow in my face. Fell in a hole. Buried up to the shoulders. Slut of a snow, at night! I climbed out again. Run? I ran, up to my knees in snow. Yes, I ran, I ran for a long time. I remember well, I said to myself, fourteen miles to Lachau, fourteen miles. I said to myself, "If I can just get to Saint-Charles it won't be so deep after that." I must have got on to the slopes at Draille, I could feel the drop. I slipped. The snow came down with me. The slut! My throat was on fire. My poor Cadet. I'm in some kind of valley. I say to myself, where are you? Nothing, not a notion. Whereabouts? Lost! And it was coming down! The slut. My poor Cadet! My poor Cadet! And what should I do? Where should I go? How to go on down? And even if I reached Lachau, how to get up again in pitch dark? The way it was coming down . . . You could hear a noise in the night. But I couldn't wait. Just get the doctor and go up again. How? On foot? Poor old Clairin. He'll never, never go up on foot. How then? I say to myself, no, no, go back. Go on back up, this is crazy. Go back, what else can you do? Go back, don't leave your Cadet all alone.

That was what took me by the hand and pulled. I went back, how, I don't know.'

'You're not cold any more?' said Violette.
'No, I wasn't cold. I was running with sweat.'
'I mean now. You're not cold?'
'No, but give me a brandy anyway.'
'And on the way back, did you know your way?'
'No. But all at once I was there. And I said to the women, "All right, clear out. Esther, you stay. Now, never mind, my lovely, we'll manage . Don't cry, in God's name!"

"He's lost!" says my mother. "It's the croup. Listen to him, he's saying it."

Sure enough, as he breathed he went, "Croo, croo!"

Valérie says to me:

"Come, Marceau, let's get out of here. It's the croup. Come, come on home, don't stay here, it's catching, think of your children."

"Those children again!" I said. "And you, mother," I said, "don't start putting your hands up to your head. If you're going to get in the way around here you can leave too."

She said to me:

"Don't get excited. Shouting doesn't help." (Yes and no. When you come in from outside, it helps.)

Oh, I'd have given I don't know what if I could have stayed like that, angry at everything. But no. Esther says to me:

"What are we going to do?"

What to do! Oh, MonCadet, oh, my poor Cadet! Cadet, answer me! But no, there was no one home. He didn't move. Every time he breathed he gave a start. Breathed? He wasn't breathing. He was drawing in with all his might, almost closing his nostrils. And hardly anything was getting through. My poor Cadet!

I said to him:

"Open your mouth so I can see. I'll clear it for you. Open your mouth."

Oh, never a move. No more than this table here. I said:

"Esther, come and help me. Here, sit down there and hold his nose."

I had my lighter in my hand.

"I want to see, do you understand? Then we'll know what we have to do. Now then, go ahead, hold his nose."

He gave a jump that knocked everything out of our hands, lighter and all.

"We have to make him open his mouth. Get up on the bed."

"I'm afraid!"

"Get up there," I say to her. "We have to hold him. We have to look, we have to do something. We have to. He's going to die, get up there, Esther."

She got up on the bed. She held his shoulders. I held his legs.

He opened his mouth.

"It's all right, I had a look. Get down, let go of him. Yes." '

'And that was on the Friday evening?'

'More like Saturday morning. It must have been on for four or five o'clock. I said to myself, "He's going to die." '

'And then?'

'Then nothing. I said, "Mother?" She was standing there, near the fire. She hadn't moved a finger. She said to me:

"What do you want? Is he going to die, then?"

"Yes."

If you could have seen in his throat! All around a kind

of rind was growing there, thick as two fingers, like ham fat.
Dirty as the dust on the road.

I remembered my mother telling me once about Faustine's little girl.

"What did they do? Tell me."

"Why shouldn't I tell you? They scraped her."

"What with?"

"A leek."

"What do you mean, a leek?"

"You peel off the outside skin and shove the leek down
his throat as you'd shove it down a lamp-chimney."

"Are you crazy?"

"No."

"Did it work?"

"No."

"Well. So much for that."

He was straining to breathe! Oh, anything but let's take
out what he has in his throat! Let him breathe! Let him
die if he wants to but let him breathe! Come, the leek it is!'

'You're joking!'

'You don't mean it!'

' "Anything. Give me anything!" I said. "A stick, a
knife, even fingers. I'm going to take it out. I won't let him
strangle here in front of me. Give me a leek."

My mother said,

"It took three men to hold Faustine's little girl."

I said,

"This time it'll take one man. With Esther."

She says:

"No."

I say:

"Yes, yes, Esther my dear, come, we're going to help him.
Come, my dear child, look, you've only to do what you did

just now, we'll do what must be done. Hold his shoulders and pinch his nostrils."

Then I get up on the bed. I kneel on his legs. I had the leek in my hand, white and clean.

"Pinch them tight, Esther, don't be afraid. Hold him fast and pinch tight. Let's not make him suffer for nothing. Ready?"

She was white as well. He opens his mouth. I shove in the leek and pull. He sent us both flying. He almost sat upright in bed. He's vomiting blood.

Then he stops vomiting blood. He falls back in bed. No more noise. Nothing. Is he dead? No. He's breathing. No, I hadn't killed him.'

'Drink your brandy.'

'No, I didn't kill him.'

'You didn't kill him. Drink your brandy.'

'And that's how it was.'

'That's all there was to it?'

'No, I did it five times. Every time, I tore out that rind. It would grow again. I'd tear it out. And throw it in the fire. Until Sunday, and then, about four in the morning, he was resting. I felt as if I'd been knocked on the head. I went to sleep. Esther too, and my mother too. And the daylight woke me up. Blinding, with the snow. I said :

"We've let him die."

I went over to him. He was breathing softly. He opened his eyes. He said :

"I'm thirsty."

Mon Cadet! I said to him :

"Mon Cadet, listen, open your mouth."

He opened it.

"Let me look."

I lit the lighter. This time there was hardly any rind. Just a little touch, hardly any. The way it was when I cleared it the last time. It hadn't grown again. I woke the women.

"Come, get up, wake up. He's better. Make some herb tea. He's thirsty. He can talk. It's all over."

It wasn't over all at once. But it was over.'

Despite the thick, slow-falling snow you could still hear the whirring, faintly muffled, of the flails threshing the wheat. The stove was roaring. It was hot in the room.

'There's nothing doing in this place,' said Marceau.

'What do you mean?' said Violette.

'I mean there's nothing doing with this weather. Nothing. You can't move. You can't do anything, that's all.'

A tiny trace of red flesh showed at Violette's mouth, and the lines that were her eyes grew a little thicker, and black.

'Well, you don't say,' she said, 'you don't know what to do, eh? No ideas at all?'

She went slowly away in the direction of her kitchen.

'I need to move,' said Marceau.

He poured another brandy, watching the brandy run into the glass.

'I want to get moving. Need to get moving.'

He drank the whole glass at a gulp. He stood up.

'God damn it, yes! I've an awful hankering to get a move on now.'

He went out.

A little later, Violette came back from the kitchen and sat down by the fire, in the place that he had left.

The Flasher

Raging, the storm spat sulphur and blood against the windows. An iron rain hammered at the walls. The wind set the barns and streets to ringing. The sudden shadow lay heavy on their shoulders. There wasn't much doing in here. Mon Cadet was silent, a little smile at the corner of his mouth. He felt an anxious tenderness for the forest, where the paths had just grown clear of snow under the dripping, black branches.

'Do you want me to tell you what I really think, my boys?' said Marceau. 'I think it's just as tiresome here as where we come from, when all's said and done.'

'You should have been here a little earlier,' said the fair-haired man.

'For more of the same? What I see is enough!'

'Don't worry, there was action for everybody, you and the others too!'

'What, then?'

'A fight!'

'The devil you say! In Saint-Charles! What next! But you're wrong, my fair-haired friend. For me, when my little boys fight it's no sport, it's a nuisance.'

'Ah, but this was no brawl. And it was no little boy. It was the Flasher!'

'And just what might this Flasher be?'

'The Flasher! You don't know the Flasher?'

'No.'

'The champion of the Rhone valley.'

'By God!' said Marceau. 'And what's he doing here, this champion?'

'Why, wrestling, what else!'

'Ah!' said Marceau.

'That's easy,' said the fair-haired man.

'What's easy?'

'To say.'

'I said nothing.'

'But you thought.'

'Who's to stop me thinking?'

'You know Costard?'

'Yes.'

'Flat on his back.'

'Oh?' said Marceau.

'You know Piégut?'

'Which one?'

'The big one.'

'I know him.'

'Flat on his back.'

'Oh?' said Marceau.

'You know Christin?'

'I know you all,' said Marceau. 'I know your precious Rhone valley.'

'He beat them. He beat them hollow. And fast. In the count of five. And even Jocelme de la Pilatte.'

'Now, that surprises me,' said Marceau.

'Surprised or no. . .' said the fair-haired man.

'Jocelme,' said Marceau, 'can carry three great sacks of flour. And not only carry them, take them upstairs.'

'Right,' they said.

'Jocelme,' said Marceau, 'can bend a penny between his left hand and his right hand.'

'Nobody says he can't,' they said.

'That surprises me,' said Marceau.

'Surprised or no,' said the fair-haired man, 'he shook your Jocelme like a rat.'

'Dirty work,' said Marceau.

'No,' said the bearded man with the straight nose, 'strength!'

And near the forest in full flight before the rain a flash of lightning struck sharply.

Marceau looked at Mon Cadet.

'Do you want some fun?' he asked softly.

Mon Cadet's little smile spread all along his mouth.

'Well!' said Marceau to the others, 'where is he, this Flasher?'

'In his doss, most likely.'

'Let's see,' he said, looking at the fair-haired man, 'you wouldn't like to go and get him for me?'

'Who?'

'Your Flasher.'

'What for?'

'To talk about the weather.'

'You?'

'Why not?'

They were nonplussed; not a word to say. The bearded man, after a moment, was the only one to speak:

'Basta! Why not?'

'Why not indeed?' said Marceau.

Zéphyrin, pushing out his lips as if he were eating waffles, volunteered:

'I'll go if you like. Now, what do you want me to tell him?'

'Tell him, tell him, "We want to see how you're put

together." That should let him know what it's all about. It's not good enough to beat the Rhone Valley, he has to beat Jason's Marceau. Full stop.'

The storm hurled three splatters of fire against the trembling windowpanes. The fire puffed among its embers.

'And let's drink,' said Marceau.

And he pulled the casserole from the fire. He was wiping off his moustache when the Flasher came in. The Flasher had put on a jacket over his sailor's sweater; but with his hands in his pockets he managed to hold it open and stick out his chest, as covered with medals as a roof with tiles.

'Well,' he said, 'what's the trouble here?'

His face was tiny, but completely surrounded by more than twenty great rings or fat; on the perimeter of all this were his chin, running right down to the notch of his sweater, and his ears which seemed to be planted in the middle of his cheeks; and on the top of his shaven pate were folded five or six rolls of fat, each one as thick as a man's arm, crowning his head like a republican cap.

'They brought you the message,' said Marceau.

'Yes,' he said, 'you're hard to convince in this village.'

'I'm not from here,' said Marceau.

'Oh, you're the one!'

'Why not?' said Marceau.

'Why not, you're right,' said the Flasher. 'And where shall it be?'

'Here.'

'Go bring us three bales of hay.'

'What's that for?' said Marceau.

'For your back,' said the Flasher.

'Pull off my boots,' said Marceau.

He stuck out his foot to the red-headed girl. The Flasher took off his jacket, he did it very gracefully. At least, as gracefully as he knew how, that is, with slow sweeps of

his arms while, from the middle of the twenty great rings
of fat that rounded out his face, he puffed with his little
mouth as if he were cooling soup. They brought the straw.

'A little more straw,' said the Flasher.

He winked at Marceau and added:

'The ground is hard.'

Marceau already had one boot off. The redhead was
holding it in her hand. And she laughed at the naked foot
she had just undressed—really a very strange foot: black,
calloused, but with very agile toes.

'Don't worry about the ground,' Marceau retorted, 'your
shoulders are well padded.'

And in fact, talk about shoulders, so far as the Flasher
went he was right. Even what you could see above the neck
of his sweater—it was like hams from a full-grown sow.

'Never you mind about *my* shoulders,' said the Flasher.

He wrinkled the skin of the heavy pads that hung like
sacks of flour on his shoulder-blades. The redhead pulled
at Marceau's other boot, and the Flasher began unpinning
his medals. He was looking for a spot to display them,
and he had three, side by side, on the flat of his palm: one
red, one green, one yellow. He asked for a hat.

'Don't worry, it's just to pin the medals on.'

And someone passed him a wide, felt hat.

'Have you ever wrestled?' he asked.

'Me?' said Marceau. 'Yes.'

'Who with?'

'Key-of-Hearts.'

'Key-of-Hearts!' said the Flasher.

He unpinned a wide, striped ribbon with a round pendant
as big and thick as a goat-cheese.

'There's your Key-of-Hearts for you!'

He held up the medal in the bundle of sausages he had for
fingers. He showed it around.

'Key-of-Hearts, beaten six times. It's written right on it. Look! This medal was presented to me at the farewell reception by the town council of Charrières-Basse.'

He remained thus for a moment, passing this porringer under people's noses. His eye, which was like a breeches-button, looked sternly at Marceau. The brief silence and the look were full of meaning.

'Let the gods decide,' said Marceau.

'Why gods?' demanded the bearded man with the straight nose, who seemed ticklish about the choice of words.

'The Good Lord, of course,' said Marceau. 'I don't know why I said the gods. I was thinking about my two paws.'

'Champion of the Rhone valley,' said the Flasher.

'Valley,' said Marceau, 'what's all this about a valley?' Do you think we give a curse for your valleys up here? What's the good of a valley? Champion of the hills, now, that's something.'

The Flasher had finished unpinning his medals, and he stripped off his sweater. Just as he was pulling out his arms, with his head still covered, he put all the muscles of his back so fully in play that those behind him began to shout, but then the sweater came off completely.

'Look at this, would you,' said big Julia.

She had pushed into the front row and had been sitting on a table. Now she jumped down and went over to the man. The fact is, everyone who saw him from the front was open-mouthed! The last time he had wrestled he had kept on a ring sweater but now, stripped down, he was somethiing to see! His whole chest was tattooed with a great sailing ship! A three-master! It was so finely done that you could see two initials on the nave of the helm. You could count the cords in the rigging and behind the stern there was even a little rope, plain to see and all uncoiled, trailing, so to speak, in the sea.

'Look,' said Julia.
'Look,' said the redhead.
'Look,' said the bearded man.
'Look,' said Julia.
A crack of thunder splashed the windows with honey.
'Look at that,' said Laurent the younger. (He meant the prow of the ship, made with a naked woman, half fish!) 'Look!'
Those who were behind came around to look.
'Make a little room so I can see!' said Marceau, who had remained seated.
'And it can sail,' said the Flasher. 'Watch this.'
On his sides he had a tremendous forest of hairs so long that in spite of their curls they hung over his hips like the hairs on a goat's leg. He combed them with his fingers, bringing them in towards his navel. He swelled his muscles. On both sides of his chest his great denticulated muscles opened their fans. He began a very slow, rippling belly-dance. The hairs frothed like the sea; a foam made iridescent by grease and skin rose to strike and fall back from the woman at the prow. The extensor muscles of his arms filled the main and studding sails with wind, and the two enormous trapezes of his shoulders stirred up a tumultuous hurricane high among the flags.
A series of thunderclaps came in quick succession: the lightning flickered from pane to pane and, at the last crack, hung for a long moment with golden bat-wings quartered against the trembling squares of glass. As its light died the tearing thunder puffed at the cinders in the hearth, and two long, iris-coloured leaves of fire whistled upward.
The Flasher had let his trousers fall. He stood there naked, in his wrestling trunks. He was surely not a man; or only part. Those around him drew back. He was built

of great, writhing serpents with no head or tail.

'Well?' he said.

'Here we go!' said Marceau, and stood up

'You're not going to fight with trousers on!' said the Flasher.

'You wouldn't want me to show my arse to the whole world, would you?' said Marceau.

Only his torso was bare.

'I warn you, this makes it easier for me. You'll get your legs tangled.'

'So much the better for you.'

'I tell you, no,' he said, 'no, no! You need trunks.'

'What a fuss about nothing,' said Marceau. 'Let's start, since it's your advantage. Don't fret about me. I'm a grown boy. . . .'

'No, no, no!' said the Flasher. 'It's not regulation.'

'You make me laugh with your regulations, the lot of you. What difference does it make?'

'I tell you, no.'

He wouldn't give in. He would only fight if the other wore trunks. He didn't want it said afterwards that he'd had an edge.

'Who's going to say it? Nobody! And if I beat you, what then?'

'We'll see about that.'

'Indeed we will. That's what we're here for. Now, let's start.'

'I tell you I won't.'

'Good, God,' said Marceau, 'now we need the cross and banner here just to have a little fun! Julia,' he said, 'lend me a pair of yours.'

It was getting silly.

'There's nothing to laugh about,' said the Flasher.

'Nothing to cry about, either,' said Marceau.

It was a simple matter. Was he champion of the Rhone valley, yes or no?

'Champion my foot!'

'I'll lose my temper,' said the Flasher.

'That's right,' said Marceau, 'lose your temper. You'll have double the trouble.'

The Flasher gripped him suddenly with one arm wrapped under his chin.

'Double the trouble,' went on Marceau.

He rolled his great boar's head against the other's chest.

'The trouble of losing it,' they heard him say, 'and the trouble of finding it again.'

Then he struggled in silence.

Julia retreated, pushing the men back with her great bottom.

'Make room,' she shouted.

On all sides they leapt up to stand on tables. The bearded man, leaning forward, gripped others' shoulders with his powerful hands. Old man Carles, drawing back as quickly as he could, had pulled the stem from his pipe: he was sucking it furiously and holding the detached bowl at arm's length. The door to the stables down at the back began to flap furiously in the crowd of men, women, girls that came in running. Some of them, stamping about near the hearth trying to see, upset the trivets: the flames died. Beer bottles rolled on the floor.

'Candles!' shouted Julia. 'Light the candles.'

Pots fell from the kitchen rack. People were clambering on stools, benches, tables, and their heavy hob-nailed boots struck sparks from the flagstones. Thuds came from the bar counter as the climbers' knees landed on it. Women were groaning. The two men had fallen, you could hear them above all the noise, writhing in the straw.

'Candles, you son of a whore!' cried Julia.

'Yes, ma, I'm getting them.'

'In the table drawer. Make a little room there, let me breathe, let me tell him where the candles are. In the table drawer.'

Two candles arrived, passed from hand to hand. The women covered their heads to keep the flame from their hair.

'Give them here,' said Julia.

'Double the trouble,' Marceau was saying, 'double the trouble: losing your temper. . . .'

There was a last plunge among the straw, as of a great carp falling in dry grass.

'And finding it again,' said Marceau, just below Julia, who was leaning over with the candle.

They saw the Flasher spread out, quiet, flat on his back, and Marceau astride his stomach.

'Maybe it doesn't count,' said Marceau. 'It went so fast.'

'No,' said the Flasher. 'It counts.'

'Do you want to start over?'

'No, that'll do,' said the Flasher, breathing heavily.

'I said it before, my boys,' said Marceau, 'and it's not this will make me take it back. It's just as tiresome here as where we come from.'

Night was falling.

'Why not?' said Marceau.

Romuald of the Square Head went over it all again.

'There's me, there's Salvador, there's Crouzier-of-the-Fine-Cravat, there's Barles-of-the-Little-Dungheap, there's Pinier, Jocelme, Tronchet, Girardin and Hauvière-of-the-Green-Collar. Nine of us.'

'And me, don't forget!' said the redhead.

'Can you ride a horse?' said Marceau.

'I ride,' she said.

'Side-saddle?'

'Man-fashion.'

'You'll show your legs.'

'What then? You won't go blind!'

'What's your name?' said Marceau.

'Autane.'

'That's ten of us, then,' said Marceau, 'and the two of us, that's twelve. But have you horses for everybody?'

'And then some,' said Romuald. 'Come on outside. You'll see.'

The storm had gone down from the mountain. It was still poking about with great crow-bar blows, striking sparks in the little valleys below. Up here it had left behind a land slaked with water, steaming between the great puddles green with evening light. Dazzling silver piping underlined all the black coral branches of the forest. The weather had grown so calm that drops of water hung immobile, as if frozen, from the tips of all the buds. The tattered west throbbed gently in the very pure, green evening sky. The air was cold as sugar.

While Romuald-of-the-Square-Head collected the cavalry the two brothers, already in the saddle, trotted slowly in circles under the chestnut trees where the forest path begins.

'Did you like it?' asked Marceau.

Mon Cadet said yes.

'It was over too fast,' said Marceau.

'Was he really trying?'

'By God, he was doing more than that! I thought you'd seen it. He tried to pull a dirty one. He wasn't holding back. Here, look! And all his talk about regulations! He tried to put my eye out!'

'Not so strong, was he?'

'He was very strong. He almost opened my grip. Do you call that strong or not?'

Mon Cadet cleared his throat.

'You're not cold, are you?' asked Marceau. 'What about your scarf? Do you want my jacket? If you'd rather go home, we won't tag along with their little game. You know, as far as I'm concerned, the fame of it! ...'

Romuald-of-the-Square-Head had even found a horse for the red-headed girl. She made no fuss, lifted her skirts, revealing her magnificent white thighs right up to her hips, and, spreading her legs as she leapt, was in the saddle. Indeed, they were all there, even Salvador, thin as always and burned on the face and body by the terrible fire of his dark eyes; and Fine-Cravat, who for the occasion was wearing a new one, a little scarf:

'See, it's got invented flowers in yellow gold on red.'

It looked handsome at his neck. There was big Pinier, a thundering, great carcass, on his mare. Jocelme, of course, and Tronchet, in fact all the great proprietors. Great proprietors of desires. Soldiers of every adventure going, up in these parts. Men chosen by the rain and the wind to create the legend of the countryside. Knights whose fief was the shade beneath the chestnut-trees, always ready to spring to horse at the first call from the spacious land, when some softness in the time of year sets loose a daemon in the hearts of men whose lives are lonely.

Hauvière-of-the-Green-Collar was a great Gaul with a tangle of blond beard right up to his eyes. He sang an old song of the mountains (ten people at the most still knew it):

> Deep in the forests of salt
> When winter seals the paths
> Her black-branched candelabra

> Light up in this our castle
> The fairest halls on earth,
> And while the snowstorm howls
> We feel our hearts beat warm.

He carried an old storm-lantern hung at his saddle-bow.

The green evening sky, struggling slowly free from the tattered clouds, with its thousand reflections from the fallen waters and the russet gum of the rain that polished the bare branches, lit the way for the cavalcade. But on the slope they soon entered the hazel groves, which whipped them with water, and riding into Pigneboeuf they had to light the lantern. They asked for matches at the baker's shop, and nine loaves, which they tied in a sack and gave Autane to carry tied over her shoulder. After Pigneboeuf came the steep descent, which they took at a walk, in single file. Hauvière, in front, picked up his song again:

> Honey of wax-lights, honey of fires,
> Honey of arms notched by the glaive,
> Honey of all that leaves its trace
> On the red tongues of the brave.

Behind him came Romuald-of-the-Square-Head who had put down the ear-flaps of his deerskin cap, then Jocelme, Pinier, Girardin, all in single file, then Mon Cadet and Marceau side by side. Marceau, crowned with a branch of holm-oak they had found at the baker's, rode behind Autane, whose shifting saddle stirred up the smell of forest.

From time to time now the moon, tearing loose from jagged shorelines of black, lit up the dancing frieze of the cavalcade moving at a walk down the steep slope over the stones. At last Hauvière, down below, was heard singing that he had reached the countryside. But at the same time they saw the fog beneath them, as high as your face. The storm leapt and flicked its tail like a hooked salmon.

They passed into the land of the groves. They had to

disentangle themselves from maples. They got lost and
went in circles in the bosquet of the Bitch. The fog played
tricks with the metal plates of the storm lantern: it hid the
road and revealed other roads where there were none. Not
one of them had ever come this way except at night and
for the adventure of it. It was not a normal route. You had
to pick your way among the canals with which the people
here criss-cross their prairies.

'Put out the lantern,' said Autane. 'I can do better in the
dark.'

She took the lead and brought them step by step,
cautiously, through high-growing mint that perfumed the
horses' legs up to their bellies.

'Here we are,' she said.

And indeed, you could hear the naked branches of the
sycamores gently switching at the night. It was the cross-
roads, and immediately afterwards hard ground sounded
beneath their hooves. They started off at a trot which
quickly grew more rapid. At Séchilienne they broke into a
gallop and went through the village like a whirlwind, with
a clatter that struck dazzling sparks from the paving-
stones. People opened shutters behind them. Beyond were
the gorges of Traverselle, full of fog so thick that despite
the black of night it made patches of wet flour of which
you could see the beads. They scarcely slowed down.

In front of them the storm was beating sulphur carpets.
They headed straight into it. They rode at full speed with a
common impetus that bore them on together all at once,
stirrup to stirrup, in fours Hauvière still in the lead, Autane
beside the two brothers, the whole of her thighs showing
white as pigeon's wings, and then they all burst into frightful howls of laughter, splitting the night.

Thus they entered the plains. At a breakneck gallop they
dashed through the marshes in a splatter of reeds and cold

water, pulling up short and taking to the road again the
other side of Agnel. After that the going was easy. The fog,
moreover, was clearing, but only because of the storm
which they had just overtaken. And they charged at a
gallop into the downpour.

Marceau had pulled his crown of holm-oak down to his
ears. There it was solid and nothing could take it off. He
held his hat in his teeth. From time to time Hauvière let
out a hoot that took the place of his song, for you don't sing
at a gallop in the rain. He would get this off his chest, clench
his teeth, put down his head and away. There was no more
need to touch the horses, nor even to worry about reins or
knees: the ten of them fused into one mass carried away
by speed. At last the storm turned off to the right, attracted
by the eddies above the great oak forest bordering Lachau
on the east. They turned left into a drizzling rain. Thin
clouds filtered the light of a pallid moon. They had slowed
to a trot, now to a walk. They stopped. The town lay before
them in the hollow, two hundred yards away, down in
front.

'What time is it?' asked Romuald-of-the-Square-Head.

Fine-Cravat struck his lighter. It was ten o'clock.

The town was sleeping behind crenelated walls at the feet
of its four churches. The little wind that swept away the
last powder-clouds of the storm was sounding its horn in
the corridors of the deserted streets. The gas lights of the
outer boulevard were haloed with a fuzz of rose-coloured
rain. The high, green walls and the pale, sea-green bristle
of steeples and watch-towers were light and transparent as
muslin.

'What do we do now?'

They felt suddenly abashed. The horses sneezed, and
Hauvière grabbed the nostrils of his mare as she was about
to whinny.

'That's easy,' said Autane, 'we've only to go to the lute-maker's. Bombard, in the rue des Agneaux. They call him Pretty Eyes.'

And just what might he be good for?

'He'll arrange everything.'

'And you know him?'

'The devil I don't,' she said.

'He'll be in bed.'

'Never worry,' she said. 'I'll roust him out. When I get there his bed will be too hot for him.'

They went in the town by the Saulnerie gate. They were still intimidated, and though each one rode quietly it seemed to them that all together they made too much noise on the paved streets. Hauvière kept an eye on the nostrils of his mare.

In the narrow rue des Agneaux, Autane leading, they proceeded in Indian file. The girl said:

'Halt!'

They were in front of a shop with a great wooden violin for a sign. The doors and windows were shut.

Autane unbuckled her belt and, standing in her stirrups, flicked at the sign with the strap.

'You swine!' she cried tenderly, 'do you want the whole street to know I've come to see you?'

The window nearest the violin opened.

'Quiet!' said the low voice. 'You'll have all the neighbours awake. And what have you done with your own key, anyway?'

'You're right,' she said. 'Just a minute. These horses have me drunk.'

'What kind of torchlight tattoo is this?' said the voice.

'Wait!' she said. 'Get dressed.'

And then, to the others:

'Off your horses, come!'

They tied their horses to the grills of the low windows. Autane, digging in a hidden pocket, had pulled out her key and opened the door. They struck matches in the hallway. Autane lit the lamp in the store.

'Wait for me here,' she said. 'I'm going upstairs to see him. What I explain to him alone, he understands at once.'

The store was a strange thing. By God, this was the first time in their lives something like this had happened to them! Marceau pinched Mon Cadet's arm with all his might.

'Are you having sport?' he said.

He himself was having sport, at any rate. There they were, the nine of them with their enormous shoulders beside the little shoulders of the violins in unfinished wood. The instruments hung from the ceiling by their ears. If you coughed, you could hear it reverberate and rumble in the little bellies. There were flutes in the window, ocharinas, harmonicas, steel triangles, cymbals; but most interesting were the violins, and they amused themselves for a good while, coughing to hear the violins cough after them with a little extra moan that followed. They had begun to feel at home on their legs again. They were no longer in the least abashed. Only thirsty. Finally they found a bugle with a magnificent lanyard whose tassels Hauvière began caressing as if it had been a little cat.

'What's she doing up there?'

But there they were, coming down! She was putting up her hair again. They were surprised at the man. He was as tall, as broad, as heavy as they; perhaps not as Marceau, but not far from it. He was pretty well fitted-out. You'd think, because violins are a delicate thing. . . but not at all, and he said to them: 'Well, a fine sort of music you make!' with a splendid bass voice and the indulgent smile of a very powerful man.

'Well, I'll tell you. . .' said Romuald.

'I know,' he said, 'where is this phenomenon?'

'Yes, but. . .'

Marceau stepped up.

'It's a fact,' said the lute-maker. 'You're bigger than I am.'

'Barely.'

'Yes, yes, at least three fingers. And broader.'

'I don't think so.'

'Yes, a whole hand broader than I am. No doubt about it. And you beat the Flasher?'

'A powder-puff.'

'Powder-puff nothing! He's a good wrestler. There may not be three others like him. Was it hard?'

'No.'

'How do you mean, no?'

'I couldn't tell you.'

'What do you mean? Did it last long?'

'Two minutes.'

'Not even,' said Romuald.

The lute-maker whistled between his teeth. He looked at Autane.

'Yes,' she said, 'it's true.'

'Did you use your full strength?'

'Not the quarter of it,' said Marceau.

'You're joking.'

'It's the God's truth, by Mon Cadet's head! As soon as I had a grip on him I knew I'd won. And it wouldn't have lasted even one minute if he hadn't stuck his fingers in my eye.'

'On purpose?'

'You can believe it. I felt his hand searching around my nose to find my eyes before he took aim. And he wasn't playing, look!'

'If he did that,' said the lute-maker, 'it's the first time in his life. Up to now he's been right as a clock. In ten years there's never been a word against him. It's a known fact.'

'He did it,' said Marceau. 'Look, if he didn't put my eye out it wasn't his fault.'

'He must have been desperate. Let's see your eye.'

And there it was, in the corner of the eye, a deep nail-wound in which the nail had even turned.

'That,' said the lute-maker, 'is more important than anything you've told me. It's just as if he'd given you a certificate. He's signed his defeat. Well, come along to the other room.'

They went in a kind of dining-room.

'Sit down,' said the lute-maker. 'Autane, get the bottle and put out the glasses for everybody. Now,' he said, 'stand up. Let's have a look at you. Take off your jacket. And your shirt.'

He looked at him from all sides.

'Not bad,' he said. 'How old are you? You're starting late. Never mind, I'm for you. Get dressed. Here's what we're going to do: now you've beaten the Flasher, there are only two left: Bel-Amour and the Sweetheart. To-morrow's Monday. . . .'

'It has to be over by tomorrow night,' said Marceau.

'You're talking nonsense,' said the lute-maker. 'You can't take these two chunks at one bite.'

'Never you worry,' said Marceau.

'I am worried,' said the lute-maker. 'Bel-Amour is a man-killer.'

'The Flasher puts out eyes,' said Marceau.

'He tries to,' said the lute-maker, 'but he misses. If Bel-Amour tries, he won't miss.'

'And I,' said Marceau, 'I suppose all this time I'll be reading the paper?'

The lute-maker was thinking.

'Monday's not a bad day. The tanners don't work.'

Good! We'd like to meet Bel-Amour and the Sweetheart both at once, tomorrow.

'That is, I mean of course one after the other.'

He could be sure of meeting them. The lute-maker would see to that. Agreed? Agreed. He'd take care of everything. In that case, then, there was nothing for it but to go to bed.

'Where?'

'At the Maltese Cross,' said Hauvière.

At the Cross they found four rooms, for the nine men. In any case Marceau and Mon Cadet took one between them. They could easily sleep in the same bed.

They were soaked to the skin, right through their shirts.

'I didn't even notice it, all the time we were setting things up. They're a funny crew, all of them, with their customs and their rules. Did you see? This one was just the same, because I wanted to fight the two on one day! You'd think I was breaking his heart.'

They undressed, naked.

'You know, you're a fair size yourself,' said Marceau. 'Let's see.'

He touched Mon Cadet's chest, his ribs, his sides.

'You're well-built, you bastard. Not bad at all. Strong as a fire, I must say. Let's see your arm, Mon Cadet!'

They measured arms.

'Just as big as yours.'

'Oh no,' said Marceau, 'after all!'

Lying down, they compared bodies. There was a mirror over the mantel, they could see each other side by side. Marceau said:

'No, you're smaller than I am, little one. It's the glass that's warped. It's only natural anyway for you to be smaller. You're only Mon Cadet, my little brother.'

They went to sleep peacefully, side by side.

Towards six in the morning someone knocked at their door.

Someone asked:

'Are you alone?'

'Who's there?' said Marceau.

It was Autane.

'What are you doing here so early?' said Marceau. 'I thought you were sleeping at the fiddler's place!'

'Not at all,' she said. 'I have a room here. You don't need anything?'

'No,' said Marceau, 'I'm with my brother.'

He bounced them on their backs as he had said he would, even better than he had said, plainer to see, more swiftly, with more finality, with a kind of joyous bounce like a cartful of harvest grapes. It took ten minutes, no more, and afterwards nothing remained to be said or done about his strength and the strength of the others.

'It seemed,' said Hauvière, 'as if you did it all to bugle calls.'

Away we go! . . . You could see nothing but whirling circles, like a threshing-floor, his flailing arms, his open hands grasping. He caught the Sweetheart; and heave-ho! . . . And you could hear the two hundred tanners roaring, and the wild pigeons fluttered up from the tall reeds, and more than a hundred little ruffians who were tumbling about among the men's legs began running right and left like frightened swallows.

'Ha! Now! . . .' And everything froze. Petrified. Except Marceau who was the only one moving, flexing his legs, lifting the Sweetheart as if he were waltzing with him, tilting him up and slamming him into the grass, flat as a pancake. . . . And there he stayed. They pulled him off to one

side. It was not until later that he got to his feet, painfully,
half-stunned, as groggy as if he had been drinking for three
days. Without a word he staggered towards the spectators,
sat down among them and watched the next instalment.

What followed was simple, even more simple.

'Next!' Marceau had said.

Next was Bel-Amour, who deserved his name: a handsome, three-hundred-pound baby with a nose like a truffle,
the forehead of a fish, the eye of those who come from the
depths of the valleys down behind, from which, in fact, he
came; hands that hung down past his knees, feet as big as
your hat and planted directly on those legs that had no
ankles: a fine lump of a lad, in short! Just one thing to
add: the hair on his head, black as ink, and a curled moustache, waxed and pointed, three sharp-glued waves in his
straight hair and a pretty kiss-curl on his right temple.
Another thing: all the aforementioned, and most likely
everything else from head to foot, was perfumed with musk
and violets—out of modesty. A third thing: his good lady-
friend, all red and green, in a rich dress like a Basque
petticoat, purple lace, feather and all, was seated at the top
of the embankment with three pals determined to cheer. She
shrieked,

'Go to it, Precious!'

He went, at one swoop. That was the next instalment.

Marceau had turned away to look for Mon Cadet. He was
grinning at him like a wolf when Bel-Amour leapt on him
from behind, with his full weight. But Marceau shook himself indifferently under him, like an ox beneath a fly. And
Bel-Amour, mortified that the man had slipped from his
grasp, retreated. He knew. He shook his head as if to say,
'No!'—silently, with his head, in the silence that had overtaken the whole crowd. When he was stretched on the
ground, his arms thrown outwards, he, like the other, stayed

there a good long minute, to show that as far as he was concerned it was over, all over. His good lady-friend, erect and motionless in her finery, was readying a sort of cry that she was not quite able to utter.

Afterwards, to be sure, there was hubbub enough. They even had to carry the woman off, stiff as a board, losing her switch of hair. Hauvière, Romuald, Crouzier, Jocelme and the others, shouting, 'This way!' put to work their shoulders and even (discreetly) their fists, in all that milling mob. Mon Cadet, on the other hand, had withdrawn to one side, and it was in his direction that Marceau sprang away, having snatched up his shirt and jacket:

'Quick!' he said, taking him by the arm. 'Run to the horses. If we wait we'll never get away.'

Already they had the lute-maker at their heels, red as a rooster, trying to explain something and shouting out numbers:

'A thousand francs! A thousand francs, I tell you, muleman! A thousand francs. Listen. . . .'

But they ran for the tall reeds and the woods faster than his words could carry.

They went into town by narrow alleyways.

'Quick, get the horses!' said Marceau. 'They'll be after me like lice. Hurry!'

They slipped in to the Maltese Cross by the back doors. Marceau slapped a few coins in the hand of a stable-boy.

'Take that to your mistress, and you haven't seen a thing. If they ask where we are, say we left.'

They threw their saddles on the horses' backs, tightened the cinches, mounted, went through the portal heads down, made off through the alleyways at a trot, came out in open country on the side farthest from their homeward route and broke into a gallop, straight ahead.

Until the sun went down—there was a brisk north wind

that evening, and a pure, clear sky even below the sun—
they galloped the wrong way. It was not until nightfall that
Marceau stopped the race, deflecting its course, and they
entered the beech-groves, beginning their roundabout cross-
country way to rejoin the path to the High Hills. As they
came out on the path someone hailed them: it was Autane.
She was sitting on her horse under the trees in the shadows,
and she didn't come out.

'Clever girl,' Marceau said to her. 'You guessed, did
you?'

'Of course,' she said. I knew you'd come this way. Are
you going up home?'

'Yes,' he said.

'You don't want to stay?'

'No,' he said.

'One night?'

'No,' he said. 'What for? It's all over now.'

'Au revoir,' she said.

'Adieu,' said Marceau.

Mon Cadet

They were in the oak forest. There was a full midnight moon.

'Now we're home,' said Marceau.

They were riding uphill at a walk.

Spring was still too young. It had awakened nothing, neither animals nor leaves. All was silent and transparent. The horses walked on ground that gave beneath them.

'I like this forest,' said Marceau, 'I like these trees, I love this smell. I like to ride slowly like this with you.'

The bark of the tree-trunks had not drunk all the rain. Swollen like sponges, they oozed an oil that glistened in the moonlight. All the undergrowth was phosphorescent, and the reflected glimmer that ran along each branch created at every step above the riders' heads a tangle of horns, of branched and silver antlers.

'Here,' said Marceau, 'I think the ground's more solid. How is your throat? Can you swallow easily? It doesn't hurt? Take care, put on your scarf. These are the best times of our life. We're alone. We can do what we want. Nobody bothers us. This could go on a hundred years.'

'How did you do it?' asked Mon Cadet.

'What?' said Marceau.

He stopped his horse. Mon Cadet rode nonchalantly on,

G

rocking with the horse's walk in the flecks of moonlight.

'How did you win?'

'I don't know,' said Marceau.

Mon Cadet pulled up across the road. His blond hair gleamed about his head like a helmet with a golden crest; the boughs of an oak, lacquered with moon-filled water, were its plumes.

'They were strong as bulls.'

'I'm stronger than they are,' said Marceau.

'There's no trick to it?'

'Not on my side, no,' said Marceau.

'They're used to fighting. Didn't you feel that they were playing foul?'

'Yes,' said Marceau.

'How?'

'It's hard to explain.'

'Show me,' said Mon Cadet.

And he leapt from his horse.

'What?' said Marceau.

Mon Cadet was waiting, standing there.

'What do you want?'

'I want you to show me how they tried to cheat.'

'Whatever put that in your head?'

'Come, get off,' said Mon Cadet.

Marceau heaved himself up in his saddle.

'What now?' he said, when he stood on the ground.

'Go ahead,' said Mon Cadet. 'What's the matter?' he asked, are you afraid?'

'Yes,' said Marceau, 'I'm afraid you'll catch cold.'

Mon Cadet had taken off his jacket and his shirt. He was stripped to the waist in the moonlight, and the shadows of the branches sketched on his rust-brown skin the articulations of a cuirass.

'Well, be quick!' said Mon Cadet.

'I hate the idea,' said Marceau.

'Then take care of yourself,' said Mon Cadet.

He sprang clumsily at him.

'Not so fast,' said Marceau. 'You're beaten already.'

'Why?'

'Your neck.'

'What's wrong with my neck?'

'Look here.'

Marceau crooked his arm.

'I take it like this,' he said. 'I squeeze. You can't breathe.
And it's all over.'

At the same time he let him go.

'Do it,' said Mon Cadet.

'There's no point, believe me. Put your clothes on.'

'That's not bad,' said Mon Cadet. 'I see now. Look, all
you do is pull your head down between your shoulders.'

'You're not a pretty sight like that,' said Marceau.

'Defend yourself again,' said Mon Cadet.

'Now, that's better,' said Marceau. 'Much better. You
see, my arm slid over your head!'

'On purpose.'

'Not altogether. But look here,' said Marceau, 'you're
going a little hard at it this time, it seems to me.'

'What about you, you're puffing,' said Mon Cadet.

'Don't worry about my wind,' said Marceau, 'that's a
small trick of mine.'

'How do you mean?'

'They think I'm tired, and they leave themselves open.
It fooled you, didn't it!'

'Yes.'

'But child, I haven't even started.'

'Start, then.'

'No, not with you, I only wanted to show you. Look, there's your neck wide open again. And here's my arm. You're beaten.'

He shoved back, and Mon Cadet slipped in the dead leaves.

'Take care,' said Marceau, 'don't fall. I pushed too hard.'

'No,' said Mon Cadet, 'I slipped.'

'You can't afford to slip,' said Marceau.

'If we'd been fighting in earnest I wouldn't have slipped.'

'For the good reason that you'd have been flat on your back for a good minute now.'

'Let's start again,' said Mon Cadet.

'No,' said Marceau, 'up in the saddle and on your way! It's late, your wife will be worried.'

'What's my wife to do with this? It's the first time you've ever mentioned her!'

'It's not the first time I've thought of her.'

The forest had grown very beautiful. The night was on its second versant. In the sky, which the two brothers could not see, the figures of the constellations disentangled their talons, their manes, their claws, their horns, scattering ever farther from each other, over immeasurable distances. The curling mountain gorges, which the full, pallid moonlight before had smoothed and levelled, now deepened into whorls, and the tingling fire of their walls unfurled enormous, glittering pennants in the fluttering of distant puffs of wind.

Under the trees where the brothers passed, side by side, at the pace their horses set, the splendour of the upturned night oozed drop by drop the length of the naked boughs. Silence, peace; only the horses' footsteps in the dead leaves.

The cold shadow slid from their faces down to their hands, and they felt beneath them the sudden shiver of the horses.

Marceau sniffed the air:

'Life is fine,' he said. 'I'm here at your side. We're riding together. We have no problems. We have no more worries. Everything's easy. Why should we go looking for trouble? If you're here, if I'm here, everything's here. When you're here there's no need for anything else. We can do anything. We can go anywhere. We can go on doing everything we're doing now. There's no need for anything to change. We can go on like this all night, if you want to. All the year, if you want to. Forever, if you want to. All's well with me. All's well with us. All's well with you!

'Duck your head, take care! There are low branches here. Cover up, button the collar of your coat: it gets cold towards morning. Hold your hands steady, don't let the reins hang loose: your mare likes to shy at shadows. I'll give you another horse. I'll give you the little bay that you like. I'll give you the red harness. I'll give you the green saddle. I'll give you my father's silver stirrups. I'll give you my sheepskin jacket. I'll give you my soft leather riding boots. I'll give you my toque of otter-skin.'

From red the summer turned golden-blond, and then to chalk: chalky, dusty scintillations that obliterated the colours of every single thing, even that of the fat ravens trying to fly to cover and disappearing in the light, whiter than snow.

They cut the grain, they carted it to the threshing-floors. They let the horses trample it.

Marceau's seven horses were circling together on the main threshing-floor. He was threshing his own wheat there, and Mon Cadet's wheat, the wheat of the Jorrisses, the Paillons, the Jacques, the Turcans and the Vargues. That was the tradition. The Jasons were related to the Jacques and the Turcans, more by common consent than by blood, but very solidly related just the same; the others were friends of long standing, without fuss or question. The eight waggons of the eight families encircled the threshing-floor, the eight stacks of straw swollen to star-points all around it piled up with absolute fairness, forkful by little forkful, from day to day. This had been going on since the Sunday, and since Sunday they had been working as a 'commune'. Five men unloaded the waggons without worrying into whose sheaves they dug their forks.

Marceau, at the hub of the circle in the full heat of the sun, was keeping the horses moving, calling on God and being very frank with each of the animals about its defects. Nearest him he had placed the little bay horse that he intended giving to Mon Cadet.

'Try the wine the Jacques brought, you'll see!' said Marceau.

'I'll see,' said Mon Cadet.

He drank and spat. He said:

'It's full of flies.'

'They're wine flies,' said Marceau. 'Little gnats as light as egg-white. They're good for your stomach.'

'No,' said Mon Cadet.

And he spat out great bluebottles, fat as meat.

'Let me look!' said Marceau.

And he left the horses to come over.

As Marceau was leaning over the demijohn Mon Cadet suddenly gripped his neck with hip and arm.

'I'm going to have your life,' he said, and made an effort to throw him.

Marceau, surprised, planted his legs wide instinctively and stiffened so hard, so vigorously, that his hob-nailed boots dug down to the pounded surface of the threshing-floor, at the bottom of the straw. At the sound the horses stopped, and the others up on the load, forks in the air, wanted to know what was going on.

'Nothing,' said Marceau laughing. 'Just the young man here having a little fun.'

'Young man!' said Mon Cadet. 'But I've got you!'

'He's got me,' shouted Marceau, laughing, 'look at him! Sure enough, he's got me.'

He was still bent double, his head pressed against Mon Cadet's stomach. The other was holding his neck between his arms and his hip, straining to get the neck deeper into the scissors of that arm and that hip.

'Look at the little devil, would you!' shouted Marceau.

He laughed, he twisted, he was more than half-strangled, but at the same time, with a little twist of his shoulders, he lifted the other off the ground.

'Hey, the rest of you up there! Tell me, are you sure he's not growing wings? Look at him, he's taking off like a partridge!'

He shook him as a bitch shakes her pups when they bite her ears.

'I do believe he wants me to flatten his shoulders on the clouds. He's got eagles' legs, my lads!'

He grasped the other's hips in his great paws, but he saw that this way he would be able to throw him down at once, and he let go, remaining with arms dangling.

'You make me die laughing,' he said. 'Go on, have your fun.'

'This is not for fun,' said Mon Cadet.

And he squeezed the neck hard enough to make his eyes bug out. He succeeded in sliding Marceau's head right up beneath his armpit. The left hand was free. He hooked it over his right wrist and began to squeeze with twice the power. Marceau, winded, pushed his great head hard into Mon Cadet's stomach.

But just as he was going to straighten up and throw him
so as to let some air into his lungs, he felt his brother's
hand clutch his shoulder in a panic. At this, he held him
at arm's length, and it was softly that he let him down into
the straw. He fell with him to keep him company in his fall.
He wanted to lay him out at his side, but the hand clutching
his shoulder leapt at his throat and squeezed. He shook his
head to get free: he wanted to say, 'You're hurting!' But
he could only cough: he had heard his windpipe crunch.
A strange noise. He fell with all his weight on the man. The
other was flat on his belly. Bending his knees he kicked
Marceau with the heel of his big boot, high between the
legs.

'Bastard!' said Marceau to himself, but as he grasped the
naked chest in his arms he felt an extraordinary heat that
came from the other and burned him, and he said to himself,
'It's Mon Cadet!'

'Let him alone!' screamed Esther.

'No, no,' said Turcan's wife, 'don't worry. Can't you see
they're only fooling?'

'Give in, Mon Cadet,' thought Marceau.

He was pushing, and all at once he stopped. He had
heard a nerve snap in his brother's shoulder. 'Oh, Mon
Cadet!'

How his mouth burned, suddenly, like burning paper!

'Give in, Mon Cadet,' said Marceau softly. 'Give in.'

'No,' said Mon Cadet.

And he tried to push back with his hurt shoulder. It
creaked. Marceau bore down on it. Mon Cadet had no more
lips, not even a thread: only his teeth bared to the gums,
clenched at first and then opened with a great, black scream
in the space between them, silent, refusing to come out. And
Marceau was the same, pushing at his shoulder. His lips
burned suddenly, there was not even a thread of them to be

seen. His teeth too were bared to the gums, first clenched
and then opened with a great, black, silent scream in the
space between them, a scream which did not emerge but
which would have burst out at the same time, with the same
pain, if Mon Cadet had screamed. Then Mon Cadet could
take no more, and turned over flat on his back in the straw.
And it had been the limit as well of what Marceau could
do in suffering the pain he was causing Mon Cadet. He
rested his great, soft face on the burning shoulder:

'I didn't hurt you?' he said.

The weather had set its heart on raining. Clouds lay
heavily on the earth of the plateau. Torrents of water
slashed through trees and mud. Herds of downpours ran in
all directions, stoned by the wind. Then they came back to
graze on the forest and on the men passing like shadows
under the grey cream of the fog. These were no longer
sheets of rain, nor even streams, they were great, smooth
masses, gleaming like new steel, under which—sheared off
as with a bill-hook—branches thick as your arm tore away.

Everyone rushed to the attics. They were filled with
drifting spray. Roof tiles were flying off one after the other.
Then the whinnyings, the racket of hooves against wooden
stalls, the crying of goats, the stampeding of sheep and the
braying of asses sent everyone running down to the stables.
Bedding straw was floating on rivers that strained at the
doors. Eddies, whirlpools, tidal waves, rattling and shatter-
ing the bundles of forks, carried off broods of new-hatched
chicks. Hens flew the length of the stables and knocked
themselves senseless against the walls. The windows shook,
the doors rattled, the putty fell from the panes. Tiny
streams of water, having made their way through the walls,
began to laugh on the rough-cast of the rooms. It began to

rain into every storey of every house. People set pots
beneath the streams that came from the ceilings. They
pushed the sheep and goats into the stairways to make them
go up. But they had to wade in to their bellies to save the
drowning hens, whirling in the water's eddies, their wings
outstretched. For the moment they left the horses where
they were. There was nothing to be done for them. They
were not in much danger, except from fear. The water was
up to their knees. You had only to reassure them, talk to
them, go to them, stay there, pat their necks, their shoulders,
and wait. The weather wouldn't stay like this forever!

You could no longer call it rain. Walls and walls of water,
slabs of steel. You couldn't go out, not even to cross the
street, the other side of which was invisible, hidden by the
gleaming metal, smooth and impenetrable, of the falling
water.

Just as the clocks struck four in the afternoon there was
a flash of lightning in the form of a sheet of red, which,
again, you really couldn't call a flash, for not only did it
last a very long time, at least a good minute, but it gave off
no light. Amid the blue darkness of the clouds (growing
ever darker as the hour fell towards night) it was no more
than a great, flapping curtain which, at the same time that it
shook the whole earth with the fracas of its flapping, lit up
no more than the monstrous black fortress of the clouds.
And then, all the time this phosphorus was sputtering away,
you could see the enormous mountains of water that were
crossing the sky. Immediately after, there remained just
enough daylight to see a thirty-year-old beech appear right
between the houses, borne along by the water with such
force that the tree, its branches and its russet leaves flayed
the whole street violently from one end to the other, like a
chimney-sweep's brush, defacing walls, tearing off doors,
breaking angle-stones. Then night fell.

And still, relentlessly, the same masses of water hurled themselves at the earth.

Valérie arrived at Mon Cadet's house, drowned, her straight hair glued to her face from forehead to mouth.

'Marceau isn't here?' she said.

'We haven't seen him,' said Mon Cadet. 'Where is he?'

'This morning when it cleared a little he left to get bedding at the beeches of Gavary.'

'I'll go,' said Mon Cadet.

He went out at once without even looking around. In front of his house he went in water to his knees, but there was an embankment on which he was able to run. You could no longer see anything but little flashes of lightning, and they only crackled softly like oil in a frying-pan.

After the embankment Mon Cadet plunged resolutely into the water. He made his way around the little square where the Martels lived by clutching the tie-rings of the blacksmith shop. As he arrived near the church there was water to his belly. The priest, who heard him floundering and saw his dark form, called to him from the sacristy doorway. He fought for a minute, bucking a current that was trying to carry him off to lower ground, and finally dragged himself out of the water like a dog, clawing the earth, to climb on to the mound bearing the cross of the missions of 1893.

It was pitch-dark everywhere; but up there to the north, barely as wide as your finger, a slip of green sunset on which a hump of the plateau was sketched gave him his direction. That fool of a Marceau, if he'd had time to turn back, must be up there on the heights.

He was running on dry land, but in a rain so heavy that it hurt as it struck his knees. He sheltered his face with his hands, opening only the middle fingers to see. The first crest along which he ran stopped short to plunge into a little valley which he recognized as Bousson. In its depths he heard the rush of water. He climbed cautiously down, the earth crumbling around him, but as he neared the bottom he realized that now the water here was too deep, too furious for him to cross. 'If only Marceau hasn't been caught by surprise in one of these holes!'

He clambered to the top again and tried to make his way to the crest of Mariande by way of Menou. By Menou it was still possible. He floundered in the fir-grove with water over his knees, already strong and turbulent but broken in its force by the tree trunks, which also gave him a handhold to reach the other side; and he set out on the long crest of Mariande which would take him a good distance towards his goal. He was soaked to the bones. His cord trousers, dripping wet, dragged heavily at his legs like iron chains. He was about to take them off when he heard the sound of galloping in front of him, then of whinnying; and finally, against a tiny, bluish clear spot in the sky, he saw the tangled silhouette of two horses running flank to flank and tossing their heads. He stopped and called to them. At once they separated, one to the left, one to the right, but as he went on calling, the one on the right came timidly up to him, step by step, stretching out its neck, sniffing with all its might, complaining with little childish moans. As soon as Mon Cadet was able to touch its muzzle the animal pressed close to him, snorting into his chest and face, desperately rubbing its forelock against his side.

He spoke to it, caressed it, patted its neck, he felt it all over to see if any piece of harness was left on it, but it was quite bare. He climbed on its back, and it made no move to resist.

The great ridge of Mariande rose high enough above the plateau to keep its whole length above water, and it went on in this way almost to the great, isolated beeches where

Marceau had gone, supposedly to get leaves for bedding.
It remained to be seen if the storm had warned Marceau in
time. In that case, he might be on the ridges up to the left
where the real road was, where Mon Cadet could not go
because the little valley of Bousson barred his way.

If this were true, Marceau was up there as if on an island,
unless, surprised in the hollow by the flood, he had been
turned arse over kettles, team, cart and all, and carried off
God only knew where. And how would he be in that case,
and what could be done, and how to find him? But surely
he had been able to get out in time.

At the tip of Mariande a sort of little gulley, full of water
of course, cut off the way to Gavary. The beeches were on
the other side. Mon Cadet urged the horse towards the
water. The animal balked. Mon Cadet spoke. The animal
refused to move, then made a leap backwards. Mon Cadet
pressed with his knees. The horse shied sideways. Mon
Cadet lined him up again. Softly, softly he spoke to him,
stroking him with his hand, scratching his ears, to make
him face directly towards the edge of the torrent below. He
struck him with his fist on the head. But the horse was glued
to the spot. It bucked, straight up, and Mon Cadet taken
by surprise rolled off among the stones. Quickly and all as
he was on his feet, the horse was already galloping back
up Mariande.

Then he heard a call on the other side. He ran, and
dashed into the water. The men of the plateau are no
swimmers. He plunged in, went under, and was bounced
up again like a ball by the brutal palm of some deep current.
A lasso of water wrapped itself around his waist, laid him
flat, tossed his legs above his head. He closed his mouth on
mud. He saw himself filled with a strange, orange light that
tore at his lungs. His side hit the bank, he dug his hands
into the earth, pulled with all the strength in his arms,

crawled out into the shadows. He tried to straighten up and run; but he fell. He spat out mud. Each time he breathed that orange light dazzled his eyes. He tried to shout. He barely managed to emit a little squeak, like a rabbit.

The rain was still falling massively. He was able to get on all fours and crawl slowly up towards the beeches. His head was heavy as a melon. Here there was a very strong smell of torn earth and sap. He tried to remember the direction of the call he had heard from the other side. After a moment it rang out again, but it was up in the air. It must have been a bird.

What time could it be? The swift battle with the torrent had taken all his strength. He couldn't clear his mouth of mud. When he breathed, his sides hurt, the air brought nothing good into him. He was burning. His head was so heavy that he stopped and shook it gently. With one hand after the other he tried to wipe it off. It seemed to him that it was encased in mud. If Marceau was not in the neighbourhood of the beeches he would have to go back across that deep and muddy water. He shivered, his arms grew weak beneath him and he fell on his face among the stones.

He lay stretched flat for a long while. Little by little he began to breathe a few reassuring draughts of good air. The orange light was flashing less often in his eyes. He was able to support himself on his hands, and again began climbing on all fours in the direction of the trees.

He clung to the branch he had found and slowly pulled himself towards it. He leaned his shoulders against it. He stretched his arms out before him in the dark with open hands and groped to feel what was there. It was a mass of fresh leaves and part of a tree-trunk. One whole beech of Gavary must have been uprooted. He would have to search in the leaves, lift up the branches, heave up the enormous trunk, clear the whole place to find his brother underneath.

Amid the flashes of orange light he saw himself rising up, hurrying, struggling, searching, running, finding, caring for, lifting up, carrying off, saving. . . . He let himself slip to the ground. He gasped for breath. The smell of blood from his bitten lips filled his nose. He began crawling laboriously on his stomach, on his elbows, on his wrists, on his knees. He forced himself to touch everything around within arm's reach. He gradually worked his way under the tangle of upturned branches.

The smell of blood was sickening. He wanted to vomit. Yet he had the impression that his lip was no longer bleeding. He couldn't have such a large wound on his lip, and in any case each time he tried to swallow blood his mouth was dry. He realized that the smell was coming not from his lips but from the earth. He sniffed about him, his nose near the ground. It was there! In some places the smell was powerful, like a filled sponge. His hand slipped on a stone that must have been smeared with it. He crawled a little farther, the despair in him suddenly extinguishing those waves of golden light that his eyes sent flickering into the shadows. Now his eyes were again seeing the true black of the night. He heard the rain falling heavily. He was so beside himself with this smell of blood that he forgot his weakness. His exhausted arms supported him again and he was able to proceed on his knees and the palms of his hands.

As he stretched out one hand he touched hair. It was a horse's tail. A cold, white fear ran from his loins to his scalp. He touched the thigh of a horse, icy cold. He began to moan, to weep, to whimper like a little dog.

'Who is there?' said a calm voice, from ground-level, near him, just ahead.

'It's me, me,' he said, 'Marceau, it's me!'

'Mon Cadet!' cried the voice. 'What are you doing here?'

'You, you, you, Marceau! You, where are you?'

'Here,' said Marceau.

'Where?'

'Gently, now,' said the voice, very calmly. 'Take care! Don't lean on the tree-trunk. It's just over my chest.'

'Are you hurt?'

'No, not even touched. I'm holding it up.'

'Wait!'

'No, no,' said Marceau. 'Listen. Don't move! Don't move!' repeated the voice very calmly. 'I don't think I could hold up a cigarette paper more than I'm holding now. It'll be almost two hours I'm holding this thing up. Listen, you're going to help me. The horse is crushed,' said the calm voice. 'Say something, so I'll know where you are.'

'Marceau,' said Mon Cadet.

'Good!' said Marceau. 'You're two yards away from me, on the left. Don't move. I'm on my back on the ground. I'll tell you what to do. Don't try to hurry. My shoulders are well-propped. And the whole trunk is on my two hands. I'm under it. I can't budge. I can just hold on. I was going to hold on like this as long as I could. Do you hear me?'

'Yes, yes,' said Mon Cadet.

'Don't move. Here's what you're going to do: if you're where I think you are, there's a big branch pointing up in the air, about an arm's length ahead of you. Try to touch it, gently, gently. Very gently. When you've found it, tell me.'

Above all he mustn't feel groggy, he mustn't have any more yellow shivers before his eyes, he must be able to get up slowly, stand solid and square on his feet, and pour all his strength into his shoulders, he must have arms of steel and hands like feathers. . . . Hands light as feathers, and his mind clear, and know this minute what he was doing.

Mon Cadet bit his lip furiously, and sucked in a good draught of his own blood, licking his lips greedily, avid for this salty taste. He rose to his knees. He bit his lips again and swallowed blood. He dug ferociously with his teeth into his lips. He drew up one leg. He pressed one foot on the ground. He must get up without leaning on anything. And above all, once he was up, stay up.

'I'm coming, hang on!' he said in a thin voice that was trying to sound calm. And it did.

He was crouching. He stood up, wavering as if in a wild wind. He summoned all his strength to balance himself.

'When you find that branch,' said Marceau, 'I'll tell you what you have to do. It's simple. You have to push.'

He was standing up, but his head was buzzing like a saw-mill. He felt that at the touch of a feather he would fall like a sack, flat on his face, any old way. In the dark he felt for the branch, but he didn't dare stretch his arms too far, their weight made him lose balance.

'There it is,' he said finally, 'I've got it, I've touched it.'

'Yes, a little too hard,' said the calm voice. 'Quick, shove!'

Then Mon Cadet let himself fall forward with all his weight, which he would have liked to be the weight of a mountain, but which seemed to him as light as down, and he lost consciousness in a white, fluffy silence.

He awoke. A dog licking his face. It was Marceau's tears and his mouth. He kissed him furiously.

'You!' groaned Mon Cadet.

And he too began licking, at the great, rough cheeks.

'Yes,' said Marceau, 'it's all right. We won!'

Winter came, crystalline. The frozen air, like a rarefied alcohol, enlarged all forms, and the few enormous birds that

crossed the deserted sky left in it long, mottled traces from
every feather-tip.

Marceau carried the new bell up to the steeple on his
back; as if it were nothing but a sack of flour, and from the
outside, on a ladder. Afterwards, as he was stepping down
from the last rung, Mon Cadet took off his coat.

'I want to fight with you,' he said.

'Very well,' said Marceau.

'When?'

'Right now.'

'Where?'

'Here. Now then, who'll bring us some straw?'

The men were masked up to the eyes in their mufflers;
they had pulled their berets down to their eyes, there was
nothing but eyes to be seen. They threw back their capes
from their shoulders. They brought bundles of straw in
their wool-gloved hands under their flapping capes, then
they folded themselves in their mantles to look on.

The two were stripped to the waist.

'Look,' said Marceau, 'aren't you cold?'

'No.'

'I'm trying to remember something. We have to do this
by the rules. Wait, I have it! We salute. . . .'

He saluted his brother, who saluted him.

'. . . and we say, "We swear that there is no private
quarrel between us, and no question of gain; and that we
will fight fair before you for the sake of the manly art. . . ." '

'I should hope!' said Mon Cadet.

'It's not that,' said Marceau, 'it's just the rule. We have
to say that. I said it, now you say it.'

Mon Cadet recited it again.

They saluted.

Marceau, arms wide, feinted to the left. Mon Cadet's

heart burned with joy; this time there was no condescending: Marceau was even using his tricks, and his eyes were darting about under his thick eyebrows like bees tangled in wool. Mon Cadet dodged the encounter with a little bear-dance. After the feint to the left Marceau came on with his right arm curved, for all the world like a professional. Mon Cadet felt the hold grip his flanks with a brutality that proved this was no child's play.

Just now, as he saw Marceau's open arms come at him, he had been afraid that it was only an embrace. It was one, but it was full of power, right to the fingertips. His heart burst into full flame. At last, peace of mind in battle. The greatest happiness in the world was to have recognition with honour. He planted his legs wide. Getting his footing, he took time to ensure that his back was well in line. Pulling his left foot to the rear to buttress himself there, he faced the other. He did better, he moved in on him. Not much. They were already almost intertwined after these first manoeuvres, but if you want to score you have to hurt. And to hurt, you have to bore into what's in front of you. For one thing, your best support is the man you're fighting. He leaned in, knee against knee, chest against chest, shoulders against shoulders, chin against chin.

Mon Cadet tried to slide his left arm to a point below Marceau's chin. If he succeeded he could push upwards and pry it out from his throat. He succeeded. The chin slipped, tightened again, slipped, grunted and flew up. Mon Cadet saw Marceau's whole face pass his eye as it turned upwards. But suddenly Mon Cadet lost sight of that red, open mouth with the black gap-teeth where bits of tongue swelled out. He butted the chin with his skull and pushed his head against his brother's gullet until he could feel the little point of the Adam's apple in the thick of his hair. His face rubbed against his brother's hairy chest. The acid smell of sweat, which the frost dried at once, itched in his nose. There were monstrous movements rumbling in this chest, and sudden waves of skin and muscle leapt hard at his mouth and eyes. He continued crushing at his brother's throat with such force that the back muscles rooting his arms in his shoulders were petrified in full play like the wings of an eagle shot in flight. At last in the tumult that filled his ears he began to hear a thudding sound, violent and fast. It came at the same time as a great wave which shook and gripped him so brutally and quickly that he quite lost his footing, and he felt himself lifted up as if he were going to be thrown to the other side of the mountains. Then he suddenly heard the thudding rhythm resound again. He fell back on his feet. He found his footing. It was only a residual violence that shook him now. Finally the thing at which his head was boring sank away and he himself fell at the same time, pulled forward and down. He rolled over Marceau whose arms were flung out as he lay flat on his back in the straw. The icy air washed the blue and green visions from Mon Cadet's eyes. And through these wriggling bits of snakes and lizards that were blinding him he saw his brother's face. He didn't recognize it: it was black as a negro's! . . .

He leapt to his feet. Marceau was up at the same time. He was trying to speak but couldn't, and was only making gestures. But his black face was beginning to redden in places, like cinders touched by a breeze.

He said:

'I'm not beaten.'

'No more am I,' said Mon Cadet.

'You!' said Marceau. 'I'll show you.'

And he leapt on him. They fell.

The whole assembly of capes rushed to form a circle around them with a flutter of black wings. Reflected gestures of the fight jerked at all the arms under all the mantles. In their great, black mantles the men jumped backwards, all together.

All together they jumped forwards, then retreated again, spreading their arms under the great woollen folds of their mantles, as crows spread their wings around a carcass, pecking apart its muscles. Turcan lifted his beret, pulled down his muffler, wiped the frost from his mouth:

'Too old!' he said, 'No wind left. He can't hold out.'

He pushed up his muffler again, pulled the beret down to his eyes, watched the fight, jumping up and down with his great, woollen wings. Paillon the younger lowered his muffler, lifted his beret:

'Cadet's twenty years younger,' he said.

Then he sprang aside, for the battle was rolling near his feet.

'And the same mother,' he said.

'What?' said Faurie.

'I said. . .' began Paillon the younger, but he was almost upset by the battle which boiled up at his legs.

He spread his arms under his cloak, forcing back the others who were pushing him too far ahead.

'I said, it's the same mother made the two of them. It's no wonder.'

But Marceau heaved a long sigh, like an ox. He was puffing, laid out at full length in the straw. Mon Cadet was holding him down with a hand that was all timid and trembling, that would scarcely have held a fly, and Marceau did not push the hand away. He clutched it, he pressed it to his heart. Then he pushed it away. Slowly he got to his knees and stood up:

'No,' he said, 'no, no! No, dear child! I'm not beaten. Not at all. He's my little brother, he's Mon Cadet! It won't do! No.'

He looked at the faces around him.

'Am I right? What do you think, the rest of you? And Mon Cadet? What do you say? Do you really believe I was beaten? Me? No!'

He shook his head.

'No, it can't be: he's Mon Cadet. It mustn't be,' he said softly.

'Rest,' said Mon Cadet, 'get your breath. It's all over.'

'What's over? What do you mean it's over? I don't need anybody to tell me to get my breath.'

And he pretended to laugh. He threw back his head with its great jowls. The grimace of his mouth swelled out his lower lip grossly, and the laugh sliced his two cheeks with motionless wrinkles.

'Something has to be set right here,' he said.

He looked Mon Cadet straight in the face.

'We have to fight,' he said.

'We just did,' said Mon Cadet.

'We have to fight again,' he said.

'What for?'

'For everything.'

'Are you ready?'

'I'm ready.'

Marceau spread out his arms at full length. Standing on the tips of his toes, he looked around him one last time.

'Hold your tongues,' he said.

But the black capes had nothing to say, the mouths were hidden beneath their mufflers. Only the eyes were alive, beneath the berets. Leaning forward, his arms spread, it seemed as if Marceau were about to fly. They rushed at each other.

Eluding the arms, Mon Cadet's head brushed past Marceau's chest. Again he heard the furious thudding sound.

He realized that it was his brother's heart. For his part, he felt lean, sound, hard, fit as a fiddle. He slipped away from the hands, he grew daring and dug his shoulder square in Marceau's belly. He tried to grasp him around the middle. Marceau took him by the hips and lifted him up. He was forced to turn to an eel, at once, from head to foot. Marceau was about to lay him over his shoulder and throw him down. At the very moment when his feet left the ground Mon Cadet, instead of resisting, flipped upwards with his toes and threw his legs in the air. Marceau's hands lost their grip on his hips for a fraction of a second. Just a fraction. Mon Cadet hooked Marceau's shoulder under his right knee, let his left leg dangle and, without using his strength, pressing diagonally with his full weight, he grasped Marceau's left thigh and threw him. He felt himself capable only of easy, graceful, victorious movements. As he fell along with his brother, his power sprang to life. Like a snake it writhed joyfully in every part of his body. He straddled his brother, resisted his flailing legs, subdued the left thigh which he had not let go, and, crushing it under his chest, he addressed both arms to the right thigh which was still kicking like a carp on dry land.

But an enormous sun of fire, red and speckled, burst in his head, blinding his eyes, filling his throat with a kind of smothering mortar that stifled him. Marceau had kicked him square in the face with the hobnailed heel of his boot. Marceau drew up his leg and kicked again with all his might. Raising his head to see if he were succeeding in freeing himself from the weight and exertions that were crushing and twisting his leg, he let fly another blow with the flat of his heel at that mask of red clay. He saw jets of blood spurting out in stars. But he heard a sound like thunder in his head, and all the nerves of his jaw spattered the inside of his head with terrible, freezing, slashing lights. Tiny,

cold bones rolled into his throat. Some he swallowed, some
he spat out. A wind of nausea carried him swiftly to heights
where his heart refused to follow. As he reached the point
where breathing stops he remained suspended, out of the
world, for a brief second, then he fell back. And all the
water of his stomach and all the warmth of his bowels came
fighting to his upper throat, and he began to vomit. It took
all his strength to keep from retching himself empty, to
harden his stomach and resist the plunging in his head
which threatened again to carry him off to the heights with
a whirring of enormous wings.

At a moment when he was no longer thinking of anything
but himself, he heard the bone of his forehead crack; immediately afterwards he saw the blow that struck him: it
was blue, like lightning, with a trembling aureole of red
ochre, but it had not yet stopped quivering when the dark
came slowly to his eyes which suddenly, both of them, lit
up with a smarting pain like a great oak turned gold from
tip to roots.

Mon Cadet had struggled to his knees and having un-
tangled his arms from Marceau's failing grip he struck with
all his force with his fists at Marceau's face, he aimed for
the eyes and struck the forehead, found the eyes, rallied
all his strength and struck. He himself was blinded by the
blood spurting from his nose and from his whole face, torn
by Marceau's hobnails. Tall, purple waves rippling before
his eyes hid the world from him. But in the middle of his
body, just at the hips where the bruises of old battle-holds
were still hurting, right up to his right side, like an enormous ball his anger rolled, lighting up another world. He
struck at the face as if it were something to be built.

Marceau shook his head, trying to shiver off the pain, but
he had two grindstones of fire in his eyes, throwing streams
of sparks. Then, all around his middle, he felt the crackling

of great, leafy trees on fire, and he himself was suddenly on fire with rage. He spat a last clot of bitter bile and blood. He lowered his head and hurled his legs and arms at the other's body with such force that his back lifted each time off the ground.

He was fighting in a total darkness traversed by hurricanes of fire. Finally, under his big, open hand he found, lost, sought and found again a crotch, an opening between thighs. He kicked at it with all his might. He heard a terrible cry that was like the howling of the wind, and suddenly he was disconcerted. Then he rallied his desire to win and slowly, very slowly, got to his feet.

When Mon Cadet took the blow from the boot—it was a little off-centre—he had been warned by a kind of presentiment of the blood and in that instant he had turned his hip. The hobnailed sole tore off a little fabric there and, slipping, harrowed with all its nails—but only with their points—the tender part of his groin! ...

Despite his evasion a sickening pain took away his breath and suddenly, gasping for air, Mon Cadet leapt upright like a spring, shouting:

'Here!'

Overcome with dizziness, he was teetering and about to collapse at full length when, through the red storm of his eyes, he saw Marceau's black form rising slowly as he got to his feet. Drunk with pain and anger, he looked at the other blind man who was heavily seeking his footing on wide-spread legs. Then, with all his heart, with all his weight, he kicked out with the toe of his shoe, just at the spot where the other bore his sex. And despite the effort he remained standing, listening for a long, long while, as to a rock-slide, to the growl of Marceau crumbling to the ground.

Chorus

At the Hotel of the West, around the stove, they're telling stories.

The time they went to the place of the man called Marc, whose wife's name is Suzanne, and they keep house at the bastide named Blanchon, at the top of Malecolle hill, in the fields of Esparron.

'I remember, that very same day I bought sheep from Chaillan, Joseph, the one they call "The Blonde Woman", who goes by the nickname of Bouffetti, at Pigoulet farm, just at the bottom of Malecolle, across the little valley that carries down every sound from the top. You could hear them singing. And that went on. . . well, the time it took to do business over the forty-three ewes and the jackass, which I've still got.'

'There was Pierrisnard, that they call Pierrette, and there was a man named François de Bras, or Saint Maximinus, and one of the Canores from Saint-Martin, and a man and a woman of forty or forty-five, all charcoal burners by trade, working in the woods of Esparron where they had a kiln burning—the man and the woman had left their six children there.'

'Wasn't Silvy with them too?'

'Which one?'

'Silvy the Hard, the one with the wicker buggy.'

'No, the time with Silvy was at the bastide they call the Grand Adroit, and it's in the fields of Esparron as well, for that matter. They used to like to go to Esparron.'

'And why would that be?'

'No reason at all, and then again because neither Marceau nor Mon Cadet gave a fig for any man in the world. Why did they go to Esparron? Because once, the first time, they'd had sport there. That was enough for Marceau. He'd do anything to give his brother a good time.'

'No, not anything. And there's proof of that!'

'That has nothing to do with it. I'm talking about a good time. This fellow called Marc, he's a funny duck, you know it as well as I do. He keeps nothing for himself, he gives everything, especially his house. And that Suzanne, tell her to whip up some pancakes or doughnuts and she's ready every time. But it's one thing to have yourself a feast by the fire, eating black pudding or chestnuts or sweets and drinking short ones, and it's another thing to see yourself forced to eat dirt.'

'By his Cadet? Why should he let that bother him?'

'You're not thinking. His Cadet was his God!'

'That's the point, Cadet could do no wrong.'

'What kind of nonsense is that? Do you know what you're saying? He could do anything he liked, except be stronger than Marceau. That's what it is to be a god!'

'It's no more that than another thing. Men have no notion of things like this,' said Violette.

'And women, what do they know about it?'

'What are the women doing today, while you're all here talking?' said Violette. 'They're crying. As long as you talk about a thing it means you don't understand it. As soon as you understand the first thing about it, you weep.'

'And how does that help?'

'How can anything help now?' said Violette. 'Everything's been done.'

'True enough. But we're not trying to bring back the dead. We're trying to understand.'

'It's clear enough,' said Violette. 'If you don't see that when you love someone you want always to give, you want always to be stronger than he is, what can you expect to see? Marceau had come to this way of thinking: he was the strongest man in the world. Because he loved his Cadet he was giving him the strongest man in the world, as well as all the rest. Suddenly, he's not the strongest any more! What do you expect him to do?'

'What do you mean, do? It seems to me he could have done a lot of things before doing what he did.'

'I tell you, he couldn't. A woman understands these things.'

'So you think he had to go sharpen a bill-hook and hide in the small hours, and when the Cadet comes along to fetch some wood open him up with four or five slashes—maybe more—any old way in his belly, the way he did? You should have seen. . . .'

'The bill-hook, maybe. Sharpened, no. Hide? It's neither here nor there; but kill him, yes.'

'If you'd seen what I saw! It wasn't pretty, I'll tell you that. I came along less than half an hour after he'd done the job. I said to myself, "What's that red over there?" It showed up on the snow. It was a length of those doings you have in your belly, but I was far from thinking that. I thought it was I don't know what, a little cat, a big rat. I was just going to kick it away and then as I looked right and left I saw a bigger lot at the foot of the woodpile. And it was Mon Cadet, or rather his Cadet. And well gutted, by God! Dead, he was that. I didn't really ask myself any questions, until I saw how. Somebody had chopped into his stomach the way you chop a tree to fell it. And what with? Then I saw the bill-hook. And I said to myself, "Why, why, why, why! ..." '

'Why? I told you why,' says Violette, and she goes off to the kitchen with her pot of hot wine and coffee.

'That must have been not very funny.'

'It's not that it wasn't funny, it was a deed I couldn't understand. Who could have done it? Not a hair of my head ever thought of Marceau.'

'It's not with the hairs of your head that you'd think of that,' says Violette, coming back with her coffee-pot.

'And what did you do then?'

'Do? I did nothing. What do you do in a case like that? You look, you say to yourself, "It's not true," and little by little you know that it is true. And then I said to myself, "There's going to be trouble over this!" and I ran to Esther's house.'

'There's nothing but women now in the Jason family.'

'There aren't even any Jasons left. Esther, Valérie—and Delphine even more, we don't count her—they're only Jasons by marriage. There's nobody left of the old stock but Ariane.'

'And Ariane, is she nothing? The whole thing came out of her.'

'She's over eighty. She's at the end of her road.'

'She's running things right now.'

'Somebody had to do it.'

'And how many in her place would have hid their heads under the sheets?'

'I can still hear Esther screaming.'

'She's screaming yet. She woke me up the other night. I looked at the clock. It was three in the morning. I got up, I went to the window. It was dark at Esther's place, no lamp, no fire, and a little scream, never stopping. I said to

myself, "What are you going to do? Go there?" I went back
to bed. She could have been sick but it wasn't the crying of
a sick person, it wasn't a scream to wake other people. It
was a scream to make the time go by.'

'The time will go by,' said Violette.

The stove is roaring. The wind rattles at the door. The
heavy flakes are crushed against the panes. The heat is
enough to put you three parts asleep. All these great, strapping fellows will spend the winter dozing around the fire
at the Hotel of the West.

'It was Ariane who straightened out Mon Cadet—that
is, her Cadet, for he was her youngest as well—he was
curled up around his wound. She pressed down his shoulders and I held the dead man's legs.'

'Dead he was, God knows. I was the one who opened
out his arms. Talk about dead! . . .'

'It was then we had a good look at what killed him. Up to
that minute we hadn't seen his face, nor how he had come
to die. When he was straightened out, we saw. He was
almost cut in two by the blows that madman had given him
with the bill-hook. . . .'

'Why no, not at all, not mad at all,' said Violette.
'Wretched. It's not the same thing.'

'He only held together by his spine. His guts were on the
ground, and a lot of other things.'

'And I almost took a kick at one of those things with my
boot.'

'And Ariane said: where is Marceau?'

'Yes, and we all said, that's right, where's Marceau?'

'There'd been uproar enough. Why wasn't he there?'

'It took me the whole morning to get it through my head.
I did the same as you: I carried him, I laid him on his bed.
I said to Esther, "What can we do, that's the way it is,"
just like everybody else, and I went home to make my

coffee. I was frozen. I made my coffee, I took my bowl. I put
in milk. I cut my bread. I wasn't even thinking at the time.
My head was in the clouds. I ate just as usual. My door
opened and Ariane came in. She said, "They'll have to go
and get Marceau." Then, all of a sudden, I understood. We
didn't have to go and get Marceau the way you go and get
somebody you need. We had to get him because he was the
one who had killed his brother.'

'Not his brother,' said Violette, 'his Cadet. It's not the
same!'

'Yes, well, I stayed on a while longer at Esther's house.
Why? I couldn't tell you. It's not that I like to hear women
wailing. Especially her, you'd swear it was a goat. I couldn't
get used to the idea that such a thing had happened. And
who could have sliced into the boy with a bill-hook? I
couldn't see it.'

'I'll tell you. I was down with the sheep. I do this and
that, I look here and there. It was warm in the sheep-pen.
I was in no hurry to leave. I go over the whole flock. I
take my time. I come back to the house. The woman says
to me, "Somebody's killed Jason." "What are you trying
to tell me?" "Somebody's killed Jason." "Which one?"
"I don't know. One of the two of them." I go out, I go to
have a look. Polyte was the one that told me: "It's the
Cadet." I thought to myself, "By God, here's something we
haven't heard the last of." '

'Take me, now, it got me by surprise, just like Baptiste.
I didn't know a thing. I was planing wood, I'm making a
cupboard. When I saw Ariane come in, the way she looked,
my mouth fell open. She said to me, "They'll have to go and
get Marceau." "Where?" I asked, like a damned fool. Then
she explained.'

'And since it was all over for Mon Cadet we had to see

how it would end for Marceau. It's against the law to cut
open your brother, or even just anybody, with a bill-hook,
on the excuse that you're wretched, as Violette says. What
was going to be the end of it all?'

'We soon found out that he didn't take the gun.'

'But he'd taken his fur-lined tunic, and his mitts, and
his fur hat. And if a man that big wanted to keep warm
after what he'd done, he wasn't going to pay attention to
the first one along that told him, "Come with us, little boy!"
—or rather the first ones, there were at least five of us
already.'

'Oh, but they're stupid!' said Violette. 'They don't see
that it wasn't Marceau any more. It was nothing but a
machine.'

'Well, old girl, a machine isn't always easy going. Tumble
into a thresher and see.'

'We thought of that, too, what Violette said. We didn't
fall with the last rain. When everything pointed to him—
the bill-hook he'd sharpened that same morning by the first
light, Valérie hearing him turn the grindstone, then finding
it there by the body; and then Ariane singling him out, and
as you say, Violette, not as a madman but a wretched man,
and telling us to go and get him, not as a criminal but a
sick man that you have to help in his last moments. When
we thought over what had happened the day before, how
his Cadet had made him eat dirt, we realized he hadn't run
to get away. What could he get away from? He went just to
walk up and down, the same as anybody having trouble
with his metric system. The only thing we wondered was
just where this little stroll was going to take him. Wasn't it
going to take him into parts where they didn't know him?
Wouldn't he end up scaring people, the way he'd likely
look, and wouldn't they treat him as if were just anybody?

That was the whole question! And that's why we went looking for him.'

'It was ten o'clock in the morning.'

'Maybe it was. I didn't look at my watch. I didn't even have it on me. It stayed hanging on the nail at the head of my bed. Ten or eleven, it didn't matter. The weather was worse than it is today. Today it's snowing, that makes you feel good. The other day it was threatening. It was dark, nothing was moving and there wasn't a sound. A man can't come to terms so easily with silence, not in wide, open space. And it was no help still being near the village and under forest, we knew we were heading for open spaces. It wasn't mind-reading. Where would a man from here head for, if he wasn't out after fun? He's not going to go down, he's going to go up. That's what we did, from ten in the morning—if you say we left at ten—to a time that's not marked on watches, when we got hungry and thirsty and our heads were dizzy with the silence. We'd been out of the trees for a long time, and for a long time we'd been climbing in the great, clear parts of the mountain, the parts that are just against the black of the sky in winter. Hungry, thirsty, and we needed a corner by the fire. Not so much for the fire as for the corner, in that space there are no corners, and anything could come at you from any direction. So far as Marceau was concerned, that was settled. We'd found his tracks. They led straight ahead of us, and there was nothing they could do but go on straight ahead. I don't know who was the first to think of Jean-Pierre Amaudric's barn. Maybe we all thought of it at once. Anyway, there was no argument, we all headed for it as one man. The snow carried well, it was crust to the bone. The barn was locked and we had to rip the bolt off. There was dry wood, all you could ask for, a cauldron, and the best of all was, we melted chunks of ice in it and brought it to a boil to hear the water

H

humming. We ate our ham. We smoked out pipes. Night
fell. I even think we smoked our pipes so night would fall.
No more question of going out again. This was better. We
laid wood on the fire and went to sleep.'

'Went to sleep, and all the time here! . . .' said Violette.

'Went to sleep and whatever you like. You were here in
your houses. Very well, we had a house too. Marceau, all
very well, Jason, all fine and lovely, and you're a lovely girl
yourself, but a man can only use the strength he's got. Whoever says different is telling stories. We only woke up to
keep the fire going. There are times when heat in your joints
is good for the heart, and ours needed tending. And then
came the morning that you're waiting for. It came, don't
worry. We ate another bit of fat and went on our way. The
weather was still on the dark and silent side. Marceau's
trail shone like silk on the crust. We didn't have to go borrowing trouble, we just had to follow him. We followed.
And that's how we came to the slope of Paleirottes, to the
house of Thomé Rebuffat. There was smoke from the chimney and we saw someone doing chores in the yard. The
Rebuffat woman told us he'd knocked at their door the
day before in the evening. That he'd stayed a good spell
framed in the doorway without coming in and without going out and never saying a word, in spite of her and Thomé
urging him to come in. That at last they'd given him a loaf
of bread he hadn't asked for, just so as not to leave him
alone in the night, as the Rebuffat woman said. He went
away. Never a word. And we went on about our business
in country that was getting very difficult now. The thing is,
after Paleirottes, there's nothing. I'd never seen Paleirottes
in winter. Those are places where unless you're obliged
you don't go of your own free will. In winter we'd never
been in what's above Paleirottes. Is there anybody here
that has?'

'No. In '16 the gendarmes went up there to look for Ferry la Blache, the hunchback's son, who'd deserted. But they were gendarmes.'

'And not in winter?'

'No, in June.'

'Did they get him, the la Blache boy?'

'No.'

'We got Marceau. It wasn't hard. He was waiting for us. Not specially for us. He was waiting for somebody that he must have found by now. We were on a slope that according to me must look out over the valley to the farms of Valbelle. I'm saying what I think, not what I saw. We were in the clouds. You couldn't see more than three paces in front of you. That was more than we needed to find him. He was lying across our way. We brought him back. The gendarmes' doctor opened him up to see what he had in his stomach. Nothing. He didn't die of sickness, nor of cold. He had bitten into his bread, just once, and he still had the bite in his mouth. The bread, sure enough, had tried to keep him company for a while, but bread isn't everything. He died of his life that refused to go on.'

Manosque, 1950.

Also published by Peter Owen
Jean Giono
The Man Who Planted Trees

This is the story of Elzéard Bouffier, a Provençal
shepherd who single-handedly regenerated a whole
landscape simply by planting trees. The story –
both parable and manual – pits the tree-planter, the
earth-husband, against the makers of war and those who
would carelessly exploit the earth and needlessly destroy
the environment. For Giono, nature was a living force in
which mankind can rediscover the depth and harmony
he has lost in urban life, and *The Man Who Planted Trees*
is his manifesto for a reafforestation programme that could renew the
whole of our planet.

Since first being published as 'The Man Who Planted Hope and Grew
Happiness' in *Vogue* magazine in 1954, Giono's profound and prescient tale
– modern in its concerns but which predated the current thinking on
environmental issues by several decades – has appeared in many editions
throughout the world as well as a cartoon feature film and a BBC radio
adaptation.

The book is illustrated with twenty-one beautiful woodcuts by Michael
McCurdy.

'This is a lovely, poignant little book by one of the most distinguished twentieth-century
French writers.' – *Sunday Times*

'Michael McCurdy's gentle woodcuts enhance this haunting tale . . . a version of
pastoral, regenerating a whole landscape and community.' – *Observer*

'This powerful story . . . can be an inspiration to us all.'
– *Broadleaf*, the magazine of the Woodland Trust

0 7206 1021 4 | paperback | £6.95

To order *The Man Who Planted Trees* or any other Peter Owen title, contact
the Sales Department, Peter Owen Publishers, 73 Kenway Road, London SW5 0RE, UK;
tel: ++ 44 (0)20 7373 5628; fax: ++ 44 (0)20 7373 6760; e-mail: sales@peterowen.com

Peter Owen Modern Classics

If you have enjoyed this book you may like to try some of the other Peter Owen paperback reprints listed below. **The Peter Owen Modern Classics** series was launched in 1998 to bring some of our internationally acclaimed authors and their works, first published by Peter Owen in hardback, to a contemporary readership.

To order books or a free catalogue or for further information on these or any other Peter Owen titles, please contact the **Sales Department, Peter Owen Ltd, 73 Kenway Road, London SW5 0RE, UK** tel: **+ + 44 (0)20 7373 5628 or + + 44 (0)20 7370 6093**, fax: **+ + 44 (0)20 7373 6760**, e-mail: **sales@peterowen.com** or visit our website at **www.peterowen.com**

Guillaume Apollinaire
LES ONZE MILLE VERGES

In 1907 Guillaume Apollinaire, one of the most original and influential poets of the twentieth century, turned his hand to the novel. He produced two books for the clandestine erotica market, the finer of these being *Les Onze Mille Verges*. One of the most masterful and hilarious novels of all time, it was pronounced owlishly by Picasso to be Apollinaire's masterpiece.

'A vigorous and highly readable translation.' – *Times Literary Supplement*

0 7206 1100 0 £9.95

Paul Bowles
MIDNIGHT MASS

Chosen by the author from his best, these superlative short stories reveal Paul Bowles at his peak. They offer insights into the mysteries of *kif* and the majesty of the desert, the meeting of alien cultures and the clash between modern and ancient, Islam and Christianity, logic and superstition. Set in Morocco, Thailand and Sri Lanka, these stories reverberate with vision and, like Bowles's novels, they are universal in their appeal.

'His short stories are among the best ever written by an American.' – Gore Vidal

0 7206 1083 4 £9.95

POINTS IN TIME

Here Bowles focuses on Morocco, his home for many decades, condensing experience, emotion and the whole history of a people into a series of short, brilliant pieces. He takes the reader on a journey through the Moroccan centuries, pausing at points along the way to create resonant images of the country and the beliefs and characteristics of its inhabitants.

'His plain and compact prose makes this a wholly

satisfying book.' – *Literary Review*

'Persuasive prose which leaves one with a very strong and distinct flavour of landscape and people.' – *Gay Times*

0 7206 1137 7 £8.50

THEIR HEADS ARE GREEN

First published in 1963, this is an account of Bowles's experiences in Morocco and his journeys to the Sahara, which influenced the classic *The Sheltering Sky*, as well as his travels through Mexico, Turkey and Sri Lanka. With his exceptional gift for penetrating beyond the picturesque or exotic aspects of the countries he describes, he evokes the unique characteristics of both people and places.

'Few writers have Bowles's skill in evocation while making of the familiar something new and extraordinary.' – *The Times*

0 7206 1077 X £9.95

UP ABOVE THE WORLD

Dr Slade and his wife are on holiday in Latin America when they meet Grove, a young man of striking good looks and charm and his beautiful seventeen-year-old mistress. An apparently chance encounter, it opens the door to a nightmare as the Slades find themselves being sucked in by lives whose relevance to their own they cannot understand. Oiled by a cocktail of drugs and dark relationships, the Slades are lured on another journey: a terrifying trip where the only guides are fantasy, hallucination and death.

Brilliantly written, with the poetic control that has always characterized Bowles's work, *Up Above the World* is a masterpiece of cold, relentless terror.

'Sex, drugs, fantasies and the machinery of derangement . . . Bowles's overpowering void descends on the mind and heart like a hypnotic spell.' — *New York Times Book Review*

0 7206 1087 7 £9.95

Blaise Cendrars
TO THE END OF THE WORLD
The narrative of this novel shifts between a Foreign Legion barracks in North Africa and the theatres, cafés, dosshouses and police headquarters of post-war Paris. The central character in this *roman-à-clef* is a septuagenarian actress whose affair with a young deserter from the Foreign Legion is jeopardized by the murder of a barman. *To the End of the World* is not pure invention. Like all Cendrars's works it has some basis in his nomadic life; but this original and often very funny portrayal of the Paris of the late 1940s is obviously the product of an abundant imagination.

'There is nothing like reading Cendrars.' — *Independent*

0 7206 1097 4   £9.95

DAN YACK
Dan Yack is an eccentric English millionaire ship owner, a notorious hell-raiser, and the envy of all St Petersburg. He is also the alter ego of his creator, Blaise Cendrars. This strange travel yarn begins with Dan Yack finding out that he is no longer wanted by his lover, Hedwiga. Regaining consciousness after a mammoth drinking bout, he impulsively invites three artists to accompany him on a world voyage via the Antarctic. After a hard winter the sun finally returns, but no one could predict the surreal disaster that is about to unfold, a scenario involving a plum pudding, whales, women and World War I.

'A kind of jazz-age super-cocktail, a swirling cauldron of the outrageous, the orgiastic and the surreal.' – *Guardian*

'Mad, vicious, amusing and beautiful.' – *Time Out*

'A virtuoso performance.' – *Observer*

'Tintin for grown-ups.' – *Irish Times*

0 7206 1157 1   £9.95

THE CONFESSIONS OF DAN YACK
This continues the adventures of Dan Yack. He tells the story of his love for Mireille whom he meets in a crowded tabac in a Paris gone mad on Armistice Night, 1918. This love transforms Dan Yack's life: he abandons his women, gives up his fast cars and debauchery to marry this convent-educated girl of his dreams. To indulge her fantasies he launches her as a film star and casts her in wraith-like roles inspired by Edgar Allen Poe. But before long Mireille is struck by a mysterious and fatal illness, the psychological origins of which raise disturbing questions about the nature of their relationship. Whereas Dan Yack's previous memoir celebrated his exploits with malicious bravado, this is a bittersweet memoir of love and loss, shot through with profound melancholy and a palpable sense of psycho-sexual disturbance.

'A beautifully written work, memorable and compelling and superbly translated. It makes one reach out for everything else he ever wrote.' – *Sunday Telegraph*

'Discovery of the year, a box-fresh piece of 1920s Parisiana.' – Books of the Year, *Independent,*

0 7206 1158 X   £9.95

Jean Cocteau
LE LIVRE BLANC
This 'white paper' on homosexual love was first published anonymously in France by Cocteau's contemporary Maurice Sachs and was at once decried as obscene. The semi-autobiographical narrative describes a youth's love affairs with a succession of boys and men during the early years of this century. The young man's self-deceptive attempts to find fulfilment, first through women and then by way of the Church, are movingly conveyed, and the book ends with a plea for homosexuality to be accepted without censure. The book includes woodcuts by the author.

'A wonderful book.' — *Gay Times*

0 7206 1081 8   £8.50

Colette
DUO and LE TOUTOUNIER
These two linked novels are works of Colette's maturity. In *Duo* Colette observes, with astuteness and perception, two characters whose marriage is foundering on the wife's infidelity. Acting out the crisis, Alice and Michel have the stage to themselves so that nothing is allowed to distract from the marital dialogue. *Le Toutounier* continues Alice's story after Michel's death and her move to Paris. There she and her two sisters live in a shabby, homely apartment; fiercely independent, reticent, hard-working, needing men but showing little sign of loving them, they speak a private language and seek comfort in the indestructible sofa (*toutounier*) of their childhood.

'Drenched with her talent at its best.' — *Sunday Times*

0 7206 1069 9   £9.95

Lawrence Durrell
POPE JOAN
In this superb adaptation of a novel by the nineteenth-century Greek author Emmanuel Royidis, Lawrence Durrell traces the remarkable history of a young

woman who travelled across Europe in the ninth century disguised as a monk, acquired great learning and ruled over Christendom for two years as Pope John VIII before her death in childbirth. When *Papissa Joanna* was first published in Athens in 1886 it created a sensation. The book was banned and its author excommunicated. It nevertheless brought him fame and the work established itself in the history of modern Greek literature. Subsequently Durrell created a masterpiece in its own right, a dazzling concoction presented with the deftest touch.

'A sharp satire . . . acutely funny . . . salacious.' – *Spectator*

'The most remarkable of Durrell's adaptations was his brilliant version of Emmanuel Royidis's novel.' – *The Times*

'One of the funniest novels ever written . . . A true classic.' – *Punch*

0 7206 1065 6   £9.95

Shusaku Endo
WONDERFUL FOOL

Gaston Bonaparte, a young Frenchman, visits Tokyo to stay with his pen-friend Takamori. His appearance is a bitter disappointment to his new friends and his behaviour causes them acute embarrassment. He is a trusting person with a simple love for others and continues to trust them even after they have demonstrated deceit and betrayal. He spends his time making friends with street children, stray dogs, prostitutes and gangsters. Endo charts his misadventures with sharp irony, satire and objectivity.

'The perfect guide in the form of fiction to Tokyo and the Japanese experience.' — Grahame Greene

0 7206 1080 X   £9.95

Jean Giono
TWO RIDERS ON THE STORM

Set in the remote hills of Provence, where the lives of the inhabitants are moulded along fiercely passionate lines, this is the story of two brothers, members of a family renowned for its brutality and bound together with ties stronger than those of ordinary filial love. Yet this affection turns to hatred after the elder brother kills a wild horse with a single blow at a country fair and becomes the local wrestling champion. As his strength increases and his fame spreads, the younger sibling's jealousy causes this bond to snap. The end, when it comes, is a violent – and deadly – confrontation.

'Giono gives us a world he lives in, a world of dream, passion and reality.' – Henry Miller

'It has a timeless fairytale quality . . . zestful and humorous.' – *Sunday Times*

'Violent but beautiful . . . a novelist of great originality.' – *Spectator*

0 7206 1159 8   £9.95

Hermann Hesse
DEMIAN

Published shortly after the First World War, *Demian* is one of Hermann Hesse's finest novels. Emil Sinclair boasts of a theft that he has not committed and finds himself blackmailed by a bully. He turns to Max Demian, in whom he finds a friend and spiritual mentor. This strangely self-possessed figure is able to lure him out of his ordinary home life and convince him of an existing alternative world of corruption and evil. In progressing from an orthodox education through to philosophical mysticism, Emil's search for self-awareness culminates in a meeting with Demian's mother – symbol and personification of motherhood.

'One of the most elevated spiritual and ethical allegories I have ever read . . . extremely readable.' – *Listener*

'A moving fable of spiritual growth.' – *Observer*

0 7206 1130 X   £9.95

GERTRUDE

Gertrude portrays the life and emotional development of a young composer, Kuhn, who finds success in his art under the sway of Heinrich Muoth, a melancholy and self-destructive opera singer, and the gentle self-assured Gertrude. Kuhn falls in love with Gertrude but she falls for Muoth, and their unhappy marriage becomes a metaphor for the opposing forces of the Dionysian and the Apollonian.

'It would be a pity to miss this book – it has such a rare flavour of truth and simplicity.' – Stevie Smith, *Observer*

'There is a freshness and authenticity about these characters.' – *Times Literary Supplement*

0 7206 1169 5   £9.95

JOURNEY TO THE EAST

The narrator of this allegorical tale travels through time and space in a search of ultimate truth. This pilgrimage to the East covers both real and imagined lands and takes place not only in the last century but also in the Middle Ages and the Renaissance. The fellow travellers, too, are both real and fictitious and include Plato, Pythagoras, Don Quixote, Tristram Shandy and Baudelaire. Like the better-known *Siddartha*, this is a timeless novel of broad appeal, with an easy lyricism and a well-composed symmetry of style.

0 7206 1131 8   £8.50

NARCISSUS AND GOLDMUND

Narcissus is a teacher at a medieval monastery, and Goldmund his favourite pupil. The latter runs away in pursuit of love, living a wanderer's life which brings him both pain and ecstasy. Narcissus remains behind, detached from the world in prayer and meditation. Their eventual reunion brings into focus the diversity between artist and thinker, Dionysian and Apollonian. Thought by some to be Hesse's greatest novel, this is a classic of contemporary literature.

'Deeply moving and richly poetic, this brilliant fusion of concepts is astonishing in its simplicity and power.'
— *Birmingham Post*

0 7206 1102 4   £12.50

PETER CAMENZIND

In this semi-autobiographical novel, Peter Camenzind is an introverted Swiss peasant boy who becomes a student at Zurich University where he seems destined for some academic post. Yet he does not choose this path: perturbed by what he perceives to be the thankless and turbulent unrest of human nature, he seeks his salvation through self-knowledge in the manner of a Romantic hero. But salvation in casual love affairs and in the bars and literary salons of European cities proves elusive. Finally he turns to St Francis of Assisi, but personal sublimation after the example of the saint still does not give his mind rest. It is not until he returns to his own village to care for his dying father that he can find the path that leads back to himself.

'Explores in frequently moving terms the early manhood of a genius.' – *Daily Telegraph*

'Liberating, fiercely undated, inimitable. Hesse should be read in chunks.' – *Guardian*

'A masterpiece' – *London Evening Standard*

0 7206 1168 7   £9.95

Anna Kavan
ASYLUM PIECE

First published sixty years ago, *Asylum Piece* today ranks as one of the most extraordinary and terrifying evocations of human madness ever written. This collection of stories, mostly interlinked and largely autobiographical, chart the descent of the narrator from the onset of neurosis to final incarceration at a

Swiss clinic. The sense of paranoia, of persecution by a foe or force that is never given a name evokes Kafka, though Kavan's deeply personal, restrained and almost foreign-accented style has no true model. The same characters who recur throughout – the protagonist's unhelpful 'adviser', the friend/lover who abandons her at the clinic and an assortment of deluded companions – are sketched without a trace of rage, self-pity or sentiment.

0 7206 1123 7   £9.95

THE PARSON

The Parson of the title is not a cleric but an upright young army officer so named for his apparent prudishness. On leave, he meets Rejane, a rich and beguiling beauty, the woman of his dreams. The days that he spends with Rejane, riding in and exploring the wild moorland, have their enchantment, but she grows restless in this desolate landscape. Though doubtless in love with him, she discourages any intimacy, until she persuades him to take her to a sinister castle situated on a treacherous headland . . . *The Parson* is less a tale of unrequited love than exploration of divided selves, momentarily locked in an unequal embrace. Passion is revealed as a play of the senses as well as a destructive force. Comparisons have been made between this writer and Poe, Kafka and Thomas Hardy, but the presence of her trademark themes, juxtaposed and set in her risk-taking prose, mark *The Parson* as one-hundred-per-cent Kavan.

0 7206 1140 7   £8.95

SLEEP HAS HIS HOUSE

A daring synthesis of memoir and surrealist experimentation, *Sleep Has His House* charts the stages of the subject's withdrawal from contact with the daylight world of received reality. Flashes of experience from childhood, adolescence and youth are described in what Kavan terms 'night-time language' – a heightened prose that frees these events from their gloomy associations. The novel suggests that we have all spoken this dialect in childhood and in our dreams, but these thoughts can only be decoded by contemplation in the dark.

Kavan maintained that the plot of a book is only the point of departure, beyond which she tries to reveal that side of life which is never seen by the waking eye but which dreams and drugs can illuminate. She spent the last ten years of her life literally and metaphorically shutting out the light; the startling discovery of *Sleep Has His House* is how much these night-time illuminations reveal her joy for the living world. The novel startled with its strangeness in 1948. Today it is one of Kavan's most acclaimed books.

'Possibly one of her most interesting books, a near masterpiece in the imaginative speculations of those whose paradise simultaneously contains their hell.' – *The Times*

'Anna Kavan's "night-time language" is in no way obscure: on the contrary, her dreams are as carefully notated as paintings by Dalí or de Chirico.' – *New Statesman*

'Her writing is magnificent. It is a fascinating clinical casebook of her obsessions and the effects of drugs on her imagination . . . in the tradition of the great writers on drug literature, de Quincey, Wilkie Collins, Coleridge.' – *Daily Telegraph*

'A testament of remarkable, if feverish beauty.' – *Guardian*

0 7206 1129 6   £9.95

WHO ARE YOU?

Who Are You? is a sparse depiction of the hopeless, emotional polarity of a young couple and their doomed marriage spent in a remote, tropical hell. She – described only as 'the girl' – is young, sophisticated and sensitive; he, 'Mr Dog-Head', is a thug and heavy drinker who rapes her, otherwise passing his time bludgeoning rats with a tennis racket. Together with a visiting stranger, 'Suede Boots', who urges the woman to escape until he is banished by her husband, these characters live through the same situations twice. Their identities are equally real – or unreal – in each case. With slight variation in the background and the novel's atmosphere, neither the outcome nor the characters themselves are quite the same the second time. The constant question of the jungle 'brain-fever' bird remains unanswered – 'Who are you?' First published in 1963, *Who Are You?* was reissued to widespread acclaim in 1973.

'To write about this finely economical book in any terms other than its own is cruelly to distort the near-perfection of the original text. There is a vision here which dismays.' – Robert Nye, *Guardian*

'*Who Are You?* is accomplished and complete . . . so fully imagined, so finely described in spare, effective prose, that it is easy to suspend disbelief.' – Nina Bawden, *Daily Telegraph*

'Lots of fun to read, sprouts with a macabre imagination and is, no question, a classic.' – *Sunday Telegraph*

0 7206 1150 4   £8.95

Yukio Mishima
CONFESSIONS OF A MASK

This autobiographical novel, regarded as Mishima's finest book, is the haunting story of a Japanese boy's homosexual awakening during and after the Second World War. Detailing his progress from an isolated childhood through adolescence to manhood, including an abortive love affair with a classmate's sister, it reveals the inner life of a boy's preoccupation with death. The books continuing appeal attests to the novel's enduring themes of fantasy, despair and alienation.

'A terrific and astringent beauty . . . a work of art.'
— *Times Literary Supplement*

0 7206 1031 1   £11.95

Anaïs Nin
CHILDREN OF THE ALBATROSS

Children of the Albatross is conceived as a series of lyrical descriptions of the experience of Djuna, a former ballet dancer, and her circle. The central account of the novel is her love affair with a seventeen-year-old youth who finally leaves her. On the surface a portrayal of the clash between autumnal and adolescent passions, this is an insightful tale about an older woman who, as the result of an unhappy childhood, rebels against male tyranny and instinctively looks for the child – one in whom 'the arteries of faith have not hardened' – rather than the man in her lovers.

'A novel that oscillates with sensibility like a cat's whisker.' – *Sunday Telegraph*

'A finely spun web of feeling and insight into the feminine condition . . . Exquisitely written.' – *Scotsman*

0 7206 1165 5

THE FOUR-CHAMBERED HEART

This continues the adventures of Djuna, the eccentric star of *Children of the Albatross*. Djuna is in love with a husky and feckless Guatemalan guitar player. They make their home on a squalid, leaky houseboat anchored on the Seine which, like their relationship, is destined to go nowhere. His volatile personality and bohemian outlook ensures that the dream of accomplishing the very something that Djuna awakes in him will never come to anything. For her part, the self-sacrificing Djuna is forced to accommodate into her home his sickly wife, to whom he is tied by a half-blind complicity in her desire to exploit all who come within range.

'Her prose is like a shaft of sunlight, a cold clear colour that can be broken up suddenly into many prismatic hues. Of her books, *The Four-Chambered* Heart is undoubtedly the most successful . . . the book expresses the destruction of poetic imagination by the hard facts of life; but the expression is done in the manner of poetry.' – *Irish Times*

0 7206 1155 5   £9.95

COLLAGES

Collages explores a world of fantasy and dreams through an eccentric young painter. A radical work when published in the early 1960s, in it Nin dispensed with normal structural convention and allowed her characters to wander freely in space and time in an attempt to describe life with the disconnected clarity of a dream in which hip and freakish lives intersect or merge. Making a rapid escape from her sick father in Vienna, Renate begins her sensation-seeking travel odyssey accompanied by a gay Norwegian man who allows her to open one of his Chinese boxes and read a chapter of his past each time she finds his absence unbearable. *Collages* is a shifting notebook indelibly inscribed with Nin's humour, invention and unrivalled gift for sensuous description.

'Perfectly told fables, and prose which is so daringly elaborate, so accurately timed that it is not entirely surprising to hear her compared to Proust.' – *Times Literary Supplement*

'Nin's writing is spare, and sharply perceptive, her imaginative vision quite remarkable.' – *Scotsman*

'A delight.' – *Independent*

0 7206 1145 8   £9.95

LADDERS TO FIRE

This poetic, sensual novel, the first in the 'Cities of the Interior' series, focuses on the lives of a group of women as they undergo a period of emotional and sexual development. They record their experiences as they struggle to understand both themselves and each other. As with most of Nin's novels, *Ladders to Fire* draws its inspiration from her confessional diaries begun in 1914 at the age of eleven. It dates from the period when Anaïs Nin moved to New York, a time also explored in the film *Henry and June*.

'It is refreshing to find a 1940s' novel so firmly situated in the realms of female consciousness and so rooted in a conviction of the validity of female desire.' – *Scotsman*

'Nin writes sensitively, with psychological training as well as insight . . . she has a subcutaneous interest in her characters and Lawrence's sixth sense.' – *Times Literary Supplement*

0 7206 1162 8   £9.95

Boris Pasternak
THE LAST SUMMER

By the author of *Dr Zhivago*, and his only other completed work of fiction, *The Last Summer* is set in Russia during the winter of 1916, when Serezha visits his married sister. Tired after a long journey, he falls into a restless sleep and half remembers, half dreams the incidents of the last summer of peace before the First World War. As tutor in a wealthy, unsettled Moscow household, he focuses his intense romanticism on Mrs Arild, the employer's paid companion, while spending his nights with the prostitute Sashka and others. In this evocation of the past, the characters are subtly etched against their social backgrounds, and Pasternak imbues the commonplace with his own intense and poetic vision.

'A concerto in prose.' — V.S. Pritchett

0 7206 1099 0   £8.50

Cesare Pavese
THE DEVIL IN THE HILLS

The Devil in the Hills is the most personal of Pavese's novels, an elegiac celebration of lost youth set in the landscape of his own boyhood: the hills, vineyards and villages of Piedmont. Three young men while away the summer talking, drinking – rarely sleeping – and there is an overwhelming sense that it is the last summer that they will be able to indulge such pleasures. In contrast to their feelings of transcience, the leisure of their new, wealthy acquaintance, Poli, fascinates them. For a while they linger in his world, in his decaying villa, half appalled by his cocaine addiction, his blasphemy, his corrupt circle of friends, but none the less mesmerized until autumn creeps upon the hillside and the moment of leave-taking arrives . . .

'In this remarkable author, the compassionate moralist and the instinctive poet go hand in hand.' – *Scotsman*

'*The Devil in the Hills* shows how ahead of his time Pavese was.' – *The Times*

'Erotic, but extraordinarily delicate and controlled.' – *Guardian*

0 7206 1118 0   £9.95

THE MOON AND THE BONFIRE

Anguilla is a successful businessman lured home from California to the Piedmontese village where he was fostered by peasants. But after twenty years much has changed. Slowly, he is able to piece together the past and relates it to what he finds in the present. He looks at the lives and sometimes violent fates of the villagers he has known from childhood, setting the poverty, ignorance or indifference that binds them to these hills and valleys against the beauty of the landscape and the rhythm of the seasons. With stark realism and muted compassion Pavese weaves the strands together and brings them to a stark and poignant climax.

'Wonderfully written, beautifully translated.' – *Sunday Times*

'Reminds us again how good a writer Pavese was.' – *Sunday Telegraph*

0 7206 1119 9   £9.95

Mervyn Peake
A BOOK OF NONSENSE

'I can be quite obscure and practically marzipan.' From the macabre to the brilliantly off-beat, Mervyn Peake's nonsense verse can be enjoyed by young and old alike. This collection of writings and drawings was selected by his late widow, Maeve Gilmore, and it introduces a whole gallery of characters and creatures, such as the Dwarf of Battersea and Footfruit.

'Deserves a place among the eccentrics of the English tradition alongside Sterne, Blake, Lear, Carroll and Belloc.' – *The Times*

0 7206 1163 6   £7.95

Edith Piaf
MY LIFE

Taped shortly before her death, this is the dramatic and often tragic story of the legendary French singer Edith Piaf. She recalls her early years in the Paris underworld, her rise to international stardom, her long fight against alcohol and drugs, and her succession of stormy love affairs – and defiantly asserts the message of her most famous song, *Non, je ne regrette rien*.

0 7206 1111 3   £9.95

Marcel Proust
PLEASURES AND REGRETS

This was Proust's first published work, appearing when he was only twenty-five, and it consists of stories, sketches and thematic writings on a variety of subjects. The attitudes reflect many characteristics of the turn of the twentieth century, yet Proust illumined them with the unique shafts of observation and gift of analysis that he was later to perfect in *The Remembrance of Things Past*. This book is a period piece of intricate delights and subtle flavours that will be relished by the author's many admirers.

'This is the perfect introduction to Proust.' – *Punch*

0 7206 1110 5   £9.95

Joseph Roth
FLIGHT WITHOUT END

A young Austrian soldier returns home after the Great War. Having fought with the Red Army and worked as a Soviet official, he arrives back in bourgeois Vienna to find that it no longer has a place for him. His father has died and his fiancée, who had waited many years for his return, has married another man and left for Paris; there is nothing for an ex-soldier in Austria at the end of the Habsburg empire. He travels Europe searching in vain for a place to belong. This is the story of a young man's alienation and his search for identity and home in a world that has changed out of all recognition from the one in which he grew up.

'Almost perfect.' — *Rolling Stone*

'A very fine writer indeed.' — Angela Carter, *Guardian*

0 7206 1068 0   £9.95

THE SILENT PROPHET

This story grew out of Roth's visit to the Soviet Union in 1926, at a time when speculation was rife about the fate of Leon Trotsky. Roth referred to this book as his 'Trotsky novel', but the experiences of the book's hero, the Trotsky-like Friederich Kargan, are also recognizably those of a less well-known Jewish outsider, – Joseph Roth himself. Not strictly a historical novel nor personal analysis, *The Silent Prophet* is a beautifully descriptive journey from loneliness into an illusory worldliness back into loneliness and a haunting study of alienation.

'A novel one should not wish to be without.' – *Guardian*

'With his striking elliptical style, which can evoke despair through real wit it would be only mildly flattering to view him as a compassionate, laconic Conrad.' – *Time Out*

0 7206 1135 0   £9.95

Natsume Soseki
THE THREE-CORNERED WORLD

A key work in the Japanese transition from traditional to modern literature, this is the story of an artist who abandons city life to wander into the mountains to meditate. But when he decides to stay at a near-deserted inn he finds himself drawn to the daughter of the innkeeper. This strange and beautiful woman is rumoured to have abandoned her husband and fallen in love with a priest at a nearby temple. The artist becomes entranced by her tragic aura and he wants to paint her. Yet, troubled by a certain quality in her expression, he struggles to complete the portrait until he is finally able to penetrate the enigma of her life. Interspersed with philosophies of both East and West, Soseki's writing skilfully blends two very different cultures in this unique representation of an artist struggling with his craft and his environment.

'Natsume Soseki is generally acknowledged to have been one of the most important writers of the modern period.' – *Times Literary Supplement*

0 7206 1156 3   £9.95

Bram Stoker
MIDNIGHT TALES

In the last decades of the nineteenth century, the Lyceum Theatre in London was the scene for brilliant gatherings hosted by the great actor Sir Henry Irving. There Irving and his guests talked of the theatre and told strange tales of far distant places. Bram Stoker was Irving's manager during these years, and such dinner-table conversations provided him with inspiration both for his immortal classic of horror fiction, *Dracula*, and for the chilling stories in this book. Opening the collection is a terrifying encounter with a werewolf, a scene from an early draft of *Dracula*. Here, too, is 'The Squaw', Stoker's most blood-curdling short story, set in a medieval torture chamber. The theatrical world features in 'Death in the Wings', a tale of brutal revenge. Also included is the dramatic finale from the 1903 novel *The Jewel of the Seven Stars*, with its raising of a mummy from the dead, which so shocked Edwardian readers that it was later expurgated. Some of the stories in this collection have not been reprinted since their original publication, and all display the fascination with the strange and the gruesome that made Bram Stoker a master of the macabre.

'A head-on collision between horror and sexuality.' – *The Times*

'Compelling . . . strictly for vampire lovers.' – *Guardian*

0 7206 1134 2   £9.95

Tarjei Vesaas
THE BIRDS

A tale of delicate beauty and deceptive simplicity by one of the greatest Scandinavian writers of the twentieth century, *The Birds* tells the story of Mattis, who is mentally retarded and lives in a small house near a lake with his sister Hege who ekes out a modest living knitting sweaters. From time to time she encourages her brother to find work to ease their financial burdens, but Mattis's attempts come to nothing. When finally he sets himself up as a ferryman, the only passenger he manages to bring across the lake is a lumberjack, Jørgen. But, when Jørgen and Hege become lovers, Mattis finds he cannot adjust to this new situation and complications abound.

'True visionary power.' – *Sunday Telegraph*

'Beautiful and subtle.' – *Scotsman*

'A masterpiece.' – *Literary Review*

'A spare, icily humane story.' – *Sunday Times*

0 7206 1143 1   £9.95

THE ICE PALACE

This is the story of two eleven-year-old girls, Unn and Siss. Unn is about to reveal a secret, one that leads to her death in the palace of ice surrounding a frozen waterfall. Siss's struggle with her fidelity to the memory of her friend, the strange, terrifyingly beautiful frozen chambers of the waterfall and Unn's fatal exploration of the ice palace are described in prose of lyrical economy that ranks among the most memorable achievements of modern literature. Tarjei Vesaas was awarded the Nordic Council Prize for this novel.

'How simple this novel is. How subtle. How strong. How unlike any other. It is unique. It is unforgettable. It is extraordinary.' – Doris Lessing, *Independent*

'It is hard to do justice to *The Ice Palace* . . . The narrative is urgent, the descriptions relentlessly beautiful, the meaning as powerful as the ice piling up on the lake. – *The Times*

0 7206 1122 9   £9.95

Noel Virtue
THE REDEMPTION OF ELSDON BIRD

Elsdon Bird is an affectionate and imaginative child raised in a family steeped in the religious intolerance of the Christian Brethren sect. When Dad gets sacked from his city workplace for proselytizing, the Birds are forced to leave Wellington and move to a small, remote town in the north. Here the family begins to disintegrate, with Elsdon becoming a whipping boy for all his family's frustrations. Driven more and more into himself, he builds a fragile internal world maintained by conversations with cows and sheep. Yet, when a sequence of disasters finally breaks up the family, the endearing Elsdon's amazing resilience and humanity see him win through in the end. Many writers have attempted to convey the terrifying world of a sensitive child in the grip of a family bent on pathological violence, but few have brought it off with such conviction.

'Little Elsdon must be the worst-treated child in literature since Smike. But Virtue never attempts to play the violin on his reader's heartstrings. Elsdon's untarnished optimism lights the bleakest landscapes and carries him to safety.' – *Independent*

'A wonderful account of childhood that touches you to the quick with its painfully funny amalgam of misery and euphoria.' – *Mail on Sunday*

0 7206 1166 0   £8.95